How to Solve Murders like a Lady

How to Solve Murders Like a Lady

Hannah Dolby

HEAD of ZEUS

An Aria Book

First published in the UK in 2024 by Head of Zeus,
part of Bloomsbury Publishing Plc

9 7 5 3 1 2 4 6 8

A catalogue record for this book is available from the British Library.

ISBN (PB): 9781804544433
ISBN (E): 9781804544396

Cover design: Meg Shepherd

Typeset by Siliconchips Services Ltd UK

MIX
Paper | Supporting
responsible forestry
FSC® C171272
FSC
www.fsc.org

Printed and bound in Great Britain by
CPI Group (UK) Ltd, Croydon CR0 4YY

Head of Zeus Ltd
First Floor East
5–8 Hardwick Street
London EC1R 4RG

www.headofzeus.com

To my friends, for making me laugh

Resolve

Build on resolve, and not upon regret,

The structure of thy future. Do not grope

Among the shadows of old sins, but let

Thine own soul's light shine on the path of hope

And dissipate the darkness. Moist no tears

Upon the blotted record of lost years

But turn the leaf and smile, oh smile, to see

The fair white pages that remain for thee.

Ella Wheeler Wilcox (1850–1919)

Chapter One

Life was good, full of recent achievements and adventures to come. I had an exemplary fiancé and a fledgling career as a Lady Detective. It was only a tiny setback to be trapped in an oast house full of hens.

A bird with black feathers and an evil expression clucked ominously near me and I shifted in case it pecked my ankle. Oast houses were built to store hops for beer and in the middle of the room, three storeys high, rose the giant furnace that was lit day and night in August and September to dry the hops, before they were taken away for brewing. It was spring now, and even though the slatted floor above had long been swept clean of the hop flowers, the hints of juniper berry and pine still mingled with the scents of hay and hens.

Ten or so were meandering around the floor and more clucking from nesting boxes lined around the circular wall. They were not my only company. Three baby goats sat at my feet, staring at me.

I was lucky. Not many women could expect a career at all in the year of our Lord, 1897. My luck had come about only last spring, when I had plucked up courage and hired a detective to find my mother, who had been missing from Hastings and St Leonards for ten years. I had persuaded Benjamin Blackthorn, a very tall detective, to let me work for him, initially as a typist. It had led to several adventures, including finding my mother and becoming engaged to him, and now, to handling cases like this one.

A brush-bearded, fustian-trousered farmer called Mr Wicken had shut me in the oast house. I had asked him if he had seen any of the little goats who pulled children along in the goat-chaises on the Hastings and St Leonards promenade, as three had gone missing, and a shrimp-seller on the seafront had told me she had spotted him walking homewards early this morning, a wildly wriggling sack over his shoulder. When I arrived, Mr Wicken had grunted a little and gestured towards the oast house, and the second I stepped inside he locked me in with a bar over the door. And here were the three little kids, one chewing my bootlaces; too little to have started pulling the chaises, white and brown with whirling tails, amber eyes and soft snouts.

Three hens were circling the smallest goat, clucking in agitation. I couldn't blame them. The kids overflowed with hapless, haphazard energy, sometimes leaping and twisting into the air as if some invisible force propelled them, pausing only to play-butt each other and my knees and trying to eat everything in sight. They had only tired themselves out enough to sit down in the last few minutes. The smallest bleated forlornly, so I took it onto my lap and stroked its soft ears. Too soft. There was a reason they were made into gloves.

Six months or so ago, I had found my mother. I had hired a shady detective to find her, a Mr Frank Knight, and attempted to replace him with the morally superior Mr Blackthorn, and then in the end I had found her myself, living quietly in Buxton in affectionate, if surprising, proximity with a lady friend.

Mr Fake-Detective Knight had died. I could not bear to call it murder, but he had chased me all the way to Buxton, revealing a long, bitter obsession with my mother and threatening both of us, and my mother's lady friend had precipitated his early departure from the world into the depths of a cave. It was a shocking moment that still woke me at night, but it had cemented the feeling I must become a detective, must face all of the horror and sadness of life. I had learnt so much in the past year, I never wanted to return to the naive, ignorant female I had been.

There were rough edges. I was still coming to terms with the fact that for ten years, my mother had not made a very great effort to let me know she was alive. It hurt with a sharpness I had not expected, but the only vital point, surely, was that she was living and in good health. I must ignore the hurt. I had more splendid things to think about.

There was my agreement with my new fiancé, Benjamin Blackthorn, for example. It was a very modern one, in that he had agreed we could mutually get to know each other for as long as I needed and if it didn't work out, we could reconsider with no blame on either side, and I would be a free woman again. We had been engaged nearly six months now, and I was very content. Maybe in ten years we would get married and settle down to raise a family.

Overall, it was not so bad to be locked in an oast house. I did not think the farmer meant injury. I was getting cleverer at discerning when people meant me harm. He had looked panicked rather than angry. Besides, being locked up was giving me a rare moment to reflect on the miracle of my life finally falling into place.

But I had had enough ruminating. It was time to escape.

It was not hopeful. I went up the circular staircase leading to the floor above, where hops were dried by the shovelful, but could see no way out. The door which led to the cooling house next door was firmly locked, and it was impossible to escape through the hole in the roof as it was conical, a giant chimney to funnel the hot air from the furnace up and out.

It was impossible to fail. I had not spent six months training to be a Lady Detective to fall at the first hurdle. But after I had perambulated the entire roundhouse thrice, each time followed by small curious goats, I had to admit the possibilities were slim.

Finally, I sat down on the upper floor, frustrated, resting my head back against the wall, looking up at the distinctive white-painted cowl at the very top of the coned roof. Shaped like the hood of a nun's robe, it spun around in the wind, propelled by a weathervane. Dimly, I thought it might be to protect the hops from the rain, but all I knew was that it looked very showy from the outside. Scores of similar oast houses dotted the countryside, each with its white peak, a distinctive mark on the landscape.

I looked at the cowl again and sighed as an idea formed. Was it the only way? Would I have to risk my dignity and my reputation for my freedom? Would it be better just to wait, in hope the farmer saw the error of his ways?

I was not the waiting kind. I went down the stairs again, picked up a long-handled rake lying against the wall, and then climbed back up. It was not long enough, so I took the ribbon off my hat and tied two rakes together, prongs to prongs.

Would I ever be allowed out in society again, even if my actions saved me? But my hat would not fit through the hole, and I could hardly take off my skirt. Instead, mumbling to myself, I removed my serviceable white cotton petticoat, which was woven with a thick cording of fabric that made it stand out stiffly to support my skirt. It had a cotton tie around the waist that I fastened as firmly as I could around the thin end of one of the rakes, allowing an opening for it to billow in the wind. Then I hoisted it up and out of the hole at the top of the roof. I had made a flag. A flag which would save me or shame me forever.

For a few seconds my petticoat inflated splendidly, silhouetted against the sky, a signal no one could miss. Then the wind picked up and the cowl spun again, knocking my petticoat clear off the end of the rake, so it flew away and out of sight, a white cotton bird against the clouds. I sat down again on the slatted floor, defeated.

Chapter Two

The farmer's face was extraordinarily red above his scrubbing brush beard.

'Miss, you've lost...' he said. 'Is it yerrs? It can't be anyone else's. You might want...' He stood at a distance, his arm stiffened out at full stretch, and handed me a folded parcel of brown hessian. I guessed it contained my lost undergarment.

'Thank you,' I said. 'Perhaps you might let me out.'

'Me wife says I should,' he said. 'But ah'm doin' it on behalf of the goats. 'Tis a protest. Goats are not horses. They shouldn't be on the seafront, pullin' along carriages for the tourists. That's not what they're for. That's usin' 'em. It's agin nature. They should be allowed to grow up, and graze in a field; become good milkers. That's a proper life.'

'You have stolen them,' I said. 'Theft is a serious matter. You took them away in a sack. And you imprisoned me among hens. I am covered in feathers. Several important people will be wondering where I am. Besides, is not keeping goats for their milk using them, in a way? They do not make their milk for us.'

He wrinkled his nose. ''Tis unnatural, pullin' spoilt brats along the seafront. Better for their lazy legs if they walk. Me wife says I've maybe gone too far this time, though. Yer... it hit me in the face, yer... yer... as I was feedin' the cows. I reckon it's a sign. I didn't mean to scare you into doing summat so... so... *unladylike.*'

'Why don't you let us all go, and we'll say no more about it,' I said.

He shrugged and stroked his beard. 'Tell Mrs Pearson she

5

needs to look after her livestock better. Make sure they aren't pulling children twice their size. 'Tis no life for a goat. But me wife is the one with the sense. Tek 'em away, then.'

He took a ball of string from his pocket, cut three pieces with a penknife he produced from another pocket, tied each piece of string round the necks of the goats tight enough they couldn't wriggle out and then tried to hand me the end of the strings.

'Good luck wi' it,' he said. 'Sorry for the trouble. Bit unusual for a lady to be harin' about the countryside sorting out troubles, ent it? Aren't you too… gentle for that sort of business?'

'I am a Lady Detective,' I said. 'Tough, decisive and when necessary, brutish.'

He turned towards the doorway as if to look at the clouds, but did he have a smile on his face? I would ignore it if so. He had touched a nerve, but he was a man who stole goats and therefore lacking good sense. 'If you will take the animals outside temporarily and leave the door ajar, I will… attend to matters.'

He shot out the door, rosy-faced again, and I put my petticoat back on before meeting him in the farmyard.

'Sorry, miss,' he said, handing me the kids on the string.

'Thank you for having me, goodbye,' I said, and stalked out of the yard. It was not quite the dignified exit I had hoped, because the three kids had different opinions about which way they wanted to go, but eventually we made it out and I set off down the hill to return them to Mrs Mavis Pearson, seaside proprietor of goat-chaises.

It was heading towards lunchtime, so once I had left the country lanes and entered the edges of town, I took the narrow twittens and back streets to avoid meeting anyone. It was all downhill, as Hastings and St Leonards was a motley marriage of hills and valleys, dropping sharply towards the sea. I zig-zagged my way until I reached the promenade, and then I picked up one kid under my right arm, pulling the other two, and walked with the nonchalant saunter of someone doing something entirely natural.

It was the first of March, and the seafront was coming to life again. It had been a harsh winter. Storms had ruined several piers further along the coast and Beach Terrace had been flooded three times, although it was generally agreed it had been built too close to the sea anyway.

Now the day-trippers and convalescents were starting to trickle back. The hawkers were out, selling whelks and periwinkles; toffee apples and sticks of rock; flowers, postcards, driftwood carvings and seashells. A fisherman was mending his trawl net in the doorway of a black-tarred net shop and another was making wicker baskets. I passed a row of bath chairs on the promenade, ready for hire, and on the beach were several rows of the new striped deck chairs that had become so fashionable last summer. Beyond them at the edge of the sea, surrounded by ready crowds, were the giant pleasure yachts, their sails billowing. The air was full of shouts, laughter and loud conversation. I had heard talk the council was bringing in by-laws to curtail the worst of the seafront's excesses and control who could sell what where, and I hoped the rules would not destroy this dramatic maelstrom of life.

Hastings Pier, stretching majestically out to sea with its onion-topped Moorish pavilion at the seaward end, had been shut for most of the winter months. The gales had destroyed the landing stage on the new St Leonards Pier, some of its timber beams driven further along the coast to smash into several of the two hundred iron columns holding up Hastings Pier, but the damage could not have been too serious, because today it was open again. People were pouring through the two octagonal tollgates to visit the numerous stalls and sundry entertainments, from fortune-telling and strength-testing machines to this week's new attraction, a hall of mirrors.

Imps of fate being what they were, as I passed the end of it, I saw the Spencer sisters coming towards me, in apricot dresses. They were a strange pair, fond of cutting me in the street. They noticed me and veered slightly as if considering crossing the road, but they were with a burly man with an unusual red-brown beard, dense enough for sparrows to get lost in, who must be their father. Not knowing me, he did not change course, so they did not have time to avoid me. They contented themselves with identical looks of horror and disdain, giving my animal charges a wide berth.

A little further along, because the angels disliked me today, I met Mrs Withers from my local church. Criticising me was already her favourite pastime, without her needing extra ammunition. She was fond of extravagant hats and today's was covered in red and purple silk poppies, a whole field flowering on her head with a startled blackbird at its epicentre.

'What in heaven!' she cried. 'Miss Hamilton, what on earth are you doing?'

'Just returning some goats,' I said, and tried to circumnavigate her, but one of the kids, fascinated by the foliage on her hat, reared up with its little hooves on her knee to have a closer look and the others became happily entangled in her skirts.

'For goodness' sake!' she said, brushing them away and stepping behind a bench to protect herself. 'Have you no sense, no decorum? Parading around town with dirty farm animals! What would your mother think?'

'My mother disappeared eleven years ago,' I said, 'Her thoughts would be… antiquated. I must be going. Good day,' and I managed to circle around her and continue on my way, not looking back, knowing her face would be unpleasantly scrunched up with disapproval. I should not have been so flippant about my mother because it was only Benjamin and I who knew she was alive and well and had not drowned at sea, been abducted by highwaymen, seduced by pirates or any of the other lurid theories eddying around town for years. But Mrs Withers deserved short shrift.

Eventually, I reached Mrs Pearson's goat pen on the seafront and handed them back. She was a small woman of some asperity, perfect for training stubborn goats.

'I shall go and give Farmer Wicken a piece of my mind,' she said, but I deterred her.

'He is old-fashioned and thinks goats should be kept for milk,' I said. 'He was attempting some grand point about liberation, and the ethics of goat-chaises. He has realised he was wrong and will not do it again. Treat them kindly, I beg of you.'

I had developed an affection for them over the morning, with their lively exuberance. But they looked happy to be home, so I patted their heads and left.

I planned to go and meet Benjamin Blackthorn, my fiancé, in our office. First, I would go home and wash off the scent of my adventure. I only wished to meet him looking my best.

The morning had been successful, if I ignored the small irritations. I was perhaps less patient than I had once been with people's foibles and failings, because I had a profession now, a calling. Surely it gave me the right to avoid the slings and arrows of those who did not suit me, and gravitate towards those who did? The last year had brought good friends into my life and I needed to find a way to excise the likes of Mrs Withers and the Misses Spencer from it.

I did not know, then, how soon one of them would be gone.

Chapter Three

I hastily completed my ablutions and set out for our detective agency, walking straight down to the seafront and then turning left to walk along the great, flat stretch of promenade running from St Leonards to Hastings. It was easier than wending my way across higher up, along the three hills and dips that made up our town, where streets or alleyways often went up when you wanted to go down or abruptly led you to a blank wall with no way through.

Just past the splendour of Pelham Crescent, a Regency street built in an elegant sweeping curve in front of the cliff face, I passed a wall of advertisements, a colourful assault on the eye and a rude mix of testimonies for hair restorer, seasickness tablets, plumbers, sanitary engineers, waxwork exhibitions, theatre and lantern shows. Past this lay Hastings Old Town, a cluttered gathering of streets lined with uneven buildings spanning two or three centuries. Set off a cobbled side street, half a mile inland from the liveliest part of the seashore, within a little square with high walls on three sides, which you might not discover if you did not know it was there, was our sleuthing headquarters.

Three months ago, my fiancé Benjamin Blackthorn had repainted the door from a dull brown to a deep forest green, and affixed a new brass sign on it saying:

BLACKTHORN ANTIQUE FURNITURE

And underneath:

HAMILTON AND BLACKTHORN DETECTIVE AGENCY

We had argued a little about it, because I thought it should be Blackthorn and Hamilton as he had been a detective for so very much longer than me, and his father before him, but he had insisted, which only increased his credentials as a gentleman. I polished it with my sleeve, as I did every day, and went in, the little bell clanging as I entered.

Benjamin was near the back of the shop, on his haunches, polishing a small oak cabinet to a fine sheen. He liked this aspect of this job, I knew, the practical side of restoring furniture, of taking a piece battered or scratched almost beyond repair in its long service of mankind and slowly, lovingly, bringing it back to life. He had set about training me to be a good detective with the same quiet deliberation. I was learning it was the way he approached most things in life.

I had first inveigled my way into his services as a Lady Typist, typing up his letters and invoices on the Remington Standard Typewriter, a gleaming modern machine with an ink ribbon and little round white keys with the letters of the alphabet on, made in America. I loved typing and I was excellent at it, and the roles of detective and fiancée had perhaps followed naturally, because once I had typed successfully, anything was possible. He had given up detective work after the death of his father, setting up the furniture shop, but I had convinced him we could do both.

'Hamilton,' Benjamin said, tipping his head at me.

'Blackthorn,' I said, nodding seriously, and his mouth quirked at the corner.

'Coffee?' he said, pushing himself up to his full height. 'How did you get on with the goats?'

'I found them,' I said. 'It was the farmer who manages Wicken Farm on the north hill. He had been keeping them in his oast house, as he had an idea it was wrong to make baby goats pull well-fed children along the seafront in the chaises. He has a point. But he saw my point of view and gave them back. I've returned them, so we can consider the case closed.'

'Excellent,' Benjamin said. He went into the back and after a while brought out the tall silver coffee pot and cups on a tray, setting it down on an ornate metal table near our two armchairs and pouring us both a cup. It was an intimacy between us. He made very fine coffee. 'Did you have any trouble?'

'No,' I said. 'It was mostly straightforward.' I would like to be truthful, but it warred greatly with my need to impress him. He should be enthralled with ingenuity, my dispatch, my efficiency; I did not want to tell him I had saved myself from imprisonment by flinging my petticoat across rooftops.

He raised his eyebrows at me, but I concentrated on sipping. My best course was distraction.

'This is wonderful coffee,' I said. 'What case is next?'

'There is no rush,' he said, blowing across the top of his cup to cool it. 'You race at life as if there is no tomorrow.'

There were not many days left in the world of sleuthing, if I were to be married. It was why I was content to be in a long engagement. I needed to fill every day with learning and investigation, adventure and action, enough memories to keep me going for the rest of my life.

'What do we have on the cards?' I asked.

'There is not much. We need to advertise. There's a chap who thinks his wife is having an affair, but I will handle it.'

'Why? Why you?' He had a habit of doing this, of taking certain cases on himself, and I suspected he was giving me the gentle ones, investigations that would not upset me. In the last six months I had rescued a lost cat, found a missing tapestry for the Medieval Renaissance Embroidery Society (the clerk had a grievance, and had been using it as an antimacassar) and sorted out a fierce argument between two competitive cucumber growers at the Hastings Country Show. These were interesting, but I had done more typing than detective work and I suspected Benjamin was protecting me from the more difficult ones. I wanted to experience all of life, to be a proper detective, not dabble around the edges. If it meant I needed to toughen up, to put some of my feminine sensibilities to one side, I would do it.

'He's not one for you to speak to,' he said. 'A rough sort. Not a gentleman. Best I deal with it.'

'I can look after it. It is about time I worked on a real case. I do not want to always be working on the light cases.'

'Slow down, my Violet,' Benjamin said. 'I have time on my hands, I can look after this one. There is time for you to learn. You will run out of steam if you throw yourself headlong at everything. Savour the coffee, enjoy sitting here with me, as I am enjoying being with you. We are not running a race.'

He was a man who took his time with everything, from the way he sanded, polished and varnished furniture, bringing back shine and life to wooden surfaces and brass handles, to the way he wooed me, with quietly determined restraint. My mother had admitted a horror of bedroom activities, so on our engagement I had asked him boldly if we could try them out to prove it was not an inherited trait. He had agreed but since teased me with an intimacy so achingly slow and innocent in its progression, it frequently left me flustered and frustrated.

I would not waste the afternoon.

'Do you think you might teach me a little about observation, then?'

'Ah,' he said, 'You have been reading detective novels again. Very well, I will share what I know. But first, I think we need to refill the pot.' He stood, stretched and ambled off to the kitchen to make more coffee, while I waited, seething with frustration, for life to begin.

'If I was the great fictional Sherlock Holmes,' he said once he had settled back in his easy chair, 'I would sniff you from afar and proclaim you smell freshly of rose-scented soap, and therefore have washed recently, which when you spent the morning on a farm makes me think things were not quite as simple as you say. But really, it's all about incongruence.'

Sometimes I thought Benjamin looked a little like Lord Byron, taller, without the poetry, the club foot and the rakishness, but the same black curly hair and handsomeness of visage.

'Incongruence?'

'We are all of us putting on a show,' he said. 'At some point between childhood and adulthood we all learn to do it, even if we do not realise. We discover we can change our facial expressions to hide our feelings, smile when we are angry, stiffen our backs to hide our hurt, wear sharply polished boots to feel more important. Often you can see that divide, the incongruence, if you look closely enough. It's what happens with a mirror when it gets old. Instead of seeing your reflection you start to see through the glass, in patches, to the board beneath.'

'How do you spot these discrepancies?' I asked. I poured us both more coffee and got up briefly to grab a piece of paper and a pencil from the desk.

'Just watch,' he said. 'See the person as you might watch an actor at the theatre, stepping back from the action. Try to see the person inside, and whether their outward appearance matches it, or whether they are struggling to reconcile the two. See if they have signs to give them away. If they rub their ear lobe when they are lying or fill their sentences with pomp and circumstance to hide an insecurity. See if their actions match their words; don't trust them if they proclaim to be excellent fellows while tying a tin can to a cat.'

'Should one provoke someone, to uncover incongruence?'

'One can,' he said, stroking his chin, 'With subtlety. But often people will give themselves away, if you allow them free reign. Be interested in them and they will trip up in their attempt to be interesting for you. Women are often good at listening – too good, when the other person is a bore. You are good at it. Use your skill cynically. Let your target drone on about themselves and take from it what you need.'

'Do I have any signs?' I asked.

'Several,' he said. 'The dimple on your left cheek when you like something I've said. The way your big brown eyes widen when you are about to dissemble... the small frown between your eyebrows right now, when you are about to argue. No... do you really think I would gift you my power over you, negligible as it is? Your weaknesses are for me to know.'

When I first met Benjamin, he had been taciturn, dishevelled; a grumpy giant of a man, and it was only once he shaved off his wild beard that I had started to get to know him. But even now, after six months as his fiancée, I did not know him properly. It was a slow process of unravelling layers. He was quietly confident and assured of his place in the world without needing to draw attention to himself, in a way that allowed me to be the best version of myself. A less discerning fiancée might not have noticed all the small things he did and said to make me feel his equal, but because it was a rare quality among gentlemen, I noticed. It made my heart knot a little bit tighter every time.

I did not know if it was love. We had not become engaged solely for affectionate reasons. Benjamin had rightly pointed out we could not work together unless we were engaged, and he had professed affection for me, but I did not quite believe it. He did not seem tortured by pangs of deep emotion or suffering from overwhelming passion like heroes in books; there was no drama or tearing of hair; he did not send me longing looks or forget to shave because he had been thinking of me. His affection had more of a quiet calm certainty to it.

'Very clever. What are your weaknesses?' I asked him.

'I have none,' he said. 'I am perfect. Have you not noticed?'

There was a grain of truth in it, in that some days it did seem he was a perfect gentleman, perfectly formed, honourable, willing to give me my due, too good to be true. It was, to my muddled, imperfect self, mildly irritating at times.

'You must have faults,' I said. 'Beyond arrogance. Maybe you are just very good at hiding them. Maybe they will pop out, one day, when we are married, and I will discover I have married a monster.'

'Another excuse to postpone our wedding?' he asked. 'I was grumpy when we met, wasn't I? Before you smoothed over my rough edges with your charm.'

'Ha,' I said. 'Fulsome flattery does not work on me. I am impervious. I am a detective.'

'That predisposes you to think I only flatter for a reason,' he said. 'Perhaps I flatter because it's true? Because I want to say it?'

'Enough flummery,' I said. I got a little… practical when he complimented me. It was safer. 'I must commence the typing.'

He smiled at me, in the wise, knowing way he had at times, my handsome, incomparable fiancé, and I rolled my eyes at him and sat down at the typewriter to type up notes from my goat-chaise case, as well as an invoice for Mrs Pearson. We took notes on all cases and filed them away in a special cabinet.

I spent the afternoon on it and Benjamin went back to polishing his cabinet. Later in the afternoon his five half-brothers and sisters burst into the shop, and it briefly descended into chaos. The littlest two, Maud and Ernest, were as lively as the baby goats and all were full of life and rambunctiousness, bonded even more closely perhaps since their father had died nearly two years ago. Benjamin had taken on a fraternal care, and the care of his stepmother Agnes, with an easy shouldering of responsibility that characterised his approach to life.

Maud was at my knees, the youngest, only six or so, with two little red pigtails.

'Can I try the typing, Violent?' she said. I liked her mispronunciation of my name. It made me feel criminal.

'Of course,' I said, and hoisted her on my lap to show her how it worked. By the time they left she had a piece of paper with her name typed on it, as well as an array of other sundry words that took her fancy, including 'cheese', 'socks', 'biscuits' and 'frog'.

An hour afterwards Benjamin and I locked up the shop and agreed we would see each other tomorrow. I took the invoice to the post box and headed for home with the glow of a day well-lived. The joy of my profession helped me fall soundly asleep and I knew it would fire anew in the morning when I woke up.

Chapter Four

At breakfast my father was reading his paper in silence again. I did not mind so much these days about the lack of conversation, because I had my own concerns. As I buttered my toast, I thought instead about what I would do if a dastardly villain broke in through the window from the garden, intent on murder. Would it stop him if I threw my boiled egg, still in its shell, straight at his eye? Would it be best to throw my knife? I had read about knife-throwers, mostly in circuses. Or I could upend the whole table instead, to act as a barrier between us, and grab some of the ugly china ornaments from the French dresser. They had belonged to some long-dead relative and would never be missed, even if they smashed into a thousand pieces. My father would not have my razor-sharp instincts, my preparedness for danger, so it would be up to me to save us.

He got up abruptly from the table, throwing down his paper.

'Enjoy your day,' he said, and then made a strange circling motion with his hand towards his breakfast plate. 'The eggs were a little... rubbery.'

After he had left, I rolled my eyes at Hildebrand, who had come in to clear the plates.

'Pay him no heed,' I said. 'He likes to have opinions.' I had realised this too in the last year. Commenting on trivial matters gave my father his place, his importance in the household, and the criticism itself was unimportant. I could accept it with more equanimity now, because domesticity was not my main role.

We lived in St Leonards, the newer side of town. The architect Decimus Burton had designed St Leonards forty years or so ago with similar lofty ambitions to his edifices in London, from Wellington Arch to London Zoo, but here his grand designs seemed less comfortable, the houses a little embarrassed by their own grandeur. Perhaps it was because they had been built so close to the hotchpotch of Hastings, its dwellings taking shape haphazardly across centuries since Roman times, its streets and narrow twittens as untidy as loose threads on a badly embroidered quilt. Mismatched bedfellows or not, Hastings and St Leonards was one town now, run by a single council, trapped in an awkward marriage of disparities and contradictions. Hastings was rude, lively, rambunctious and poor; its new neighbour had pretensions to better things. Even the day-trippers to St Leonards were more refined.

Our smart red-brick house was in the new suburb of Silverhill, set around a triangular private, shared garden for all the houses, a triangle because it had been built between the junction of the two roads leading out of town towards London. To the north was open farmland, with a steam mill and a windmill I could see from my bedroom window; to the east was Shornden Wood and two reservoirs which supplied the town with its drinking water. Below us were the steeply sloping streets leading to the sea. Our small household consisted of my father, manager of Hastings and St Leonards Bank, and our servant, Hildebrand. Millie came every day to assist with the cooking and cleaning and Mrs Fitzimmons came every second Thursday to punch our laundry into cowering submission.

Hildebrand had joined our household six months before, at my invitation. She had been plying her trade at a brothel in All Saints Street, in the old town. I had met her on my first ever detective case and again when she purloined some knitting wool from a local shop, and after coming up against her terrifying madam, as densely muscled as a boxer dog, I felt Hildebrand would be happier and safer with us. Hildebrand's essential character was good, I was certain. She had settled in quickly, seemed content, was far, far better than the perennially cross servant that I had had before; all the same, our backgrounds were so vastly different I could not help but feel foolish in her company. I knew very little about the darkest tragedies which beset women, whereas Hildebrand must know it all, must surely secretly laugh at me for my naivety. I had never asked her about her background in case I appeared all agog, a prurient visitor at a zoo.

My father and I lived in mild disharmony together, as the time was long overdue for me to leave. I was twenty-nine, woeful at domestic matters and had spent too many years refusing the suitors he had arranged for me. It was not all for frivolous reasons. My mother had left me in woeful misapprehension of marital relations and I doubted my own attractions, because how could I know whether suitors wanted me for who I was, or for the mystery of my beautiful, absent mother? It was only more recently I had grown up a little and seen some men had actually cared, and then it was no longer a lark.

Six months ago, I had found my mother living in secret sin in Buxton with her lady friend, Evelina Joyce. She had not contacted me, beyond a brief early letter my father had kept from me, for more than a decade, claiming it was difficult to build a new life with a woman and she was worried we would hate her for it. But however sincerely meant, none of her excuses seemed important enough to leave me ignorant of her wellbeing. I was not finding it easy to forgive her.

Benjamin had asked me to marry him, and I had accepted, on the train home from Buxton. My father had initially expressed mild doubts as to whether my prospective fiancé was an equal match in financial and societal terms, but Benjamin had impressed on him he was a successful antiques dealer as well as an investigative agent and once quite high up in the Royal Navy, and my father had conceded quickly, weary of matchmaking. He was as self-satisfied about my engagement now as if he had arranged it himself.

I hadn't shared two salient facts with my father; firstly, that

I had found my mother alive and well, and secondly, that I was working for my new fiancé as a detective. He suspected she lived, because of the letter, but as their marriage had latterly been unhappy and he had recently met a lady of ample affections called Mrs Beeton, he was unlikely to be delighted about it. I also felt it was my mother's role to take responsibility for such seismic news, as otherwise I would be the only person in the immediate vicinity he could shout at.

As for being a detective, I was not convinced he was liberated enough to understand. He knew I was working as a Lady Typist and had begrudgingly accepted it, anticipating I would quit on marriage; it was enough. Peace had been declared, although sometimes he still looked at me over his newspaper and frowned.

Neither of us were free from keeping secrets. The letter my father had kept from me had provided a final, vital clue to her whereabouts, its postmark matching one on a postcard I had found between her bedroom floorboards.

Today there was a letter from my mother on my bedside table, the direction written in handwriting unlike her own. Hildebrand was primed to take them straight to my room. I would read it tomorrow, perhaps. She had been writing to me since I found her, twice-weekly, long, rambling letters telling me details of her life, her thoughts, her opinions on world affairs, gossip about those she knew, scandals from the newspapers, questions about me. Less often I sent back polite little letters, updating her on the weather and the height of waves. She had not been in my life for ten years and she wanted to be too much involved in it again, to advise with the same joyous intensity she faced the rest of life. I was not ready.

Once when I was seventeen, shy and self-conscious, mumbling my way through an unmemorable social occasion, worried whether I blushed too much or said the wrong things, as always feeling overshadowed by her, she had lectured me quite sternly.

'Forget how you feel,' she said. 'Forget what other people think. Pretend you are an actress on the stage. Speak with confidence, do not care how your words land and they will land well. People are mostly thinking of themselves. Decide who you want to be, who you want to show the world, and be that person. You can be anybody, my Violet. You have the power to present yourself to the world exactly how you wish to be seen.'

I had not listened to her at the time, certain she had never felt as I did. But she had disappeared a year later, and without her I had been forced to deal with people and life face-on. Her words had crept back, and I had adopted a mask of bravado and chutzpah to deal with the gossip and speculation. A mask similar to the one Benjamin had described. The person I showed the world was perhaps too forthright for a young lady, because I was a little angry, but it had served me well and I had been cheeky for so long I was not certain my shy self was still there. Perhaps if my mother had stayed, I would never have had the courage to become a detective. Perhaps her words and her absence had helped me to become one.

I gave myself a shake and got ready to go to work. I would persuade Benjamin to let me operate alongside him on the case he had mentioned, or another might arrive on our doorstep; life was mostly like that these days, full of serendipity and good fortune.

But when I arrived at the detective agency, I saw instantly something was up.

Chapter Five

'Violet, I'm glad you're here,' he said and smiled distractedly. He had his outer coat on and there was a travelling bag on top of the wooden sideboard I had perched on when we first met.

'What's happened?' I asked.

'I have to go to Scotland,' he said, and ran his hand through his dark hair, leaving it sticking up at odd angles. 'Some old business has reared its head. I won't be long. A few days perhaps.'

'What is it about?' I asked.

'I have to run and catch a train,' he said. 'I'll tell you all when I get back. But hopefully I'll prevent a man from being hanged. I'm glad I saw you before I left.'

'Of course,' I said. 'I will make sure everything runs well in your absence.'

He ran his hand over his face again. 'You can't, Violet,' he said, gently. 'You can't run an agency, a single woman on your own. I know you love it, and I am sorry. We'll need to close it up for a day or two and pick it up when I get back. It would be too dangerous for you to work alone. It will not be long.'

'I can keep the furniture shop open then,' I said. 'People will still need bookshelves. I will simply run the furniture part of the business, until you get back. And type, a little.'

'You can't,' he said. 'You can't, as an unmarried woman, run a shop on your own without a gentleman present. You know it isn't done. People would try to take advantage, without my protection. We are skating around the edges of respectability already. I won't push marriage on you before you are ready, so we will have to shut up shop for a bit. I am sorry. I will be back as soon as I can, and then we will get life on track again. Our life.'

'Of course,' I said. 'You are quite right. I will wait, then, until you get back. Do not worry about me. I will be well. You must go and sort this out.'

'Will you lock up the shop?' he said, and when I nodded, he took his bag and headed out the door, and the bell clanged behind him.

I stood alone in the shop for a while, turning around in a slow circle to look at all the furniture and my little desk in the corner with its smart black and silver typewriter, and contemplated keeping it open despite his words. But it might cause friction between us and if I was brutally honest with myself, if someone bought the heavy travel trunk in the corner, I could not help them carry it out the door. I was still female, despite wanting always to prove I was more.

And I could not operate alone as a detective. I had been foolish even to imagine it, but it felt as if the door to my glorious future was shutting abruptly and I was back to the greyness of life before I had met him, even though it was only a few days and I was being ridiculous.

I locked the shop up safely and went home.

What on earth was I to *do* for the next couple of days? Tapestry? It was not in my nature to sit still. Perhaps it was time I learnt how to wait. I would be humble, self-sacrificing. Patient. Even though I was only mildly religious, I imagined myself on my knees before the altar in my local church, praying for his return. Knitting socks for soldiers. Reading improving texts, crying a little into my pillow as I prayed. Perhaps affection changed one fundamentally as a person. I could join a nunnery, briefly, until he came back. I contemplated my possible futures glumly and then shook myself back to common sense.

I tried to keep myself busy. I went on long walks along the flat promenade and up East and West Hill as speedily as my breath would allow. East Hill was wilder and less frequented while West Hill, with its fancy funicular lift, neatly tended gardens and the ruins of the Castle, was more popular with the day-trippers. On the second day I went further and walked all the way to Fairlight Glen, which included the romantic Dripping Well, set amid rocks clad with lichens and mosses, and the Lovers' Seat, a ledge just below the cliff face, once thought to be the site of a forbidden love story between an officer and a wealthy gentleman's daughter. It was a pretty place, but unfortunately wagonettes came several times a day from Hastings, so there were too many romantic couples looking longingly at the view and cooing at each other for me to stay long.

I hoped to meet with Maria Monk and Miss Turton, whose cases I had once solved and whom I thought I might call friends. Both ladies were such happy spinsters, their lives full of interesting hobbies, and it occurred to me 'spinster' was a poor word for women who did not choose to be with a man. 'Lady Bachelor' might be better, or perhaps 'Sprintster,' which held a delightful, bouncy sense of freedom and forward motion.

I missed Benjamin more than I had expected to. He had only been in my life a year and yet he had dextrously chiselled out a space for himself if not in the centre of my heart, then very close to it. He was a large man and the world seemed much emptier without him, as if a certain quality of goodness in the world had gone. But I was not going to moon about for him. I was not that kind of woman. I was a detective.

Chapter Six

On the third day there was no sign of his return.

I tried for a while reading one of the books in the front parlour, but they were deadly dull, so I lay on the couch upside down instead. Hildebrand came into the room and I righted myself so quickly I ended up sitting on the floor.

'Are you well, miss?' Hildebrand asked. I said I was exercising, and she did not look at me as if I was a fool, as her predecessor would have. Hildebrand was far more domestically adept than I was and seemed content, which was pleasing if worrying, as my previous servant Edith had been consistently dissatisfied and there must have been good reason for it. What if I came down to breakfast one day and Hildebrand was like Edith, simmering with suppressed irritation? It was best to savour her contentment while I could.

Then I struck gold. On a shelf he had a few bound volumes of The Strand newspaper, brought back from his regular visits to the capital. I took them to the parlour and sat cross-legged on the rug by the fire to scour them. I turned the page and came across *The Adventures of Miss Cately*. a series of fictional tales about a singularly independent woman who decided to live a life of adventure. She was not ready to be married! She had splendid adventures all over Europe! She was witty, strong-minded and clever. Her ripostes were superb. She saved an old lady from having her diamonds stolen, and then she travelled to Switzerland to sell *bicycles* and won a bicycle race across a mountain, against two men! She was a lady to be greatly admired. Miss Cately did not bother with chaperones or listen when people told her what to do. She was wonderful. I had to get my own bicycle.

After that I lay on the rug for a while in a starfish shape and stared at the ceiling.

In the afternoon, I decided to take a walk along the seafront to Bexhill, where there was a pleasant pavilion and new scenery. And as I reached the De La Warr Pavilion the Misses Spencer came towards me, arm in arm in puce. I decided this time, they would not cut me. Perhaps part of the cause was mine. I had neglected our acquaintance, not troubling to get to know them at school. I would be gracious and offer them my friendship.

They had always been prim to the point of ridiculousness. Once in the classroom I had recited a love poem by the esteemed seventeenth century poet Andrew Marvell and got no further than the line: *'A hundred years should go to praise Thine Eyes, and on thy Forehead Gaze. Two hundred to adore each breast'*, before they had stood up in unison and walked out of the room, noses to the sky. The teacher, befrilled in white lace, likely as innocent as I, had blushed and said the poem was best kept for married gentlemen. I needed to re-read it, now I understood more about marital relations.

The sisters' rejection was consistent at least, and I had begun to find it entertaining. I had thought it because of my mother's disappearance, which had made me an oddity in society, but my wise fiancé had suggested there might be wider reasons, unrelated to me, and they themselves might be a little lost in life. They were indeed forever burling around town without obvious purpose, and although a year or two younger, were not yet married. Were they reluctant, like me?

I stared at them as they came towards me and did a little dance on the pavement to stop them walking past.

'Good day, ladies,' I said.

They held their parasols in front of their faces, but I still did not let them by, and eventually they had to speak if they were not to make a scene.

'Miss... Hamilton,' one of them said.

'Miss Spencer, Miss Spencer,' I said.

There was an awkward pause.

'Delightful to see you. The weather is fine today, is it not?' I said, although it was blustery, with cold sprays blowing over the balustrade from the sea.

'Middling,' the other sister said. Janice? Jane? Oh, this had been a bad impulse of mine. I was about to get badly frosted.

'I hear you are selling... furniture?' the first one said, her mouth pursed, as if I was odorous.

'I assist at my fiancé's antiques emporium, yes,' I said. 'It is very successful.'

'Hmm... original,' she said. 'And have you been invited to the Harvest Ball?'

'Of course,' I said. 'But I am unlikely to attend. I have another engagement.'

It was not true. I had not been invited. After my mother's disappearance they had gradually dried up. Balls had been first to go, followed by soirees and evening parties, and then, eventually, afternoon teas and musicales. It was perhaps because an absent mother was an odd sort of scandal, or because my company was dour rather than cheerful. I briefly felt the wrench I had felt back then, when I had longed to attend parties while knowing I would be miserable at them.

'You must call on me,' I said, remembering too late how haphazard and old-fashioned our front parlour would look.

One of them made a short sound in her throat, of agreement or ridicule, and the younger twirled to look away, across the street, but that view, of the wall of multifarious advertisements for health cures and sundry entertainments, seemed to please her no better, and she swung back towards me with a huff of sound. There was a pause.

'Let us not pretend,' she said, sharply. 'We do not hold you in high esteem. We never have. You are self-centred and insufferably smug. You engage the affections of men frivolously and you dress five years out of fashion. How can you not care about such things? You do not behave as a lady should. You are hardly even a woman. You wander about town, expecting sympathy for a mother, who abandoned—'

'Pray stop,' I said. 'That is a sour enough recipe of dislikes. I hope you enjoyed cooking it up.'

The older one drew a sharp breath and then said, 'Come, Mabel,' and they circumnavigated me swiftly to continue along the promenade.

Well, then. It explained the snubs. I had not realised the Misses Spencer harboured such strong feelings against me, when I had barely thought of them. At school I had been preoccupied by adventures that might lie ahead, perhaps neglectful of my companions. Life had seemed golden, so glowing with potential, before my hopes had been roundly squashed by my mother's unfortunate revelations of the horrors of marital intimacy, swiftly followed by her disappearance.

At least I had learnt one of the sisters' names. They were an enigma. Last summer, when my friend Mrs Monk had taken me to spy on naked men bathing in the sea to fill a much-needed gap in my education, I had seen a flash of beige skirt and wondered if it was the Spencer sisters, also spying. If so, it was likely they had seen me too, but had given them no sense of solidarity.

It hurt. Insufferably smug? Barely a woman? Well. I had not tried to attract the attention of gentlemen over the years, but they had tried to court me anyway. I did not, it was true, pay as much attention to my dress as other ladies did, because I was above caring about outward appearance. My mother had been all about fashion and beauty, and I was not her. I was practical, forthright, determined. Who dictated what a lady should be? They were foolish girls, the two of them.

I walked home very fast up the hills, seething with indignation and a determination not to care and to never, ever think about the Spencer sisters again.

Chapter Seven

'Did you get an invitation to the Spring Harvest Ball?' I asked my father at breakfast.

'I always do,' he said. 'Come to think of it, you are on the invitation too. Would you wish to go? I did not think you were much interested in parties. In that, at least, you differ from your mother.'

I thought with a pang of all the years he must have received the invitation and not thought to tell me.

'Yes,' I said. It would be something to do, at least. 'If you would escort me. I need to purchase a dress and accessories.'

'Very well, very well. Perhaps Mrs Beeton would like to attend,' he said, and coughed into his cup of tea, to hide his embarrassment. He was still apt to act like a youth in the flush of his first romance whenever her name came up. I liked him for it.

Mrs Beeton, the widow of a local farmer, had come into our lives last spring. I liked her. She was large, loud and loving, bringing the softness into my father's life he sorely needed. She ran Little Ridge Farm with the help of her brothers-in-law and had five daughters, some grown, who she loved abundantly. I wished my father could marry her, even fraudulently.

He spoke with her regarding money. She had had a greatly softening effect on him. Prior to her arrival last year he had been somewhat sparse with household expenses of all kinds, not believing my girlish brain could handle accounts, treating me like an irresponsible client at his bank. But as a consequence of her advice he had raised my household expenses and now gave me a quite remarkable sum for a dress, and it was arranged the three of us would go to the ball.

I sent notes to my new friends Miss Turton and Mrs Monk, whom I had met through solving cases last year, to see if they were planning to attend. Miss Turton could not as she had hurt her leg, but Mrs Monk was planning to go. Perhaps it was for the best they did not meet, as Miss Turton was the soul of innocence and rectitude and Mrs Monk had once been a lady of the night, but somewhere underneath, I felt they might get on.

The Spring Harvest Ball was one of the most anticipated events in Sussex. Lady Brassey was known for throwing balls of exquisite excellence, partly because her husband was an Earl and the Member of Parliament for Hastings. My heart was gladdened to read she had hired a full Hungarian band.

I usually adopted only the bits of fashion that allowed me to move about freely and left off what didn't, such as bustles, but now I wanted to wear a beautiful dress oozing femininity and charm, that would inspire princes to rescue me from high towers and dragons to cry salty tears. I made an appointment with Madame LeFevre, who had been my mother's dressmaker. We argued, because I wanted it to be all frills and furbelows.

'Mademoiselle, you must not look like a Christmas tree,' she said. 'A lady can dress with subtlety, with charm, and look all the more feminine for it. Show the bosom, accentuate the curves, encase them all with simplicity; there is no need for excess.'

We agreed on a dress based on a Paris design of deep blue satin overlain with a design of tiny gold chrysanthemums. It had a low neck, a bodice trimmed with fine lace, and a skirt gathered up at the side with a little trail of dusky pink silk roses. She would make me a black satin cape to travel in. If an evil villain broke into the ballroom intent on destruction, it would be entirely impractical for me to fight him in it. But perhaps it was a test, to see how agile I could be.

There was money left over, so I also asked her to make me a detective dress.

'Made of a hardwearing material like serge, with lots of pockets,' I said. 'Hidden pockets, in the skirt and inside the bodice, where I can put lots of important things, like lock-picking tools. And not too heavy or warm, so I can jump about easily and run up mountaintops.' And because that still didn't use up the budget (I thanked Mrs Beeton silently with all my heart), I also ordered a pair of Turkish trousers in brown velveteen, like the ones Miss Cately wore for cycling. Surely these two items would make up for the frivolity of the evening dress.

It was only one night, I told myself. It would not make me a fribble. And even if it did, at least I was showing people (whose opinion I did not care about) I could be a lady if I chose.

Chapter Eight

My bosom, not small at the best of times, looked buoyant.
I felt very naked.

'What if it gets cold?' I asked Hildebrand, who was coiling my
hair up in intricate curls. She was very competent, and I guessed
she had probably learnt how to do it when she was working in
the brothel, but it did not seem polite to ask. I hoped she would
not accidentally make me look like a wanton woman, too.

'Pish, miss,' she said. 'It will be glad of a night out. Besides,
you will have the silk scarf, and the cape over the top until you
get there. You are like Cinderella, I tell you. All this luscious
chestnut hair, and that figure... I tell you; the men will flock
tonight. Smile at them, and they will fall at your feet. You are
not so good at smiling, but if you do, your Mr Blackthorn had
better watch out.'

I wished with a pang Benjamin could see me at my finest. I had
not heard from him again. He had not seen me in anything but
my day dresses, and even the kindest people would admit they
were past their best. I would like to stun him into a romantic
declaration, even though he, like me, was a pragmatic sort and
not likely to be stunned into passionate words. All the same, I
would like him to see me, stepping round a pile of overcome
gentlemen on the ballroom floor. But he was in Scotland, with
far more serious things on his mind.

'Some rouge for your cheeks,' Hildebrand said.

'No, no need,' I said, shaking my head, and I pinched my
cheeks instead. I added some amethyst earrings and a simple

pearl necklace my mother had, if not exactly given me, then left behind when she fled.

'What a picture!' Hildebrand said, and she clapped her hands together.

'Are you sure I should not put it away?' I said, looking down at my chest, but she shook her head, and it was really too late to do much about it. Perhaps I could balance my cake plate on it.

'I will never be as gorgeous as you, Hildebrand,' I said, 'But I think I am in good form tonight. I hope I get to dance a little. My father should dance with me at least.'

'Enjoy it,' she said. 'You will have plenty of dances. Gather some stories for me while you are there. I shall be glad to hear them.'

I wanted to apologise for living in such a different world to hers, but such conversations could never really be had without awkwardness. I patted her arm instead.

'I am away, then!' I said. It occurred to me those were the last words my mother had said before she disappeared from my life ten years ago. Perhaps I would do the same, vanish in pursuit of joy, abandoning all those who cared for me. Was I heartless enough? I suppressed the brief stab of hurt. 'Don't wait up.'

There were Lords and *Lords*, and Lord Brassey was one of the highest-ranking ones, at the highest level of the peerage. He and his wife could have hosted their ball at either of their grand homes at Normanhurst Court or Beaufort Park, but as both were a long carriage ride out of town, they were hosting the ball in their town mansion, a grand building called Caple-ne-Ferne in Albany Street.

Even though it would only be a twenty-minute walk for us, my father had hired a carriage to pick up Mrs Beeton, who lived further out of town, and then ourselves. It arrived outside our home in St Matthew's Gardens at the appointed hour, the horses snorting and stamping in the damp air, and Mrs Beeton peeked out of the carriage door. She looked splendid, if a little nervous.

'I am not used to occasions as grand as these,' she said when we were settled in the coach. 'My husband was always looking after the farm, and one cannot leave abruptly to help birth a calf. But now my sons-in-law have it all under control, so I am free to go out and about. Isn't it wonderful?' She beamed at us both, so hopeful and so set on seeing the best of life, I felt a sudden rush of fondness for her, and reached out to pat her hand.

'You must dance with Violet first,' Mrs Beeton said to my father. 'I am content to sit and watch mostly, and if I am very lucky, there will be some good cakes at supper.'

'You will dance with me,' my father said. 'At least once, if not twice. We can think about whether propriety will allow us another. But of course, I will set Violet off on the dance floor first.'

As always, there was a slight sting in the way my father spoke about me, as if I was livestock that needed unloading from a cattle cart, but tonight I did not mind. My heart was glad to see how much Mrs Beeton meant to him, because she deserved to be appreciated.

It was a long and impressive path up to the house and we were joined by other carriages, the horses proceeding at a slow walking pace up the drive. The house was lit spectacularly, with light pouring from the windows. I felt an unfamiliar rush of excitement and realised it was because I could freely enjoy the evening without worrying about any missing mothers. Mine was very much alive and in cheerfully good health.

A footman took our wraps and coats, and then we went to the head of the staircase, where Lord and Lady Brassey and their two daughters greeted us. Lady Brassey was Lord Brassey's second wife. She looked composed and confident in her role, greeting us all kindly and dealing with Mrs Beeton's excited effusions with perfect equilibrium. Mrs Beeton could be a little loud, but it spoke of a big and loving heart. And then finally, we were free to descend the staircase into the spectacular ballroom and our evening began.

Chapter Nine

I t was a scene to impress. Exquisite glass chandeliers, lit by electric light, hung from a soaring domed ceiling and sconces along the walls reflected shining warmth into gleaming gold-framed mirrors. There were Greek-inspired columns, temple-like alcoves, silk drapes looping every window and a gleaming parquet floor. Showy gladioli, trumpet lilies and ivy curved up the walls.

The finest of Hastings and St Leonards were here; several lords, viscounts, squires, the town mayor, clerk, alderman and chamberlain, sundry councillors, and more than a gaggle of captains, commanders, majors, lieutenants and lieutenant-colonels, because Hastings and St Leonards was a magnet for those retiring from the army and navy. And of course, their wives.

My dance card was full within minutes. Perhaps it was my dress, or because, affianced, I was safe to dance with; or because I was smiling, or a novelty; for whatever reason, gentlemen flocked. I felt the triumph of it, smiling at the Spencer sisters at the edge of the dance floor. They looked a little wan, in yellow too pale for their complexions.

I danced first with my father, who led with great correctness, whirling me around the floor as if I was a wooden puppet with my joints on hinges. It had perhaps been a while since he had danced with anyone too. After that, was a gentleman so lavishly paunched I could only dance with him at some remove; then Septimus Patmore, an eye surgeon who had once ogled pictures of my mother and tried to blackmail me into marriage, and Jeremy Parchment, whom I had rejected last year and who still looked woeful about it. The guilt struck me anew, as he danced me droopily around the ballroom. 'Seize happiness!' I wanted to say. 'Forget me!' But it was not my place to comfort him.

The next man could not catch the rhythm and believed it to be my fault, trying to jig me into submission to dance out of step. 'It takes time, you'll learn,' he said wearily at the end, heading off to find his next victim. I realised I was not enjoying the dancing as much as I had anticipated. The final straw was when a gentleman, narrow of chin, said, 'Miss Hamilton! You look quite, quite, hmmm hmmm hmmm,' with a sideways smirk, before grabbing my hands too tightly and spinning me onto the floor, and I felt like a piece of juicy steak, oiled for frying, and looked across the floor to see the Spencer sisters smirking too, behind their fans. I had forgotten their other insults. All I had proved was that I flirted with men for the fun of it.

I managed to find respite behind a pillar but – 'You dance too freely in the absence of your fiancé,' a voice said in my ear, and I knew without turning it was Mrs Withers from church, ready to proffer her opinions. From the corner of my eye, I sensed vivid purple and green and a hat proclaiming she had fought with a peacock and won.

'Are you unable to keep your opinions to yourself?' I exclaimed, driven to rudeness because she had hit a nerve. However freely I had danced, I had not enjoyed it. But I had never dared to speak to her so sharply before, and for a second she did not respond. I turned to look at her. Her hat sprouted not only peacock feathers, but a harem of tiny hummingbirds. She was staring out across the dance floor, frowning.

'If I do not moderate your behaviour, who will?' she said, and then was silent.

The dancing continued, fast, a Highland Schottische, ladies and gentlemen skipping frenetically around the floor and occasionally crashing into one another. I was glad not to be part of it. I missed Benjamin fiercely. As well as all his other perfections, he would likely be a good dancer.

Mrs Withers turned to go, a rare thing. I always left her first if I could.

'I am sorry,' I said. I had overturned the dynamics of our relationship, which consisted of her issuing scathing opinions and me ignoring them. I felt a pang of guilt.

She shrugged her shoulders a little and smiled. 'Your bosom is too bare,' she said. 'Your mother would not have dressed so wantonly.' She walked off and left me staring after her. That was patently untrue. My mother had always dressed far more daringly than I, flirting on the edge of what was acceptable; but because she was who she was, she had been admired instead of condemned for it. I wondered what Mrs Withers would say if she knew my mother had once posed for pictures in her underthings.

It was an unsettling exchange. I did not like being rude to Mrs Withers, however rude she had been to me over the years. It brought back a time, not long after my mother's disappearance, when I had attended an afternoon tea party and sat, silent, among the chattering ladies and the teacups, thick tears trapped like a headache behind my eyes, unable to think about anything but where my mother was, if she was alive, hurt or lost; the tea party as unreal as a dream, and Mrs Withers had come over and told me to go home. She had not been unkind then, I remembered. She had merely told me to go home, that no one would mind if I did, and I had gone. She had been the only one to notice I was sad.

I shook off the memories. Mrs Withers' sins outweighed a single kindness a decade ago, and she did not deserve a second's thought. This ball was not going to plan, although I had not had a worthwhile plan at all, in retrospect, beyond proving to the Spencer sisters I was a lady. That had failed, so if I truly wanted to rescue the evening, I should take Benjamin's lessons on board and observe the guests.

There was a group of young people milling around near one of the large windows overlooking the garden, chatting and laughing, and I watched them for a while, assessing the eddy and flow of social interaction. A lady languidly drooping against a pillar, doing not much at all, was the main focus of their attention. Preternaturally pale, she had a mass of thick black hair pinned back loosely at the sides and large, startled eyes. She was not talking much, not smiling, but looked vaguely frightened, like a woodland nymph plucked from a forest unawares and dropped in the ballroom. Her stillness made the activity of the ladies and gentlemen around her look frenzied, as they jostled for space at her side, cracked jokes she did not laugh at and offered refreshments she refused with the tiniest shake of her head. My mother's beauty was a fire warming everyone who came near; this lady's attractiveness lay in a fragility hinting she might snap in two, if people did not rush to save her.

Then I spotted my friend Mrs Monk and forgot nymph lady.

Chapter Ten

Mrs Monk was in her later years, patrician of feature and elegant in bearing. She had sent me to visit Hastings' least salubrious brothel last year, partly out of revenge because I had accidentally insulted her, partly for her amusement. The brothel – also where I had met Hildebrand – was one in which Mrs Monk had worked herself, many, many years ago before attaining respectability in later life. I had retrieved a love letter for her from Hastings Museum and we had forged a friendship because of it. She was clever; she was not to be messed with; and she had also told me everything I desperately wanted to know about marital intercourse. A debt like that was not to be forgotten.

'Are you well?' I asked.

'I am always well,' she said. 'If I am not, it is because I have not eaten an elegant sufficiency or I have walked too far or chosen to imbibe. My health is entirely my responsibility.'

She always talked like that, with a sharp edge, but I knew underneath she possessed a deeper streak of kindness than many, and possibly her asperity came from a life of having to defend herself before she had scarcely begun to live it. I wondered briefly if any of her former clients might be at the ball, but she seemed unconcerned about it.

'Of course,' I said. 'And what do you think of all the advertisements for pills and ointments proliferating around town at the moment?'

'Tosh,' she said. 'Absolute tosh. Do you know Lady Laxton?' And when I shook my head: 'That lady leaning against the pillar over there, interestingly languid and pale. She takes more wonder pills than any other woman in this town, and she looks as if the pillar is the only thing holding her up. Although it's the paint as well.'

'Paint?'

'It's why she looks so white and isn't smiling. The paint might crack. Very fashionable. I think she's used perfume or citrus in her eyes too. Or she actually has consumption.'

So, the sprite was an actual Lady. Her eyes were watering a little at the edges and red rimmed, now I looked. It was mildly fashionable to appear near death, but painful eyes seemed a little extreme. There was a slight flutter among her acolytes when a spindly gentleman bearing a glass of lemonade came to her side. He was older than the rest of the group, not tall, but very thin, and when he offered her the glass, she took it and lapped at delicately with her tiny tongue, like a kitten, as if more than a drop might kill her.

'Her husband,' Mrs Monk said. 'He is very proud of his ornaments.' I glanced at her but she did not elaborate. 'And are you well, Violet? How is your fiancé suiting you?'

'He is everything good,' I said. It was true. I had laughed at his self-confessed perfection, but sometimes I did feel he was a little too much, too big and gentlemanly and everything a man should be. It was daunting, when I was just Violet.

'And your mother? Have you seen her again?' I had told Mrs Monk the story of my frantic race to save my mother from the evil Mr Knight in Buxton, about how she was living with a lady. Mrs Monk had laughed and said, 'good for her', as if it was not shocking at all, which made me think perhaps it wasn't.

'We write to each other,' I said, cautiously. 'There is no rush to meet again.'

'Don't leave it too long to forgive her,' Mrs Monk said, and I looked at her sharply, as she was too perceptive, but then, 'Ah, Mr Twite, you are looking for a dance? I should be delighted,' and Mrs Monk was swept out onto the dance floor, and I was alone again.

I was content. The evening had been more sociable than I had experienced for a long time, and I was a little overwhelmed. I decided to escape to the garden for a little peace.

But there was no peace to be had. As I headed down the terraced steps leading onto the lawn, I heard the sound of someone imitating a duck.

'Quack,' a woman said. 'Quack.'

I should not have stayed. It was obviously a very private, bizarre moment. But I was training to be a detective. I crept closer, hid behind a conifer and listened.

There was a pause, and then the gentleman said: 'Madam. I care greatly for humanity. For people. I am no such thing. Calm yourself.' There was another pause.

'You are a fake. I have the proof, here.' There was a rustling of paper.

'That does not prove anything, Mrs Withers,' he said. Mrs Withers again? Having an argument, in a garden, with a gentleman? Her behaviour this evening was unprecedented. 'Give it me, let me read it. I will explain it all, and you will understand.' His voice was deep, calming, as if he was trying to reason with her.

'No, you are not having it,' she said. There was a rustle. 'I will tell her. I will tell everyone what you are up to.' There was defiance in her voice.

'But it is all nonsense,' the man said. 'You cannot spread such ridiculous rumours. People will think you are unstable. Surely you would not want anyone to know… your emotional state?'

And then Mrs Withers, shockingly, swore at him.

'You bastard,' she said. There was utter silence. I thought the unknown man must be as shocked as I was.

'All I can say is, madam, you will regret it,' the man said, and then there were footsteps moving towards me, so I shot around the conifer and deep under another tree. But it was only the man who passed me, going back into the ballroom, squat and stocky. I could not see his face, but in the light flaring from the sconce outside I saw the tip of a beard, a bushy one, the colour of burnt orange. It was the man I had seen walking with the Spencer sisters on the seafront, whom I had thought must be their father. Several seconds later Mrs Withers passed me. She paused just at the end of the hedge, withdrew a piece of paper from the bosom of her dress, and stuffed it in her reticule before also heading inside.

All was silent. I did not like the note of threat I had heard in the man's voice. Did Mrs Withers need my help? Would she ever? I would have to admit to listening to her private conversation and might get my ear bitten off for the pleasure. But she had sounded so unlike herself, a far cry from the woman who had judged me so gleefully for years. Had they had an affair? It seemed so unlikely, the two of them such odd candidates for romance, but what did I know about romance? I was uncertain of the affections of my own fiancé.

I waited for a few minutes, then went around the terrace and back into the ballroom myself through the main entrance.

I drank a glass of dandelion and burdock and lurked on the fringes of the dance floor. Mrs Monk was dancing. The Spencer sisters made a beeline towards me, and I girded my loins to speak to them, but at the last minute, as if to make a show of it, they took a swift swerve to my right, and spoke instead to a surprised-looking dowager. I did not mind. I found it funny.

'Do you know much about the Misses Spencer?' I asked Mrs Monk on a rare break, but she shook her head.

'Not much,' she said. 'The youngest one was enamoured of a young man once, but I don't think it came to anything. They could do more to occupy themselves. They are forever haring about town with nothing to do.' It was the same assessment Benjamin had made.

'Do you know their father?'

'Dr Spencer? Vaguely. He runs the Hastings Hydropathic

Establishment up in the hill. Fond of getting people to pay for water cures. If I want water, I drink it from the tap or swim in the sea.'

'You are very wise, as always, Mrs Monk,' I said.

'Call me Maria, for goodness' sake,' she said. 'I'm not your schoolteacher.' Despite the sharpness to her tone, I knew it was another step in our friendship. Despite the significant gap in our ages and our experiences of life I felt at some deep level, we understood each other; in her presence I was no longer the foolish ingenue she had met a year ago.

Mrs Beeton was also having a splendid time and was not short of dancing partners. Her delight was infectious. She came back flushed and breathless after each dance, and almost hugged me in her elation. My father was delighted by her joy too. I could practically see years of ice dripping off him. But the matriarchs of good behaviour, grouped like harpies around the buffet table, did not like to see a middle-aged widow enjoying herself too visibly. I saw them muttering and hoped Mrs Beeton did not notice. They were such unimportant curmudgeons and, as the widow of a farmer, she was one of the very few people here actually responsible for a spring harvest.

Mrs Withers would have been the worst to judge, but she was nowhere to be seen. I thought I spotted her husband, a small man with enormous whiskers, patrolling the ballroom, but it was hard to see him properly because he had goblin-like qualities, slipping in and out of the crowds. Had she been accusing Dr Spencer of being a quack doctor? There were plenty of them, peddling fake cures and wonder pills, but not usually at this level of society.

By the time my father called for our carriage, I was very ready to leave. It was one-thirty in the morning, and we did not stay for the last dance, the cotillon. I said a warm goodbye to Mrs Monk. Something of the joy seemed to have left my father, but perhaps it was tiredness. None of us were used to the late hour.

At home, I stretched out full on the bed and stared at the ceiling, contemplating. I had told Hildebrand not to wait up for me, so the challenge lay ahead of unhooking and unravelling myself from my dress, and I needed a few seconds to prepare myself for the battle.

I was not sure if I needed to go to balls again. There were too many currents of emotion eddying around and at times, I had not liked myself much. Then again, I had seen my friend Maria Monk, and her company had gladdened my heart. And as for the other guests, beneath their society faces human beings were not so very far removed from animals, beset by hunger, thirst, the need to belong, to impress, to be noticed and admired. Their behaviour had been fascinating. Perhaps I should frequent balls purely to observe.

I managed to extricate myself from my dress, fell into my nightdress and into bed and into an uneasy sleep.

At approximately three o'clock in the morning I sat up straight, hit by a revelation. I had not entirely enjoyed the evening because I was trying too hard to be a lady, when of course, I was more. I was a Lady Detective, an entirely unconventional beast, a member of a profession which required me to be as ladylike or unladylike as circumstance required. I could embrace femininity only as long as it served me; at other times I would need to forsake it to be brave and bold, daring and agile. Cold-hearted and ruthless. To dispatch criminals efficiently; face life's horrors staunchly without weeping; run, climb, argue, shout and fight; wear trousers or old dresses; forget good manners and do all the things that ladies should not. I was sloughing off the bars of the cages in which women were expected to dwell. I was a lady with a purpose, and if it meant I did not always have the right parasol to match, well, so be it.

The Misses Spencer did not have a purpose, and therefore they despised me. Mrs Withers thought my only purpose was to be a lady, and therefore she tried to clip me into that shape, like a hedge. Their opinion did not matter any more. It was more crucial I cemented my opinion of myself, so it did not wobble about with the wind. What kind of a Lady Detective was I, if I veered off course at the slightest insult?

I lay down again and fell into a mildly better sleep.

Chapter Eleven

The morning after the ball was a Sunday, which meant church, no matter how tired anyone was. The only acceptable excuse for not going was the eruption of giant boils from the plague. My father and I met wearily in the parlour at nine for breakfast and then walked to church together.

It helped that the Reverend Bartle had been a family friend since we had moved to Hastings when I was ten. A gentle man, he had long supported me and guided me in life. Six months ago, I had been hurt to discover he had known my mother was alive and well for many years, and not told me. But I understood he believed it was not his confidence to break and also, because his heart was soft, I knew it had hurt him to keep the secret. He had tried over the years of her absence, I could see now, to comfort and sustain me. When I had told him I had found her, his face had shown joy before it crumpled with guilt, his conscience torn. I was trying to forgive him and succeeding, because he had always been dear to me.

It took me a while, in my weariness, to recognise the rest of the congregation were not merely suffering from the after-effects of the ball or the envy of not being invited. People were whispering to each other, gathering in groups, crossing the aisle to talk to each other when they should have been seated. A couple of young girls were crying and hiccupping, their mothers shoving handkerchiefs into their hands and bidding them be quiet, because emotion was not polite in church. Some tragedy had happened, but because my father and I had arrived late there was no time to ask before the Reverend Bartle took to the pulpit and asked us all to sit down.

He too was worried and white-faced, his hair askew, and he shuffled through his book of sermons for quite a while before he began.

'Mrs Withers. You will know... some of you will know... it is my sad task to impart that... our neighbour, our friend, a member of this congregation for over thirty years... Mrs Withers has left this world. It is with great sadness we must reflect on the suddenness of God's will. We must take comfort in each other, in the knowledge that God is looking after us, walking by our side in this time of distress...' he frowned at his page as if it was not quite right, rooting through it again and coming up with a sermon that tried to comfort, but none of us were ready to be comforted. It was too early, too much of a shock.

Mrs Withers? What on earth? She had been fit and well at the ball, not dancing, but certainly marching around with the same verve she marched everywhere. Was it apoplexy? A coach accident on the way home? I cursed the convention which meant the reverend discussed death without revealing the cause of it. How could she have died? I had spoken to her. She showed no sign of being unwell.

I felt for the Reverend Bartle, because I knew he truly took seriously his calling to help people and felt every ripple of pain in his congregation as deeply as if it was his own. There was something innocent in him too, in that despite dealing with death more than most, he dealt with each one with fresh feeling, as if it was his first.

The service was too long, because all the way through it I wanted to understand. Her threatening conversation with Dr Spencer... what had it been about? Surely it could have had nothing to do with her death. And yet... we had to sing two hymns, and I seethed with impatience to find out. But even when the service eventually ended, there was not much to discover. Nobody knew anything, beyond that she had been found dead on the beach, early in morning, by a fisherman. Anything else was speculation.

We left the church not long afterwards, my father silent by my side. I never knew how he was affected by life's tragedies, because he rarely talked about them. My mother's disappearance had not merited much more than half-a-day's conversation, in eleven years. It was incumbent on men, I supposed, to lead by example with a stiff upper lip. Then again, he had perhaps not felt any great affection for Mrs Withers. On reflection I could not remember him ever having spoken to her, beyond greetings. It had been me she popped up for, with dispiriting regularity. I felt a pang of guilt for the uncharitable thought.

My father bought a later edition of the Sunday newspaper on the way home, so perhaps he had some curiosity. It was short and likely added at the last moment. Her body had been found early this morning among the fishing boats on the Stade, by a 'tanfrock', the name given to the fishermen due to their tanned canvas smocks. So far away? It was a stretch of the beach nearly an hour's walk away from the Ball.

Why on earth had she left the ball and wandered to the beach? It was not a warm night. Had she had her coat on? Where had her husband been? I was fiercely glad I had apologised for being rude and she had topped it with another criticism; otherwise, I would have been left with everlasting guilt.

But what had the fraught conversation with Dr Spencer been about? He had questions to answer, I was sure. Maybe she had left the Ball because of his threats, marched off into the distance and somehow met with an accident. But why had her husband not been with her?

How had she died? Death was not uncommon in our small town of fifty thousand people or so. These were dangerous times still, with so much illness, sickness and death, even though medicine had improved remarkably. The new world, our great British Empire of innovation and invention, was not without its dangers. Only the week before a waiter had been crushed by one of the new service lifts installed in the Queen's Hotel. But there was nothing so obvious about this death. Mrs Withers had been so rudely alive at the ball. It did not seem possible for it to end so abruptly.

Why had she travelled so far? It made no sense. She lived barely a street away from us and, to my knowledge, rarely willingly ventured to the rougher side of town. She was a St Leonards lady through and through, despising anyone who needed to make a living in the open air. Why had she even left the ball?

I had seen death a few times, but usually only in a coffin, the person neatly curated to look their best for visits. My grandmother, who had died when I was five, had not looked much different in her coffin than out. And then there had been the evil Mr Knight, who had threatened harm to me and my mother and been dispatched to the bottom of a cave by my mother's lady friend last summer. I had not stayed long to see his body. I would need to get used to such things, if I were to be any good at my profession.

I had not expected death so close to home. I remembered her quiet, unassuming husband, a small man with whiskers, who had often appeared at my side and whisked her away just after she had made a particularly choice insult. Had he known her ability to offend? Had she offended others? I wondered what his life would be like without her forceful presence.

The resolution slowly formed in my mind. Even though I had not been employed to investigate, would likely never be, was currently forbidden to operate as a detective, it would behove me to find out what had happened to poor Mrs Withers. I had a duty, perhaps, to find out a little more, perhaps as compensation for being impolite to her the night before.

I went to the beach.

Chapter Twelve

It was close to lunchtime by the time I made it to the Stade, where the fishing boats lay. Hastings was rare in not having a harbour. The council had attempted to build one only the year before at great inconvenience to everyone, but the unevenness of the seabed and rising costs had led to failure; now only half a harbour arm stretched like a half-buried skeleton across the shingle, the project abandoned. For centuries past the fishermen had had to pull their lug-rigged sailing boats at least ten feet down the shingle each day and back up again, a feat only achieved with the power of a horse or several men, sliding the boats across greased wood.

The narrow black-tarred wooden net shops, built tall to save space and store the fishing nets, stretched below the East Cliff, and before them on the brow of the beach lay the fishing fleet, hundreds of small boats, their sails sharp triangles against the sky. Opposite the Queen's Hotel were heaped the barrels and fish-boxes of the open-air fish market. This part of the beach was crowded, less popular with day-trippers but full of the day-to-day bustling business of the town.

The fishermen caught herring in winter and mackerel in summer. Today there was a herring auction on the beach, several piles of them in front of each boat, bantered and argued over by public and shopkeepers alike. Further along, a group of men were pushing a boat out to sea, their backs up against it, shouting instructions and complaints. Another crowd were sorting out a pile of drift nets entangled together by wind and sea. There was washing strung out to dry between some of the boats, as the fishermen's wives took in laundry from the guest houses. It was full of life and activity and it felt impossible someone's life had ended there only earlier this same morning.

The seagulls were loud, whirling and shrieking overhead and perched on the railings of the promenade. The late morning sunshine was turning the paving stones red-brown, and there were the usual smatterings of Old Town smells drifting through the air: burning wood, drying fish, frying bacon, horse manure, bleach and below it all, the scent of the sea.

I did not know any of the fishermen and I felt at a serious disadvantage. They were strong men, weathered by storm and sea. I had never needed to struggle for life and survival as they must do on a daily basis; never had to face the harshness of storms and shipwrecks; spend days at sea at a stretch or seen relatives drown. To add to it I was not only female but a lady, covered in a delicate fairy dust coating of gentility and ignorance. I was doing my best to shake it off, but in comparison to the fishermen, I was a frivolous flibbertigibbet.

I approached a man who looked less intimidating than the rest, perhaps because he was not a fisherman but a boatman, repairing the rudder of the pleasure yacht The New Skylark. I asked him if he had heard of the tragedy and if he knew where it had taken place.

He shrugged his shoulders further down the beach. 'Over there,' he said.

'Do you know what happened?'

'Lady died,' he said, and turned back to his work.

'Where exactly?' I said, and he put down his chisel and looked at me, long and hard, and then pointed further down the beach again.

'That way,' he said. 'Though as far as I'm aware, they're not selling ice-cream,' and I realised I looked like a day-tripper, coming to admire the gory scandal of the day.

'Thank you most kindly,' I said, cringing at my own words,

and tripped off down the beach, feeling exactly as if I were twirling a parasol even though I had not brought one.

I approached a man drying a freshly treated oilskin on the outrigger of his punt, and another sewing a sail, and by slow perseverance I managed to find out exactly where it had happened and where she had lain, but nothing more. No one was keen to talk to me.

Mrs Withers had been found lying near two small boats called the Swiftsure and the Mary Jane, whose owners were nowhere in sight. The area was not marked off and there was no sign to show she had been there. I supposed it was because the business of the day had to continue, and the police must have done all the necessary investigations, but it felt strange, all evidence removed so completely within hours of her discovery. The boats were moored above the high-tide mark, so the evidence could not have been washed away by the tide. It was an area of shingle exactly like all the shingle stretching for miles on the beach. There was plenty of dried seaweed and some pieces of old burnt rope, but nothing else.

I felt a mild shame overwhelm me, a not unfamiliar feeling that nothing I did could be as serious as the lives of these men. Especially the one who was sitting in the door of his net hut, his face brown with sun and weather even though it was only early March, smoking his pipe and watching me.

'Curious, aren't you?' he said, eventually. 'Did you know her?'

'A little,' I said. 'She was… an acquaintance.' My every word sounded prim. 'Do you know who found her?'

He shook his head. 'I don't know why you're here, miss, but the police have taken her away and there's nowt else to see. Best you go and keep your pretty frock away from the fish, if you're not planning on buying any.'

My frock was not pretty, it was very old and serviceable, but I got his point and left.

★

Feeling the full force of my uselessness, I decided to take a detour from my enquiries and call on the second friend I had made last year, Miss Turton, who lived in a tall apartment further along the seafront, near the pier, and ask after her wellbeing, because she had hurt her leg.

'It is entirely my fault!' she said cheerfully, when I was admitted to her parlour, which was full of chirping caged birds. 'I have bought a bicycle. Oh, it was quite wonderful, until I fell off! I will try it again just as soon as I am better.'

She looked pretty in lavender chiffon, her fluffy grey hair interspersed with a small garland of purple flowers, her expression showing she was (as always nowadays) hugely excited by everything and glad to be alive, despite any injury to her leg. She was in her middle years, happily unattached, well-off and living alone, pleasantly occupied with living life fully. I had helped her last year to rid herself of a mildly crooked suitor whom she had never really wanted to marry, and friendship had followed.

'It is SO delightful to see you!' she said, beaming with genuine pleasure and taking my hands in hers. 'I was so sad to miss the ball, and the dancing. I do hope a gentleman or two would have asked, even though I am no longer in my first flush of youth. I do love dancing. I sat here and thought of you all.'

I smiled because in her company the world was a lovely place, purely because she believed it was.

'Please tell me about your bicycle,' I said. 'I have long wanted to ride one. Did you feel very free on it? Did you cycle very fast?' I had thought for some time a Lady Detective should know how to ride a bicycle. If I solved a lot of cases successfully and could afford it, I would even consider purchasing one myself. There was something so very business-like and professional about a bicycle. There had been a lot of kerfuffle in the newspapers in recent years about whether women's cycling dress (divided skirts or knickerbockers) was unwomanly and whether cycling gave ladies unattractive levels of independence, but Public Opinion, always the arbiter of good behaviour, seemed to be coming round to the idea. I had even read an article by a doctor who said he saw no physical harm in it.

'It is a safety bicycle,' Miss Turton said. 'It is so impressive. It has brakes to stop the bicycle wheels from spinning when you want to stop. I am planning to learn to ride it properly just as soon as I am able. The promenade in the early morning is perfect, as it is so straight and flat. Perhaps you might like to come and try it with me? So many ladies cycle nowadays, it must be entirely respectable.'

'I would love to,' I said fervently. 'My friend Mrs Monk might like to try too. Do you think the three of us could have a bicycling morning one day soon? I am sure you would like her.'

Miss Turton agreed, and then we had lunch and cake, which this morning was Strawberry Toasts – bread soaked in cream, covered in strawberries and fried in butter – and Frangipane. I felt mildly ashamed enjoying myself when Mrs Withers had died so recently, but I was reluctant to disturb Miss Turton's contentment.

Eventually I told her.

'Oh goodness!' she said. 'That is terrible. I confess I did not know Mrs Withers, but I knew of her. I had heard she was a lady of... robust opinions. A very good quality to have, isn't it? To be entirely certain of one's view of life. I confess I am often quite unsure of things. My views are like clouds, scudding across the sky.'

'There is merit in both approaches,' I said. 'Did she make enemies, do you think?' Why did I ask the innocent Miss Turton, when I did not even know how Mrs Withers had died? I was not sure. I only wondered what other people thought of her.

'Oh, I hope not!' Miss Turton said. 'She was never nasty. She just knew how the world should be. I had a small contretemps with her once – not even a contretemps really, just a slight inconvenience – without ever meeting her, because I had ordered some silk ribbons for a hat in a lovely shade of rose, and when

Mrs Withers saw the ribbon at the milliners, she insisted on having it. The milliner was most distraught about it. But I forgave Mrs Withers quite easily, because hats were very important to her. And one has to admire someone who loves hats.'

I envied Miss Turton her charitable views. I had always, if I was honest with myself, been privately disparaging about Mrs Withers' enormous hats. It had been amusing.

I took my leave of Miss Turton and headed home, to find a letter from Benjamin waiting for me.

Chapter Thirteen

I t had been nearly a week since I had seen him. I curled down in our most comfortable chair to read it.

He had very strong, confident handwriting, and I could see him clearly in my mind as I read it. The letter felt like him, and yet not him.

> *Violet,*
>
> *Things are moving slowly here. I have to give some evidence to a lawyer, and he is keeping me waiting. I shall stay only as long as I have to, and then hasten home to you.*
>
> *Meanwhile, it occurs to me that because our relationship began on a business footing, I have not wooed you enough, my lady.*
>
> *Therefore... know I miss you, your cheekiness, your laughter, your firm opinions, the way your mouth quirks when you disagree with me. The way you hold yourself straight against the world, determined to face any challenges in your way. The strand of your chestnut hair which comes loose from its pins to curl against your neck.*
>
> *You make a very fine sleuth, I think. You are fearless, and curious. You make my heart stop with the risks you take, but please remember you are not just looking after your own wellbeing now. You risk mine, because you are precious to me.*
>
> *Yours, Benjamin*

Was it a love letter? It was certainly an affectionate letter. He had said the first time I met him he was a practical man, but this was not a down-to-earth letter. His proposal had been lovely, but part-born out of necessity, because we had to be engaged at the very least to work together. He had not thrown himself at my feet or shown himself to be suffering great and painful transports of love on the train back from Buxton. And I was generally a pragmatic lady too, who did not expect great romantic declarations and wooings. My mother had been the dramatic one. I was resigned to life being a little less... flowery.

All the same, the letter made me feel... flushed. I took it upstairs and hid it in my bedside table.

Later on, I wrote a reply.

> *Dear Benjamin,*
> *Thank you for your wooing. I think you will find my hair is mahogany rather than chestnut, but you can examine it on your return. You have very fine eyes.*
> *I know I will make a good sleuth. I will not be content to be anything else. I am frustrated not to be sleuthing with you now.*
> *I hope you are well and everything is going to plan.*
> *Kindest regards,*
> *Violet*

He did have fine eyes, although I did not know how to describe them, other than he had long dark lashes, too long for a gentleman perhaps, and I liked them, especially when he was laughing. I drew him a little heart at the end of the letter, and then I scribbled over it and made it into a small bird singing, because really, was he a man to appreciate hearts? Was I? For a long time, I had not anticipated, had actively avoided romance in my life, and to find it coming from such an unexpected quarter – from a man I was already engaged to, no less – was discombobulating.

*

I was still determined I would look into Mrs Withers' death. Even if I could not impress the fishermen, there must be some point to my being female, some advantage to it. Benjamin said women were better at observation, so this might give me an avenue. I was not widely known in town as a Lady Detective yet, so I could watch people and ask a few questions. The police would be looking into it all very thoroughly of course and might already have answers... but no one would suspect a curious woman of being anything but a busybody.

I decided to visit the library first to read more newspapers, although such a trip usually filled me with heavy dread, because I had once refused the head librarian, Mr Gallop, in marriage, and the injury remained in his memory as painfully as if I had sawn off his left leg.

The library was on the ground floor of the Brassey Institute, and at first, I thought I would be successful, as it was the deputy librarian, Miss Lipscombe, on duty. But then Mr Gallop appeared from nowhere, sidling in front of her. 'I will handle this, Miss Lipscombe,' he said. '*Miss* Hamilton. How may we help you?'

I could not see his mouth, as it lurked under a handlebar moustache as big as the hoof of a cart horse.

I had made a list in my head. 'I am just here to read the daily newspapers,' I said, 'The Police Gazette and the Strand' – but he was already shaking his head in a familiar way.

'The newspapers are already being read by a gentleman, *Miss* Hamilton,' he said.

'Well, he can't read them all at once, can he?' I said. 'I can read one of them, while—'

'No, no,' Mr Gallop said. 'He comes in every day at eleven, and reads all the papers, one after the other. I wouldn't want to disturb his routine. Perhaps if you come back this afternoon, although Mr Harper reads them then.'

'You surely cannot make your newspapers available to only two persons a day,' I said, 'That is not economic.'

It was a mistake. I had given him fodder for argument. He smiled.

'We are a public library, not a shop,' he said. 'We do not hire out our newspapers by the half-hour. Although I anticipate you would be slower to read than the gentlemen, as there are a lot of serious articles in them. Perhaps one of the ladies' circulars might suit better?'

'No, it is the newspapers I want,' I said. 'How about over luncheon?'

'We close for an hour,' he said. 'But this is an academic discussion. There are other reasons. I would not want you to muss them up.'

'Muss them up?'

'Get powder on them and suchlike. Loose cosmetics. I know what ladies are like. You will open up your powder puffs, fold up the corners or doodle on them as you read. No, I think not. The gentlemen must not be disturbed.'

I was not going to engage with his nonsense.

'Books, then. I would like to withdraw a book on ju-jitsu, two of the latest detective fiction novels,' I said, 'Any books you have on locksmithing and one on theatrical make-up.' It was an eclectic selection, but I was under pressure.

'You can only get four books out at one time,' he said, 'And sadly, you are over fond of asking for books on alarming subjects. None of these topics are in any way suitable for an unmarried lady. I can recommend the horticulture section. Or perhaps, to return to magazines, The Ladies Gazette? It is instructive as to how the gentler sex should conduct themselves.'

His smirk was so triumphant it peeked out of the edges of his hoof. But he was not usually quite so irrational. There was an air of anger about him today, as if he was spoiling for a fight.

'I thought libraries were supposed to be for instruction, for enlightenment?' I asked. 'You lock up your books as if knowledge is dangerous.'

'Women's minds are as delicate as unfurling flowers,' he said.

'Allowed to explore the dark forests of knowledge alone, they are easily corrupted. Especially if there is a tendency towards instability. If you had a husband to guide you, I might consider it, but you do not, do you? So, there we are.'

A wave of rage surged up inside me and I straightened as tall as my five foot four would allow. 'You will not deny me books,' I said, stabbing my forefinger in the direction of his chest. 'This is a public library, and I will have them.'

'Bold words,' he said. 'But pointless. You will not.'

I clenched my fists. 'You have let our past affect your professionalism, sir. Mark my words, the time will come when I will have any books I choose.'

He simply smiled again and fluffed his moustache upwards, as if stroking the bottom of a baby rabbit, and it was his final gesture, the smugness of it, that led me to commit the worst mistake of my life.

Chapter Fourteen

I stewed in bed for three whole hours before giving up on sleep. Who did he think he was, denying me books? What gave him the right, simply because he had a moustache, a deep voice and a job I would have cherished and done better myself, to decide what I should and shouldn't read? All he was doing was proving wholeheartedly how right I had been not to marry him.

I had seen, even six years ago, his pompous pomposity, his need to make up for his own defects by squashing other people's joy. I had met him only once or twice before he had proposed, without prior courtship or indication of his affections, by taking gifts to my father in my absence; a solid silver watch for my father and a silver bracelet for me, the ugliest bracelet I had ever seen, thick and heavy, entwined with awkward swans, a manacle around my wrist. I had returned them both, to my father's disappointment, as he had liked the watch.

After he had gained parental permission Mr Gallop had proposed to me, expecting instant acquiescence, and made somewhat of a fool of himself when I declined. Spittle had formed at the corners of his mouth and he had lost his dignity. I felt he resented me as much for those private, mortifying moments as anything else. I had tried to ease matters by sharing as many defects as I could invent, hinting I was likely to disappear from the marriage much as my mother had done, but he had seen the whole matter as an insult to himself and his magnificence, ranting at my ignorance. But he was married now to some unfortunate woman, his moustache larger and more impressive.

It had all happened so long ago. There were so many reasons he should let the past lie.

Public libraries were a great modern innovation; there was no subscription fee nowadays, and prime ministers had trumpeted about their benefit to the masses. There was no decree for librarians to behave like moral guardians. The fury grew in me, a rage fostered by injustice. I had glimpsed a better life as a lady detective, when I could control the wheels of my fate, and even in Benjamin's absence I did not want to clamber back in my cage again. I knew I would not sleep unless I did something about it.

Last year I had broken into Hastings Museum at night-time, with Benjamin, to solve a case for Maria Monk. It had been easy, a child's game; a window with a broken latch, and we had climbed in, taken a love letter hidden inside a ship (not stealing, as it was a letter rightfully belonging to her) and climbed back out again. The museum, by coincidence, was in the same building as the library, just across the corridor.

It would be no hard task, surely? To nip in, and take a book or two, and then hand them back casually a few weeks later, at the front desk, to show Mr Gallop that when I wanted a book, I got it. I would only take one or two. Or five, perhaps, because he had said I should not have more than four. I would take five of the books I wanted and saunter up to return them, never explaining how I had got them. I could envision it now, the confusion in his face, the bitterness. It would be glorious. But it was foolish of course. I was being utterly foolish, and I would never do it.

The frustration would not go away, though. I had been insulted by the Spencer sisters, danced with unsavoury men, spent hours locked in an oast house, and none of it had affected me on such a visceral level as Mr Gallop had, with his edicts. It was power, wielded so carelessly, just because he was a man and could.

An hour later, at one o'clock in the morning, I got dressed in my new detective dress, found my lock-picking tools, which

Benjamin had kindly taught me how to use, and went to burgle the library.

It was a cold Monday night and lonely to be running through the dark streets without Benjamin. But I was propelled by anger and determination. I was a detective, an adventurer. I kept close the anticipation of Mr Gallop's face, crushed by my victory. Maybe his moustache would shrivel a little when I laid out the six books on the desk, one by one – yes, six, because it was best to have a goodly, visible number – and when he asked where I had got them from, I would smile, just smile, and walk out. Or maybe I would say something clever like, 'Did you even miss them?' or 'Am I late in returning them?' or… but no. A simple, mysterious smile, perhaps a quick raise of my eyebrows, would work best.

A fox crossed the road ahead of me, lit by the moonlight, and it stopped and regarded me for a second, pricking up its ears.

'I am working too,' I said to it, nodding as if we were two night-watchmen on duty. I thought it acknowledged my place in the night-time world before it slipped away smoothly into the trees.

I was a foxtress too, a brave night creature stalking silently through the streets of St Leonards to hunt down my prey. I was a detective on a mission, solving a case of an obnoxious librarian. I was fighting for the rights of all women to read what they wanted, at any time. I was fierce, and feisty.

My bravado lasted as long as it took to break in.

Nothing was as easy as the time before. There were no broken latches or easily accessible windows on the library side of the building, so I had to clamber in through the same window as before, thankfully not repaired, which led into the museum, and it was harder in a skirt. Then I had to work out how to get out of the museum and across the corridor into the library in relative darkness. As I clambered in through the window, I got entangled with the catch and tore my new skirt at the bottom, a tragedy I felt deeply.

I had brought my lock-picking tools with me, but they were big, heavy locks and it was difficult to see, and it took me too long to unlock my way out of the museum and into the library. My fingers were sore, and the silence of the whole place seemed oppressive. I dropped my tools and the clatter of them on the floor made me jump out of my skin even though I watched it happen. It had been so romantic last time, so much of an adventure, because I was with Benjamin. Nothing serious could happen with him at my side. Being alone also gave me too much time to reflect too deeply on my stupidity. But eventually, I managed it.

The moon had gone in, so the whole library was cast into murky gloom. I had not thought – had I really planned anything? – I would need light to see the books. I had not even thought to bring a box of matches. Instead, I worked my way down the shelves, pulling out random books and taking them nearer the windows to see the titles, but it took too long, and suddenly the fright came upon me that Mr Gallop might live above the library, or opposite it, see the movement and come to investigate, and then I would have deal with him and his angry moustache, trotting out of the darkness. It was terrifying. After several more minutes I took three books I wanted and two I didn't look at, bundled them into my satchel and made to leave the quicker way, through the library windows. I didn't want to go back the way I had come. There was a book on the desk near the window, so I took it too.

Sadly, the windows opened straight onto empty air, with an open basement a storey below. Clambering out required either a substantial drop or a balancing on railings to reach the pavement, neither of which seemed wise. I thought about it and then chose the far window, nearest the steps leading up to the library, where if I was clever, I could perhaps dangle a little from the windowsill and stretch out a foot to the uppermost step. It was a risk, but I would rather be impaled on railings than risk going back through the library and seeing Mr Gallop.

I managed it. Or would have managed, if I had checked my surroundings more carefully again before I chose to exit the window. As my foot reached the upper step and I manoeuvred myself carefully over the railings to stand, like a ballerina doing a pirouette, I found myself in the arms of a policeman, and my satchel caught on his shoulder and tipped on its side, scattering books across the steps.

Chapter Fifteen

Constable Carruthers was confounded. He put me down quite quickly.

'Madam,' he said. 'Are you stealing library books?'

I crouched down to pick everything up and thought things through, fast.

'I am just borrowing them,' I said. 'I plan to return them. I got them out, legally, earlier today, and simply forgot to take them with me. So, I'm just collecting them. I don't sleep very well without a book.'

He raised his eyebrows at the weakest excuse ever known to womankind but did not ask for another. Then he showed he was a better class of man.

'Best put them back,' he said. 'If you've only gone one step outside the museum, I don't think anyone can call it theft. Here, put them through the letterbox, and then no one needs ever know. I don't know why you're taking them, madam, but if you're going to commit a crime it's an odd one, and I'd rather not arrest you. Anyone can see you're a lady.'

It was the best solution, because it didn't involve informing Mr Gallop. I would rather be tortured to death by a horned devil or eaten by rats than imagine the satisfaction in his hairy librarian face. There were some benefits to being a lady, then. They were purloined in panic and probably no use for my investigative work. I relinquished them, and he put them in the box.

'I will take you home,' he said.

'No, no, there is no need,' but he would not hear of anything else.

'It is not a town for a young lady to be wandering around late at night alone. Did you not hear about the lady who was found on the beach last night? I'll see you home, and whatever reason you were running around the streets, best forget it.'

'Mrs Withers?' I said. 'I knew her. Do you know what happened to her yet?'

He did not answer, only frowned across the whole of his face, and something about his expression told me he did not think it was an accident.

'It's a sad business,' he said. 'Best not to trouble yourself about it. Let's get you home. Do you still live with your father? I will have to speak to him.' He would not be swayed on it and he took me right to my front door and knocked the knocker very loudly, so it thundered through the house.

Hildebrand answered and I hoped my father might not wake, but he was right behind her. His face still crumpled with sleep, he looked at me as if I was a changeling.

'Violet, what have you done?' he said.

'I was just getting some books out of the library,' I said. 'There is no damage done. All the books have been returned already. No one needs ever know.'

My father and the constable exchanged a look of incomprehension.

'The library at night?' my father said. I wanted to tell them both Mr Gallop was a dictator but bringing his name into it might encourage the Constable to contact him in some way and I wanted nothing more than this whole sorry episode to be forgotten.

'She is a little naive...' my father said. 'Probably just wanted books, although why not in the daytime...' and I felt the hopelessness of being a sex automatically lacking in reason. 'But if this comes out... it will ruin her. She is respectable, of good breeding... her reputation would not recover. Need watching, of course... the doctor... a period of rest... do not think there was any malice... Can I perhaps, persuade?' and he was rifling in his pockets for his wallet, but the constable proved he was a good man again by shaking his head.

'No, no,' he said. 'I will keep it quiet. I can see how something like this would damage the young lady's reputation. But she will need watching, as you say... And if anything like this occurs again...' They looked at each other and nodded in silent accord, and then the constable took his leave.

'What in God's name were you doing?' my father said, once we were alone.

'I was only borrowing a few books,' I said. 'Mr Gallop is a despot and will not let me have them.' It did not sound convincing, but I did not know what else to say.

My father frowned and shook his head. 'Violet, you are a grown woman. When will you begin to act like one?'

I shrugged in an unladylike manner and went to bed. I was tired of him, of his relentlessly unloving strictures, his rules, his narrow-mindedness about who I was and what I could be. We had thoroughly outgrown each other. There had to be a solution in life which meant I did not have to live with him or be forced to marry my fiancé before I was ready.

I was exhausted and humiliated, and worst of all, the truth was beginning to dawn. I had been an idiot.

Chapter Sixteen

The morning dawned grey and bleak, rain lashing the windows. I rose late, washed in the tepid water in my pitcher, and donned my most respectable dress, at least three years' out of date. I needed to repair the skirt of my new detective dress, perhaps order another, if I could afford it. When I had eaten breakfast and reassured Hildebrand I was well after my midnight adventure, I got up to go out. I thought I would feel a great deal better for being buffeted about in the foul weather, to wash away the embarrassment. But as I passed my father's study, he called out my name.

I did not go into his domain very often. It was a gentleman's study, full of books, the walls covered in maps, a barometer, a cabinet of gentlemanly ornaments.

He looked weary.

'We need to talk about last night,' he said. 'I will ask the doctor to come and speak to you, to see if there is something... amiss. But this was wild, Violet. What on earth possessed you?'

I had thought, overnight, of a hundred and twenty lies more believable than the truth. I could lie well, when life required it. I had thought it might make me a good detective, but today I was feeling far from confident.

'Mr Gallop never allows me to get any books out,' I said, instead. 'He is resentful I did not accept his proposal of marriage nearly six years ago, and he will not permit me to withdraw any books. It is a public library; I should be permitted to read the books in it.'

'But can't you see,' my father said, 'how utterly out of

proportion it is, to break into a library in the middle of the night? How discovery of such a matter would ruin you, completely ruin you? It is the kind of act to land you in the asylum. It goes against all decency, all—'

'All right,' I said. 'It was perhaps a little in excess. I was just feeling... angry.' But now my father was looking at me as if I might foam at the mouth. 'I will not do it again. I am quite calm now. I didn't really want them after all. I am just going out for some fresh air...'

'No.' He stood too. 'No, you will stay at home. Today is not a day for gallivanting. You need to rest and reflect. I will ask Dr Button to come and speak to you. I hope young Mr Blackthorn returns soon. The sooner you are back under his influence, the better.'

'I am twenty-nine,' I said. 'You cannot restrict my actions as if I were a naive eighteen-year-old. I may have made a mistake—'

'Yes, you have,' he said. 'This behaviour will have consequences. When it comes to your welfare, I cannot allow you to destroy your own reputation so carelessly. As I say, I will discuss the matter with those who care for your wellbeing as I do. From now on, you will be accompanied when you go out. Meanwhile, content yourself with reflecting on your behaviour.'

I was furious my father still thought he could speak to me like this, as if I were a wayward child rather than a grown woman, and I thought the time was near when I would not allow him to. But meanwhile...

'If I must see a doctor,' I said, 'can I see Dr Spencer?'

My father was well aware our family physician Dr Button was past his best. The esteemed doctor was fond of ferreting through a tattered manual forty years old to prescribe leeches and botanical concoctions from the Regency era. His primary cure for women's mysterious ailments was forced bedrest. Women were not ill if you couldn't see them.

'Dr Spencer seems good enough,' my father said. 'Works at the Hastings Hydropathic Establishment. Likes a decent brand of cigars. I'll enquire. Perhaps you could take a rest cure there.'

'My friend Miss Turton has stayed there for a few days and found it very healthful, I believe,' I said. 'I don't need to rest, but I would be happy to stay a day or two.'

Miss Turton had mentioned being hosed down with cold water, which was not so appealing, but I was sure I could face any treatments womanfully, if it would help me in my goal.

I stayed at home all day and despite best efforts, self-reflections on my behaviour were numerous and harsh. What kind of a professional detective was I, to break the law for no other reason than spite? To risk all I had gained over the past year, for revenge on a man who was fundamentally unimportant? I had been foolish and naive. I needed to prove I was somebody the world could take seriously and I had gone entirely the wrong way about it. I had heard of women's suffrage and the battle was not best fought by being a fool.

The *Hastings Observer* finally arrived to distract me, the whole third page dedicated to Mrs Withers. It said more about her standing in the community than her death. It talked about how much she would be missed; her role as Chairwoman of the Hastings and St Leonards Society for the Rescue of Itinerant Travellers; had regularly helped organise the Harvest County Fair; was a stalwart supporter of her local church (would the Reverend Bartle agree? She had been very argumentative about the flowers).

Who would mourn her? Her husband of course, but who were her close friends? I realised we had always been at loggerheads since my mother disappeared; Mrs Withers chiding, me resenting, and I could not remember what our relationship had been like when my mother was around or if I had even noticed her. Had my mother liked her?

Her husband was a retired colonel in the army. I wondered

what he made of her, his bullish wife, with her opinions on everything and everybody around her.

The obituary included comments from the great and the good of St Leonards: the mayor, the town alderman, an army major, sundry other military and marine gentlemen. They described her as the mainstay of the community, a stanchion of good causes, a bulwark of her local church, as if she was a ship sunk in a storm. There were not many comments from women, but perhaps they feared an outpouring of the same mawkish sentiment that forbade women from attending funerals.

I wondered if Benjamin might come back in time to attend instead and watch the mourners. Now why was I thinking that? It was only the look on the constable's face when I asked what had happened, and the conversation she had had with Dr Spencer. She had not lasted very many hours after that conversation. It made me wonder.

And as if I had conjured my fiancé from the sky just by thinking of him, the next morning I received a note to say he was back.

Chapter Seventeen

I raced to the shop a little faster than a lady should.

He was inside. I paused for a second, irresolute, a little shy, because I had not seen him for two weeks and he had sent me a very romantic letter. He was already hard at work, sitting at an oak desk repairing a small carriage clock. He had a hint of stubble, and his sleeves were rolled up to his elbows. Flaunting his strong forearms, as he often did. I was very fond of his forearms.

He looked at me and his face lit up.

'Ah,' he said. 'I've missed you. Come here, wench.'

'I think you may have mistaken me for someone else,' I said.

'Light of my life, woman of my heart, goddess of my most fervent dreams. You have captured my soul and my spirit. Come here.'

'Those are lovely words, cleverly arranged, but most unlike you.'

'Violet Hamilton, Lady Detective, exemplary typist, will you come over here and help me with this carriage clock? Some of the springs are too small for my fingers.'

I gave in and wended my way over to him, and he pulled me onto his lap and kissed me with unexpected fervour. For a short while I forgot about time, about everything, except this large, surprising man, and my feelings for him.

'Coffee,' he said after a while, and went to make it.

I occasionally, quite often in fact, battled with a desire to open his shirt, button by button, until I could see his chest. I was beginning to be very certain I would not find marital intimacy with a man distressing in the way my mother had. Benjamin had dark hair on his chest. I had seen it once, when we had been a little overcome with passion and I had unbuttoned the top two buttons, just the first two, before he had called things to a halt for propriety's sake. It would never do for me to be too forward and insist. Which was a shame, because today, I would really like to unbutton more.

'You have gone quiet. What are you thinking?' he said, bringing the coffee. 'What have you been up to?'

'Oh, this and that,' I said. 'But tell me first about you. What happened in Edinburgh?'

'There's a story to it. When my father was alive, around a year-and-a-half ago, he was given a case to watch a woman who was living in Bexhill, report on her movements, where she was going, who she was with. It was an Edinburgh man, an advocate, similar to a barrister down here, and she was his wife. He wanted every detail, too much, almost – I was working with my father then, and we had to follow her everywhere. It seemed a straightforward case.'

His coffee was the best, as always, and I sipped it slowly, savouring the bitterness and the warmth.

'She did nothing out of the ordinary. Her name was Mrs Fraser. Ellen Fraser. She went to the beach, to the teashop on Rock-a-Nore which all the ladies go to, she bathed in the sea occasionally, from a carriage and always on her own. She did nothing untoward. She didn't seem interested in making friends. She was a quiet woman, younger than him, timid, almost. She mostly seemed glad to be on holiday by the sea.'

'What happened?' I asked.

'After about two weeks of sending daily reports showing she was behaving exactly as a married lady should, he told us to bring her back. Because she had left him, and he had given her her space, let her have her fun, he said... but now he wanted her back.'

'And?'

'Most detectives would have done that. Most do anything they are paid to do; some are just thugs for hire. My father, of course, was not like most. He sensed something and spoke to the lady.'

'Spoke to her?'

'He did not like the tone of the gentleman's correspondence. His words were bullying, so my father went and spoke to Mrs Fraser and she told him all about her marriage, and how her husband treated her. They had only been married two years, and it was not a kind story. She showed my father her bruises.'

'Oh no,' I said. 'Tell me she didn't go back.'

'Because my father is – was – who he was, of course not. The gentleman would not have agreed to a divorce. My father arranged safe passage for her to France, a place to stay with someone he knew, enough money to live on for a short while and he told Mr Fraser his wife had disappeared, and we could not find her. My father cancelled the account and did not chase payment for those two weeks of work. It cost us. The lady is still, as far as I know, living free.'

'So then?'

'Mr Fraser was incandescent. I think he suspected we had helped her. For many months he harassed my father, and I did sometimes wonder whether my father's death was linked. But last week I had word that Mr Fraser had been charged with his wife's murder in Scotland, and he would be hanged for it.'

'Did you save him?'

'It was a pointless trip. There was never any danger he would be hanged. He put a fake story out to get me up there and then he and his lawyers bombarded me with threats, affidavits and legal papers to try to bully me into revealing his wife's whereabouts. It didn't work. He also hired a couple of thugs to grab me in the street, but I was missing you and in a bad mood, so I threw them in the Water of Leith. I have a fine bruise, though,' and he pulled up his shirt from his waistband to show me and his lower abdomen was a map of bruises in yellow and purple.

'I am sorry,' I said, and I put out my hand and stroked his bruise with my thumb. He put his big hand over mine and then dropped his shirt abruptly, took my hand and kissed the palm before returning it.

'I have the sense revenge wasn't his only reason,' he said, 'That there was some other reason to get me up there and keep me hanging about, but I can't work out why. Did anything happen here when I was away? It's been well over a week.'

'Mrs Wilhelmina Withers was found dead on the beach, on the Stade,' I said. 'Did you know her? She was a chairwoman of many charitable committees. I have been looking into it.'

'I don't know her. Have we been hired?'

'No, but – I went to church with her. For many years. I feel I have to investigate a little.'

'It is always better not to be too emotionally involved in cases and if we have not been hired...' Benjamin said, but he saw my stubborn expression and stopped. 'Very well. I don't like that it happened on the Stade. The fishermen will be under suspicion and they have enough on their plate. It's not been good winter for herring. I'll speak to them.'

'I am not emotionally involved,' I said. 'If I am brutally honest, I didn't... like her. She was full of derogatory judgement. But... she did not deserve to die. Something about it doesn't feel right. I tried to talk to the fishermen, but they would not speak to me.'

'They won't speak to anyone they don't know,' Benjamin said. 'Do you want to come with me?'

'I think it would be best if I go to the Hydro,' I said and explained the conversation I'd overheard with Mrs Withers and Dr Spencer. Benjamin did not know him. I did not mention the ridiculous episode at the library, or that it was my father's idea to see a doctor, because I did not want to see the look that might come into Benjamin's eyes, of disappointment or incredulous disbelief I could do something so foolish. I made it sound instead as if visiting the doctor was all my own idea, for a rest-type holiday.

'Are you certain you wish to get involved in this?' Benjamin asked. 'It may be dangerous. If it was murder, there will be people looking to save their skins. I can take it on, if you would prefer.' I could see he was anxious for me but did not want to forbid me outright, and I felt a warm rush of emotion towards him for being so very different from my father.

'I cannot see any harm in it,' I said. 'After all, what can happen at a hydro? And who would suspect me, an unmarried woman? We can investigate together.'

I liked the idea. We would be a team, properly for the first time, each with our own skills, working alongside each other, his immense capability and my amateur, bumbling enthusiasm.

'There will be a funeral,' he said. 'I will go along and let you know if I observe anything untoward.'

'I will do the same at the Hydro,' I said.

'Are you sure you will be able to come and go as you please, and not be locked in there forever?' he asked.

'No, no, my friend Miss Turton went there and found it very healthful,' I said. 'Lots of water treatments. Hastings' water is full of minerals, apparently, sulphur and magnesium and calcium.'

'Do not imbibe too much sulphur,' he said. 'Doesn't that fuel the fires of hell? It might make you fiercer than you are already,' and I threw a tiny clock spring at him, an unwise move, because we had to search all over the floor for it.

Then his brothers and sisters exploded through the door to welcome him back and there was much consternation from Benjamin, because little Maud had been playing on the beach barefoot a few days ago and had cut her foot so it bled. It was healing well, but it made a dramatic story which her brothers related with relish.

'There was a length of cheese wire running halfway across the Stade, some of it hidden under the shingle, and she was skipping along and sliced her foot open,' her brother Arthur said. 'It bled everywhere, like a fountain.' Maud looked as if she felt she needed to cry again to relive the horror of the moment, so Benjamin gave a big bear hug and told her she was the bravest girl he had ever known. 'But none of you must run around there with bare feet,' he said severely. 'You all have good solid shoes and the fishermen are always mending netting and their boats and leaving their tools around. If you must take your shoes off, go to the public part of the beach and head further towards the sea where it's sandy.'

'We have the wire,' Ernest said, and he handed it over a coil of wire for safekeeping to Benjamin, and I hugged Maud too and told her she was a brave warrior woman, and then they all erupted out of the shop again and we got on with the rest of our day.

At home, I went to find Hildebrand. I was always glad to see her. She was a world away from Edith, my previous servant, who had been understandably frustrated by my inferior skills at running a household. Hildebrand did not seem to mind. She was baking bread in the kitchen and singing a ditty in which the chorus was 'a little bit of what you fancy does you good.' When she saw me, she stopped abruptly.

'Beg your pardon, miss,' she said.

'Don't stop singing for me,' I said. 'You have a good voice, and it's a nice cheerful song.'

'It's rude, miss,' she said, and I blushed, because of course it was, if one hadn't been brought up more ignorantly than a baby. I had learnt a lot in life, but the gap in my learning would apparently never be filled.

As I was leaving the kitchen, a thought occurred to me.

'Would you mind going to the library for me, and reading a few newspapers?' I said. A hot flush of embarrassment ran through me. 'Do you... can you read?'

'Of course,' she said. 'I have neat handwriting too. My mother taught me when I was young. She was bright, me ma. She could have had a different life if it weren't for me and the consumption. Not much call for writing in me last place though.' She smiled, sunnily, quite as if she hadn't just mentioned the death of her mother and her life in a brothel, and I felt my vast inferiority of life experience once again.

'I am sorry about your mother,' I said, and she shrugged, but I sensed a wariness there, as if it had never done her much good to show sadness about it. 'If you would be so kind as to go to the library and read the newspapers for mentions of Mrs Withers' death, and take notes of what's important?'

'Of course. How will I know what's important?' Hildebrand's eyes lit up, much as mine must have done when Benjamin first allowed me to use his typewriter.

'Any details of how she died, where, when... how, etcetera. Benjamin and I are looking into her death, informally. Please don't tell my father,' and she shook her head as if such a thought had never occurred to her. She was a wonderful person to have on my side.

'If you need to ask permission, try to speak to Miss Lipscombe,' I said. 'If it's Mr Gallop, stab him with your hatpin. I jest, of course. If it's Mr Gallop, do not mention me, or you may not get near the newspapers. I turned him down in marriage years ago, and he has not forgotten.'

'Bitter gent, is he?' Hildebrand said. 'The worst kind. Hurt by one woman and likely takes it out on all women till the end of time. Not that I'm saying you're responsible for him being a bastard, begging your pardon, being a—'

'You can call him a bastard, I don't mind,' I said. It was the first time I had ever said the word and it rolled around my tongue, unfamiliar and powerful. Had Mrs Withers felt like that, when she cursed Dr Spencer, wicked but powerful? Language was a wonderful thing.

'All right, I'll go now,' she said, taking her apron off. 'The bread needs to prove anyhow. Am I helping you with your detective work?'

'Why yes,' I said. 'You are.'

Chapter Eighteen

When Hildebrand came back, she was all agog.
'I took notes from The Police Gazette, The Times and the Hastings Times,' she said. 'But Miss, there was drama! Miss Lipscombe was crying and arguing with Mr Gallop, and then she went and got her coat and left. It was so loud an older gentleman got most annoyed and told them both to shush.'

'What was it about?'

'Something about a piece of paper,' Hildebrand said, and I thought it was the end of her story but then: 'I couldn't get the gist of it, so I went after Miss Lipscombe. She sat on a bench looking out to sea and I sat next to her and asked her for why she was crying, and she said it was because Mr Gallop had accused her of stealing. She said she'd worked there five years with never a problem, and she is as honest as the day is long, and she would never steal. I comforted her a bit, till she didn't feel so alone, and then I went back to the library to read the papers.'

'What was stolen?' I asked. I felt an involuntary flush of shame followed by relief because it could not be me, could it? I had not stolen anything. The books I had briefly taken had all been safely delivered back through the letterbox.

'A letter or list or something. She said Mr Gallop kept calling it different things. "As if I would want that!" she said. "He wouldn't even tell me what it was!"'

'Has she lost her job?'

'I don't think so. She walked out on him, and is threatening not to go back.'

'Interesting,' I said. It was probably, knowing Mr Gallop, a list of all the women he disliked and why, or an inventory of his knives and forks. But all contretemps were worth noticing, so I filed the incident away in my mind for later.

'Did I do right then, miss? I like to know what a drama's about, and she needed a bit of an ear. Oh, and here are your notes.' She pulled a sheaf from inside her coat. 'Mr Gallop barely noticed me. He's a cross walrus isn't he? All moustache and heavy breathing.'

'He is. You have done excellent work today, Hildebrand. Thank you. Please call me Violet, if you will.'

'Don't know as that's right, miss,' she said. 'But glad to have been of help. Bread!' and she scampered off to the kitchen. She was so young, only eighteen or so, but so full of spirit and optimism. I still had optimism, but occasionally it was more determination than belief.

The newspaper articles were long, but not terribly useful. They all talked about it being an accident, which at least gave me some comfort. The Police Gazette, though, revealed she had been found under a capstan, the device set into the beach to help the sailors winch their boats up out of the water; there had been a heavy wooden one set in the shingle near the Mary Jane, I remembered. Perhaps she had tripped on rope, fallen and hit her head on it.

It was a conundrum. I wished, not for the first time, I was a man and could simply ask questions and receive answers. Instead, I had to dabble around the edges of life, trying to see truth through cobwebs.

I spoke severely to myself, because self-pity helped no one. I would need to be dextrous and imaginative. I remembered Edith, who had worked for our family for many years before decamping to work for Mrs Withers. She would know something, surely. She might speak to me, woman to woman, and reveal information she would never share with a gentleman. Or she might not, because my consistent incompetence had led Edith to hold me in fairly immoveable dislike. But I would try.

I would also think about writing to my mother. There were three letters now on my bedside table, nagging on my conscience, but I really did not have much to say. Her letters were very needy. I did not need her any more.

Chapter Nineteen

It was already the third week in March, and the sun was getting warmer, the wind less likely to slice through clothes and freeze bones. The walk to Hastings Hydropathic Establishment took a brisk hour across the hills, as it was quicker to go up and over than down, along the seafront and back up again. I walked past the reservoirs, through Alexandra Park and along the stretch of Mount Pleasant Road, glimpsing spectacular views of Hastings and St Leonards below. I was briefly led astray by the windows of a very fine chocolate shop but held firm and was quite out of breath when I reached the Hydro.

The building had once been called Hastings Lodge and been home to a lady called Marianne North, who had achieved some fame for her botanical drawings. I had heard she travelled far to exotic countries and hoped her pioneering spirit might linger within its walls. It might have been beautiful when she lived there, but now it looked large, squat and white, uneven extensions jutting out on either side to accommodate the spa.

A flight of stone steps led through the open front door straight into another flight of steps, carpeted, leading sharply upwards, and I wondered if it had been designed that way to induce all guests arriving to immediate exercise. At the top, out of breath, I came face to face with a reception desk, manned by a weary woman in white.

'Madam,' she said. 'Welcome.' Her face said quite the opposite, and she sighed.

'I am Miss Hamilton. Violet Hamilton,' I said. 'I am here—'

'Yes,' she said, running her finger down a list. 'For a week.'

'No, only three days,' I said.

'A week,' she said, her eyes half shut with endurance. 'Booked by Dr Spencer himself.'

'I do not have enough clothes for a week,' I said.

'Most of the time you will be wearing the bathing dresses we provide,' she said. 'You are in Room 29. Up the stairs, two flights, turn left at the top. Here is a list of rules. You will find the daily schedule in your room. Two towels.'

She handed me two very old and rough towels that had dried a hundred people before me and turned her back on me.

'Enjoy your stay,' she said.

It was the first indication I should not expect any kind of holiday.

My room was also blessed with spectacular vistas through the small dormer window, but there the luxury ended. The space was furnished with a small chest of drawers, a washstand with a pitcher, a single bed and a rag rug worn to rags for a second time. I sat on the bed, with a scratchy blanket and a mattress and pillow with the softness of brick. There was a schedule attached by a nail to the back of the door:

6am – spritz bath

7am – breakfast

8am – walk

9am – cold tank

10.30am – scriptures

11.30am – walk

12.30pm – luncheon

1.30pm – reflection

2.30pm – cold tank

3.30pm – walk

4.30pm – consultation Dr Spencer

5.30pm – improvement lecture

7.30pm – dinner

8.30pm – bed (lights out)

Goodness, it was a regime. What was a spritz bath? What should I reflect on? I should not complain. I had been privileged in life so far, I knew. Maybe this spartan treatment would improve my essential character. And I would be treated to the joy of glorious sunsets from the window.

There was a splat of liquid from above, and a pigeon flew off into the sky, leaving a grey and white stain on the glass. Even my view of heaven was marred.

But I had arrived just in time for my first appointment with Dr Spencer, which would require some clever manoeuvring on my part. I left my bag on the bed and went downstairs.

Chapter Twenty

Dr Spencer was exactly as I remembered, an ordinary man with an extraordinarily dense red-brown beard. It was as if it had grown like a hedge hemmed in tightly on all sides, so it had only been able to grow inwards.

His office was decorated with a great many certificates acclaiming his medical expertise, as well as more advertisements for medical ointments, tinctures and potions than the street outside.

'Miss Hamilton,' Dr Spencer said. 'Come in. Please sit down.' We were alone. It was odd all considerations of chaperones were abandoned when it was a medical man. I might have preferred one.

He was seated behind a large oak desk, and he pointed to a red leather chaise-longue in the corner of the room. I sat on it. I was not going to argue with him until I found out what I wanted to know.

'So,' he said, steepling his hands together and resting his chin on them. His beard was really a very unusual shade, almost orange. Did he dye it? There were plenty of advertisements for miracle hair-dye on the wall. 'Your father is a little concerned about your recent behaviour.'

What had my father told him? 'Yes,' I said. 'He is a good and caring father. My spirits have been greatly affected by the passing of Mrs Withers—'

'I hear you tried to break into the Brassey Institute in the middle of the night?' he interrupted. 'The library? To steal books?'

'No,' I said cautiously. 'I met Constable Carruthers outside, so I didn't even make it inside. It was just a whim. Sometimes I cannot sleep—'

'And why could you not go in the daytime?'

'I just like to read at night when I cannot sleep, and I had run out of books.' It was a flimsy answer, but he likely thought I was capable of ridiculous behaviour already.

'Hmmm. So,' he said, switching tack abruptly, 'Have you had a grumbling in the bowels recently?' He pointed downwards.

'Grumbling in the…? No,' I said. 'But as I say…'

'A windiness? Have you felt any excess air… down there? A peculiar feeling, perhaps, of suffocation, stupor? Have you felt like laughing for no reason, or crying? Has your sleep been interrupted by sighing or groaning? You must forget any feminine delicacy and answer honestly.'

'No,' I said.

'Your monthly torments are regular, I take it? There is no greenness to your complexion.'

'Yes,' I said. 'I am quite well, thank you.'

'Do you find it… exciting to take things that are not yours? Intoxicating? You can freely tell me if so. I am not here to judge, just to understand. Kleptomania is common among the fairer sex.'

'Not exciting, no,' I said. 'I did not want to take anything, just read, but it looked very dark in the library, so as soon as I arrived, I realised it was a foolish notion, and then I met the constable.'

I examined the walls again as we spoke. The advertisements were all in identical wooden frames. There were cures for chapped hands, thin hair, absent hair, grey hair, too much hair, over-indulgence, baldness, blushing, weakness, tiredness. Halls Coca Wine would restore anyone suffering from mental and physical fatigue. Something would make women beautiful, although it was unclear if it was a potion, an ointment, a pill, face soap or bosom padding. There was an eye battery to help with eyesight, and even a machine which copied the action of riding a horse inside your home, to '*bring all the vital organs into inspiriting action*'. There were several products endorsed in spectacular lettering by none other than Dr Spencer. Surely this must be what Mrs Withers had meant, when she said Dr Spencer was a quack. I had always held a healthy scepticism for ignoble cures, and here there were far too many of them.

He leant forward. 'Let me be clear, Miss Hamilton. I am different from other doctors. I am interested in *women*. Your father has done well to send you here. The fairer sex deserves tailored treatment, because you are made differently. Female bodies (forgive the indelicacy) are created by God solely for the bearing of children and are therefore less robust, physically and mentally. You cannot be blamed for being more emotional, more confused, as a sex.'

'I beg your pardon?'

'Is it not an oversight that until recently medical men have not thought women's minds worthy of study? It is only now eminent men are beginning to fill the gap and are coming to understand your brains are physically different; smaller, more delicate. This explains so much in your behaviour. Hysteria; your susceptibility to influence; why you struggle with intellectual pursuits; your natural tendencies towards caring, kindness, submissiveness; so many of the feminine qualities are because of the physical makeup of your minds.'

My eyes widened. Was I, then, less able to be a detective because of the frailties of my mind? I refused to believe it.

'This all may be too academic for you. I will not tell you too much, then, about the doctor from Vienna who is studying what he calls the unconscious – the thoughts that lie so deep in your mind you may not even be aware of them. But let's see if we can uncover them, by talking. I will ask questions, and you must answer them honestly.

'Looking at you, I see a young woman of spirit. I see a desperation in you, to live your life beyond the domestic sphere.

Is it possible going to the library in the dead of night was an expression of your frustration, because you want more from life? Am I right?'

I looked at him. It was a perspicaciously unsettling comment. My instinct was to run, but it would not help Mrs Withers. I had a second to choose whether I would speak honestly or dissemble.

I chose to dissemble.

'Yes,' I said, opening my eyes wide at him. 'That is exactly what I am looking for. It must be why I went to the library at night. I am searching for something I am missing.'

He smiled. 'It is not hard to see. I understand your mother disappeared some years ago. Lie back. Close your eyes and relax. You can tell me all about it.'

I did not want to lie back or close my eyes, but the former seemed safer, so I lay back cautiously and kept my eyes open, poised to spring up if necessary. I was in my detective uniform, and I had a small metal nail file in one of the pockets if I needed to stab him. I did not want to give him an ounce of unnecessary power over me. Instead, I concentrated deeply on working out what he wanted me to say and diverting his attention.

He had a notebook on his desk and opened it at a fresh new page, his pencil poised. His voice was deep and calm, exactly as it had been when he had been arguing with Mrs Withers in the garden. 'There are many thoughts and memories you are not conscious of, stemming even from childhood, that can cause distress even as an adult. My goal here is to reawaken them. Was the disappearance of your mother a seismic event in your life, Miss Hamilton?'

I would categorically not go there. It felt as if he was trying to undress my mind. 'Somewhat, but it is a long time ago. The recent death of Mrs Withers has greatly saddened me, though. It is why I could not sleep the other night. She was very… concerned about my wellbeing and gave me a great deal of life advice. As a doctor, do you know what happened to her?'

He shook his head like a horse chased by a fly and waved

a dismissive hand. 'Mrs Withers was suffering a great deal of distress and confusion. Death is a part of life, and we must all deal with it as we can. In such a case, we should leave the grieving to those who have a right, such as her husband.'

'But how?' I said. 'How did she die? As a doctor, do you know?'

'This is not about that woman,' he said, impatient all of a sudden. 'This is about you.' He ran his hand over his face and took a deep breath, visibly controlling himself. 'I beg your pardon. Of course, any death is a tragedy, and she was greatly esteemed by the community. But you must understand this session is about you, and the reasons for your kleptomania are likely to go much, much deeper than such a recent event. I wonder, perhaps... it is old-fashioned... but mesmerism...?' He was talking to himself now.

'But I can't have kleptomania,' I said, 'Because I didn't steal anything, or intend to. You have a lot of advertisements on your walls. Are all the cures efficacious?'

Dr Spencer shut his notebook abruptly and stared at me. There was a small drop of brown dye running from the left-hand side of his forehead down to where his beard met his ear.

'Of course they are,' he said. 'In fact, we have a new one, trialled most effectively in Berlin, that arrived only yesterday. I think, perhaps, you might benefit from it. Would you like to be our pioneer? It is the electric corset.' He stabbed his finger at the wall to the right of his desk, where there was an advertisement for a corset powered by electricity, illustrated by a line drawing of a lady with sparks coming off her.

'An electric corset?' I said. 'There is no need. I am better already.'

'It has enormous health-giving properties all around. Often women's internal organs become misshapen and disarranged by wearing a normal corset, but the electrical charge in this corset helps them align again. It helps cure weak backs, hysteria, organic affections, kidney disorders, dyspepsia; the most awkward figure becomes graceful. I think, on reflection, your symptoms are those of hysteria. Yes, it will be perfect for you. You will be the first woman in Sussex to wear it.'

'No, thank you,' I said.

'Yes,' he said. 'We'll see you at my lecture later, and then tomorrow we will get you laced in tightly. There is a battery with it, not too heavy, so you'll still be able to move around and take part in some of the other treatments. Not ones with water.'

'I think I might go home,' I said. 'I feel perfectly cured, thank you. Your talking cure has worked wonderfully.'

He smiled at me, a little sadly. 'Miss Hamilton, your father has not sent you here lightly. You will not leave here until I say you are better, even if it takes weeks. I do think you are showing some signs of latent hysteria and possibly an unconscious desire for attention or even punishment. We can explore further. Come here tomorrow at ten o'clock. I will attend the session, as it is a new innovation, and we'll get you strapped in.'

He pressed a bell, and two burly women walked in, who looked as if they were very angry about life and looking for someone to take it out on.

'Miss Hamilton will go to the improvement lecture, and then bed,' Dr Spencer said. 'I do not think she needs dinner. Please show her the way.'

In the battle of wits, I had definitely lost.

Chapter Twenty-One

I did not want to go to any speeches. I wanted to flee and never come back, but it turned out the Hydro was not far off a fortress.

I could not – would not – allow myself to be experimented on with electricity. It was a new and magical power, witness the telegraph and street lighting, but it was dangerous. There were regular deaths reported in the newspapers from accidental electrocution, and in the United States of America they had even started using an electric chair to execute criminals. No, an electric corset was not for me. I suspected Dr Spencer thought I had asked too much about Mrs Withers, and a faulty medical device might be the fastest way to remove me from the picture.

I would have to escape, but how? First, the improvement lecture to get through, then dinner, and then it would be back to my sparse room, which was very far up from the ground. If I fought anyone, I risked being declared disturbed and locked away more securely. I would not be frightened, because I could not in all seriousness be a Lady Detective if I allowed myself to be, but I was... anxious.

I would escape.

The improvement lecture was held in a timber-beamed hall with rows of metal chairs. It was a mixed event, men and ladies sitting on opposite sides, all chairs facing a podium under the stained-glass windows at the far end of the room. Some of the men were husbands, but they only nodded awkwardly at their wives and sat at the opposite side of the room, as if hydrotherapy precluded marital intermingling. There was no heat in the room, and all of us looked chilly.

Dr Spencer gave the lecture, and it was fascinating.

'What are we,' Dr Spencer said, 'if we cannot rise above animals? If we cannot think higher thoughts than the lower classes, or set ourselves up as the moral guardians of those who are blessed with less understanding? We have a responsibility, nay, a *duty*, to avail ourselves of opportunity, and to share that good fortune, that higher *wisdom*, with those less fortunate.

'Hydrotherapy is just one of the many wonders of our era that allows us, the privileged class, to see the world with greater clarity. By coming here, you have chosen a path, like those great philosophers Hume, Locke and Rousseau, of enlightenment. By coming here, you have already set yourself above those who simply endure life's toil and never look up from treading its weary path.'

There were at least six women in the audience who were staring at Dr Spencer, wide-eyed. It could have been devotion, except in several cases, their husbands were sitting across the aisle.

Dr Spencer's voice was very deep and calming, his every word imbued with authority and confidence. 'Hastings and St Leonards have a seafront of nearly four miles. It is one of the most attractive retreats for invalids and their visitors in the whole of the British Isles. Medical authorities of repute say our climate is better here than anywhere else, warmer in winter as it is sheltered from north-east winds, with an agreeable bracing climate in summer and the highest amount of sunshine. Our resort has a lower mortality rate from consumption than any other seaside town. The area has iron-rich springs, great water purity, and the seawater is more greatly impregnated with salt particles than anywhere else.

'For that reason,' Dr Spencer continued, 'some of you will know our ambitions for this town. I say let us make St Leonards a new Eden, let us sweep away the old to welcome in the new, for everyone who wants to benefit from the water of life. For women, especially, who deserve for the first time, for their particular frailties to be looked at.'

As he spoke a shaft of sunshine came through the crenelated windows behind him, lighting up his red-brown beard so it glowed.

'This town we live in, this glorious town, was built by an architect with a vision,' Dr Spencer said. 'Like his father before him, Decimus brought high ideals to this place, in buildings and landscapes that inspire with their beauty and magnificence. These are not mere dwellings for the common type. But like all grand aspirations, there are challenges. St Leonards is hampered by the shabbiness of its neighbour. We offer a world-class seaside resort, with a grubby hotchpotch of buildings on the side. Do not be ashamed of it. Man will always look to rise up. It should always be our aim to flush away the dirt. We do not need to be surrounded by those who scrabble for a living, when there is space for everyone to thrive.

'This is not about me,' he said, frowning. 'I do not ask for praise. Call me a conduit, if you like, to help you to reach that higher place. I too, consider it my *duty* to share all I have learnt, so you may flourish from it. Listen.'

Several people in the audience leant forward, spellbound, and the shaft of sunlight reached a stained-glass window on the far wall, sending a ray of bright colour across those sitting in the front row.

'Water,' he said. 'Water is the source of all our life, all our energy. It feeds us, it refreshes us, it sustains us, it can *create us* anew. I am of the opinion we not yet comprehend water's full miracle. Its *capacity*. You must go forth to your treatments with a knowledge of the *power* lying behind it. You are experiencing nature's most powerful life-giving force. Experience it fully, let it rush through you, gush through you, and you shall be renewed.'

He went on this vein for some time. His voice was really very powerfully persuasive, and I felt myself a little swept along with it too. He poured a glass of water from a small tumbler into a glass and drank it, the glass glinting in the sunlight, and several women gasped.

'Go forth,' he said eventually. 'Go forth, and experience all the joys we offer here. Be content in the knowledge you will leave here enriched, however many secrets we share with you, however deep you are prepared to go. We are humble here, and we will not compel you to enlightenment. If you are ready, we will know, and you will come. Let the water flow through around you, cleansing, renewing. Go forth!'

He left the stage, disappearing through a small door at the back of the hall. Several people sat in the audience quite still, but I got up and left, as I had other pressing concerns.

Other ladies had the same pressing concerns too, as there was quite a long queue at the lavatories. I was not sure this was exactly what Dr Spencer had meant by 'go forth', but all that talk of water had certainly had a salutary effect.

Chapter Twenty-Two

It was a beautiful evening, red gold sunset hitting the brown-tiled rooftops, and far beyond it, the white-gold blue of the sea, herring gulls swirling and eddying above it, black silhouettes against the sky. An amber shaft of evening light ran across the rag rug and the wooden floorboards, bringing a romantic elegance and warmth to the sparse room. It was beautiful, but I did not plan to stay and admire it.

I had stupidly not brought my lock-picking tools with me. And even if I had, I was not convinced I could get through those well-manned corridors. Could I write a note to Benjamin and throw it out of the window? I had nothing to write on. Was there anything in the room that would help? I began to search the room, methodically, walls, floors, furniture, looking for anything that might help save me. The threat of the corset was looming larger in my mind each second, and I knew if I had to face it, I would turn into a gibbering, shrieking harpy and then they would have all the confirmation they needed I was mad. I could not do it.

Of course, there was nothing in the room. Why would there be? My fingertips were sore, and the sun was dipping below the horizon by the time I found it.

It was a small folded up piece of thick paper, levelling the left leg of the washstand on the uneven floor. When I unfolded it, it was a beautiful, rough pencil drawing of a brown butterfly, not more than six inches wide. It was drawn so carefully, with so much delicate life and energy in it. It was resting on leaves, at the edge of a flower, but these were just outlined, not coloured in, as if someone had painted the butterfly and not been satisfied enough to finish the rest. Although it was dull-coloured, with little round black and brown spots on its wings, it was exquisite, and it felt like a message. Could it have been begun by Marianne North? She had lived here for over forty years in between travelling the world on exotic voyages and died only six or so years ago, although she had not lived here then. The washstand looked old. It was possible.

I folded up the drawing in its original folds, so as not to damage it, and then I put it in my breast pocket for safety. I had read stories about Miss North. She was one of those ladies who filled one with awe, travelling to some of the most unexplored and dangerous countries across the globe – Borneo, Chile, Hawaii – often alone, ceaselessly painting rare and wonderful wildlife and plants. She had been brave, foolhardy and adventurous and she had left behind a sketch of a butterfly. Her drawing would give me courage, like a talisman. In my heart I knew there was only one way to escape. This brown butterfly would try to fly. I had to climb out of the window.

My room was three floors up. Below my window was a narrow-tiled roof, on a gentle slope. If I could walk, crab-like, along it, holding onto the windowsill and then the rooftop, with the guttering to hold me if my foot slipped – if the guttering was strong enough – and then clamber sideways, I could drop onto a balcony on the extension jutting out below, and then onto the balcony below it and then – I could not see my way after that, so I would have to work it out when I got there. I would need to wait a little longer until it was completely dark as there were windows everywhere, and I did not want to come face to face with Dr Spencer. It would be awkward in my skirts. I wished fervently I was wearing the trousers I had worn to break into the museum with Benjamin.

I looked down, and it was a long way. I would not survive if I fell. But smashing onto the cobblestones was still more appealing than an electric corset. I gathered my meagre possessions into my knapsack, pinned my hair back as tightly as it would go, and sat on the bed to wait for darkness.

Chapter Twenty-Three

I waited an hour, until I thought most people would have gone to bed. It was dark at last, clouds covering the sky, but with enough light I could hopefully see my way, once my eyes adjusted. Had I had a good life? I had had an eventful one, if one did not count the first nine and a half stagnant, empty years after my mother's disappearance, I thought, as I eased open the sash window. It opened easily. They must think no one would be mad enough to try to escape this way. I had good people in my life, whom I cared about, as well as some I did not, so much, but might do, if they behaved better in the future. I pulled the bed over to the window and clambered on it to put my knee on the windowsill. I had a fiancé I cared about, who I thought cared for me, although I felt very unqualified to judge these things, never having had one before. I hauled myself up, balanced precariously on the windowsill on both knees, and then extended one leg out, cautiously.

I could not do it. It was crazy. I would fall in seconds. My skirt was hampering me already.

'If you want to be any good at this job,' I muttered to myself, fiercely, 'You have to stop being a ninnyhammer.' I turned my back on the world below, and brought out my other leg, so I was kneeling on the slope of the roof, my feet perpendicular against it. It was not too steep a slope. Then I gritted my teeth and began to shift myself sideways and outwards, keeping a grip on the windowsill with my left hand, swinging my other one round and down to the triangular-shaped roof lying to my right, abutting the window below. I moved my right leg along so it was kneeling on the slope of the triangle, and then tried to persuade myself to release the hand holding the windowsill. It wasn't listening to me. It obviously believed my death-grip on the frame was my last chance of survival. My left foot, resting purely at an angle on the tiles, slipped on a mound of moss that scuttered off the roof with a shower of earth and my foot scrabbled in thin air for a second, before it found purchase again.

I was about to mutter again to myself, when a light flickered across the grass far below. The French window opened, and a man came out into the garden.

It was Dr Spencer. I could recognise his squat form and his beard silhouetted in the light shafting the lawn, even from above. He clipped the end off his cigar, throwing it into the bushes, and then lit it. The acrid smell drifted up towards me, dissipating into the night air.

If he looked up, he would easily see me, spreadeagled. He might even see an ankle, although it was no time for modesty. My right foot was resting in the gutter, although I had tried to take some weight off it by resting my knee sideways on the slope of the triangle. If it broke... if the moss had scattered down seconds earlier. Terror was a rat gnawing at my insides. Would I kill him, if I fell on him? Would that be better, than falling to a solitary death at his feet? Or would I survive, or half-survive, and have to face him? Perhaps he might still strap me in his corset, crunching my broken ribs together.

My imagination was flapping about too wildly. I tried to get control of it and ignore the fact that my left hand, holding the bulk of my weight, was starting to feel weak.

'We have sold five hundred and fifty shares, at five pounds each,' Dr Spencer said, to someone inside. 'You and I own the remaining fifty. But imagine how much more lucrative a proposition it would be, if...'

The person inside was too quiet for me to hear. I heard the

words 'It will happen,' and then there was some mumbling.
I strained to listen. My hands were getting cold. Or hot? I
could not tell the difference. The view across the rooftops was
beautiful, I noticed, even at night, the sea glowing silver-blue in
the distance against the darker sky. The moon had come out. Oh
God. Would moonlight make me easier to see? 'Has Gallop gone
mad?' I heard those words clearly. The man inside must have
moved nearer to the window. Perhaps he would come out too,
and they would both look up and clap when I fell.

'That man is worse than a cat on hot coals,' Dr Spencer said.
'Spooking at nothing. A liability. Perhaps we should cut him
loose.'

'Mrs Withers...' the other man's words drifted off. An ant was
wending its way across my right hand, up across the knuckle,
down into the darkness of the gap between each finger and then
up again. If it chose to run down my sleeve, I would have to let it.

'Maybe she was crushed by the weight of her giant hat,'
Dr Spencer said. 'I'm treating Blackthorn's fiancée, by the way.
She was asking about Mrs Withers today. She's a funny one...
tried to steal books from the library at midnight.'

There was a mumble from within and then Dr Spencer said:
'As a detective? That's no job for a woman. He's a fool to let her.'

Was it a threat, or an observation? How long would they
chat? How much strength would fear give me until my fingers
gave way and I plummeted to the grass? Perhaps I should take a
risk and edge crab-like across the rooftop.

'Come in, blast you, it's cold,' the man said from inside. I
could not identify his voice. It was more refined than Dr Spencer's
perhaps. At last, I saw Dr Spencer head inside, and the sound
of the door shutting. The lawn went dark, so they must have
closed the curtain on the inside, and there was silence.

I was frozen against the roof, through fear and cold. It took
me several seconds to persuade myself to move and even then,
it was only because of exhaustion. I took a leap to my right,

landing on the sharp point of the roof, which jutted out from the main roof enough to allow me a brief moment of respite, and I flopped across it face-first like a rag doll, legs dangling one side, arms the other, the point at my middle, until the feeling came back into my extremities and I could breathe. But shortly the fear hit again and I had to move.

All was quiet and dark below. A grim determination took over and I did not look anywhere but where I needed to, to place my feet and hold on. My hands were trembling and my heart jumping wildly in my chest. I clambered onwards over the triangular roof, and then followed the main roof around the corner of the building towards the extension, step by step. This part of the building was stepped a whole floor lower, with its balcony that might offer a way down.

No more moss scattered from the roof, although a starling squawked and flew off into the night. My skirt wrapped itself neatly around my legs and I had to cling on and shake myself free, one leg at a time. But eventually I made it to the top of the pediment leading down to the first balcony below. The room leading off the balcony was in darkness, and all was quiet. It was too far for me to jump, but I managed to half scramble, half fall down the wall, holding onto a drainpipe. I knocked over a wicker chair as I landed, and it fell with a clatter. I crouched, frozen, in the darkness. Nothing moved.

An owl hooted far off in the distance and there was the sharp call of a fox, sounding like a human scream. I stood carefully and peered over the balcony to the floor below. There was a light or two flickering in the main building, but below me was darkness. I swung myself over silently, wide of the balcony, and dropped in a crouch to the grass.

I had made it, and I straightened to run. Would I have to climb over the gates? I eased out from behind the bushes, backed slowly out of any possible line of sight from the French windows, then crawled across the grass behind the trees and shrubbery to reach the gates. And then I had to silently thank the angels, or providence, or whoever was on my side, because a little gate beside the main gate, likely for the servants' entrance or deliveries, was ajar. I shot through it and began to run.

Chapter Twenty-Four

I ran without stopping up Old London Road until I reached the top of the hill, and then I took a sharp left and carried on running. It was dark, but I was getting used to it. It was the third time now I had run fast through the streets at night. There was enough moonlight to see my way, and it felt much less scary than what lay behind me. If fate sent another challenge now, it was cruel indeed. The hardest part was passing Shornden Wood and the two reservoirs, the trees a wall of dark shadows and rustlings, the reservoirs behind them, hidden. I thought about werewolves and monsters.

I had grazed my knee as I slid down the pipe, I realised, and torn my chemise in the same place. As I cleared the forest, I had to stop to gasp my breath and give respite to my weak legs and I felt my leg throb. It didn't matter. I had escaped. I had escaped and I didn't think they knew, yet. What would Dr Spencer do when they found out? Would he demand my return, by force? Or would my father?

Some creature made a strange calling sound in the woods behind me, a deep whining growl, and I jumped out of my skin and began running again. My questions could wait. Part of me wanted to run to Benjamin, but I did not know what he would think of me turning up announced on his doorstep. Of the proprieties. I would go to my father's house for now.

By the time I reached home I was exhausted. I went round the small alleyway leading to our back garden, let myself in through the back door, thanked providence Hildebrand had not put the big bolt on, and crept wearily up to bed. I was safe for the moment. I slept the sleep of the dead.

I woke at my usual time of seven-thirty, aching and tired. I could have stayed in bed, hiding; waiting until later in the day when I had more energy to face my father, but something had resolved in me overnight, hard and cold, and the confrontation might as well happen now. After traversing a rooftop, other battles must surely be tame. I would forget the matter of my female brain and its fragility for now.

He was eating his usual kippers, reading the paper, folded over so he could read it one-handed as he liked. His eyebrows rose when he saw me.

'Good morning,' I said and sat in my usual seat. Hildebrand came in and served me some scrambled egg on toast – she was magnificent in all things – but my father gestured her out of the room with his head, a movement I did not like. She left.

'You are impolite,' I said to him. 'You should not treat her like that.'

'Violet, why are you here?' he said, pushing his chair back and throwing his paper down. 'You are not due back from the hospital – Hydro – for some time yet.'

'You told me I was booked in for three days,' I said. 'When I got there, I found it was for a week. In fact, I found out it was for as long as it would take for Dr Spencer to decide I was better, which might be weeks. Perhaps months. What do you think my malady is?'

There were spots of colour high up on his cheeks, and the slight pinching around his mouth may have been shame. But he straightened in his chair, and I could see him summoning up his authority, a god calling a thundercloud to his aid.

'Your behaviour has been wild,' he said. 'You were wandering around the streets at night, trying to break into the library. I have to take responsibility—'

'You do not,' I said. I was shaking inside, with anger or trepidation, I did not know. I had never spoken to my father thus. 'My fiancé is my keeper now, if I must have one. Do you know what Dr Spencer did, in his consultation room? He talked about kleptomania, even though I did not steal anything, and hysteria, although I have not had fits or thrown myself on the floor or shown any of the symptoms of it at all.'

'You are uncontrollable,' my father said.

'Is that it? I cannot be controlled? Do you want to know his cure for it?' I was angry, angrier than I had been when I discovered he had kept my mother's letter from me for nine years, the one showing she might be alive.

My father held up his hands as if to ward me off.

'An electric corset,' I said. 'Yes, he wanted to strap me into an electric corset. They are good for women's problems apparently, weak backs, hysteria, not, as far as I'm aware, for being uncontrollable, unless someone plans to add water to it or increase the voltage, in which case I most likely wouldn't need to be controlled by anyone, as I would be dead.'

'I am sure he did not mean…' My father for once looked lost for words.

'I am a Lady Detective,' I said in a rush. 'The reason I am wandering around the streets at night, the reason I need to go out without a chaperone, is I am working with my fiancé as a Lady Detective. I must be allowed to,' – no, that was too weak – 'I will be carrying on with this profession, with the full support of my fiancé, and I will not ever, ever be locked up against my will again. I will not allow it. You, if you care about me, if you ever cared about me,' my voice broke a little, 'if you care about my wellbeing, you will never, ever do that again.'

The silence was long, and I wondered if he might get up and leave the room as he was fond of doing at difficult moments.

'It is an utterly ridiculous, utterly impossible profession for a lady,' he said at last.

'I know,' I said.

'It is dangerous and low class. You will destroy your reputation.'

'What is reputation?' I said. 'Being shut out of drawing rooms? I never wanted to be in them, anyway.'

'You will destroy mine,' he said, and I could tell it mattered to him, had always mattered to him, even more since our mother had shamefully, embarrassingly, chosen to run away from us.

Was it too much to put on his shoulders now, to tell him she was still alive? It could wait. Instead:

'I am going to move out,' I said. 'Not immediately, but soon, I am going to move out, not marry immediately, but to live with other gentlewomen perhaps, somewhere respectable, independently, until I am ready to marry. And then... I do not mind, if you write me off. If I become the daughter you do not talk about, except in disparaging tones. The scandalous daughter who works for a living. Then I will not be such a burden to you.'

'You are not...' he said and ran his hand over his face. 'Violet, that too, is not done. For a woman, to live alone, when she has two gentlemen in her family who can support her. Protect her.'

I raised my eyebrows at him.

'I am sorry,' he said. 'For the corset. I did not know... he does not sound like a reputable doctor. I will speak to—'

'There is no need,' I said. 'I do not ask you to raise the matter with him. Just please do not ever place me back in his care again. Ever. If he asks you, I am cured.' My father's meddling would not serve to do anything but raise Dr Spencer's suspicions, and he was still crucial to my investigation. To Mrs Withers. I had almost forgotten her in all of this.

'I am not the child I was when my mother left,' I said to him. 'I can run a household if I choose, I simply get bored of domesticity. I am a grown woman, and I will run wild no matter how many times you try to stamp on me. Please let us be harmonious for as long as we live together. I will do my best not to shame your reputation, if you will let me live as I choose.'

I was proud of my little speech. I hoped it had an effect.

'You have become as feisty as your mother,' he said. I was not sure it was a compliment, but I decided to take it as one.

Then my father simply nodded and taking his usual course of dealing with our differences, left the room. He was not happy, but if I knew him at all, I did not think he was planning to call Dr Spencer and hand me straight back into the good doctor's clutches. He was hopefully planning to employ his manly wisdom and come to a rational conclusion which involved setting me free.

I still had not told him my mother was alive and living with her lady love in Buxton, but that revelation could wait.

Chapter Twenty-Five

After all the excitement, I needed the peace and quiet of Benjamin. He was my lodestar of calm. I would never need to worry he might impose his judgement on me, or direct me about; he was just there, solid, kind and all that was good, if I needed to rest on him for a while. To recover.

'You must never, ever, put yourself in such danger again,' he said. He had been working with a lathe, shaving neat strips off a plank of wood to make the lid for a trunk, but now he put it down and straightened, hands on his hips, regarding me with a frown. 'You must never do such a foolhardy thing as to clamber across rooftops in the dark. You could have got a message to me somehow, or I would have come and found you eventually, or… you must never do it again.'

'It was the corset that hastened me on,' I said. 'Benjamin, are you directing me about?'

He picked up the lathe in one strong hand, then slammed it down again on the worktop, took a great huff of breath and turned to face me.

'Violet, you may be a New Woman,' he said, 'but I am not a New Man. I am not sure they even exist. I let you do what you want to do, because my father was an exceptional man. He brought me up to see a woman's lot can be harder than a man's, and she deserves respect. That life can curtail her freedom more easily, so she should have it while she can. And my mother died too young, before she had had the chance to live life to the full. I can see how happy being a detective makes you, so I encourage you. I let you be who you want to be, go where you want to go, but I do not say it is *easy*. I am still a man. I still want to protect, to cherish, to guide, to tell you not to clamber over rooftops when you might fall off and hurt your precious self. I still have *instincts*. I am not perfect.'

The last part was almost a growl and as I watched him, usually so implacable and under control, it struck me for the first time he really did care for me. That I was not just a silly woman who had inveigled my way into his life and existence so thoroughly he could not work out how to get rid of me, but that I had entangled myself in the region of his heart too. I started to believe the words in his letter, and I realised he needed some of my calm for a change.

I went over and encircled him with my arms, resting my head on his hard chest, until he relaxed too and hugged me back.

'Do not worry,' I said. 'We are both precious to each other. I will look after myself better, and I am very thankful you are the man you are.'

He rested his cheek against the top of my head.

'Do you understand, Violet, exactly what this job is? Sometimes I feel as if your head is full of adventure novels rather than real life. It is not an easy job, and more often than not you are going to come smack up against painful reality. You will always have less physical strength than a man and be in more danger for it. If you are going to succeed you have to take less risk and more care, and work on ways to protect yourself. You can't just career out into the world as if everyone will treat you like a lady.'

It touched a nerve, as it was too close to Dr Spencer's words, although my physical deficit I could not argue with.

'I cannot help the way I am made. I'm aware of the disparity between being a lady and a detective,' I said. 'I may need to work harder in all respects because of it. But I refuse to tiptoe through life insisting I be cushioned from it. I would rather die facing danger than live in a glasshouse. But I understand what you are saying. I will learn everything I need to defend myself, if you will help me.'

'I want us to live long lives together,' he said.

'So do I,' I said, and I hugged him tighter.

He was silent for a while.

'Very well,' he said eventually, 'I'll get you a gun.'

'Excellent,' I said. 'Shall I type up some invoices?' And that was how we spent most of the afternoon, him stripping wood with his lathe and me at the typewriter, asking him the occasional question. We even stopped for a coffee break and I did not mention Dr Spencer or corsets for at least three hours, until we were both fully restored.

Once we were back to our normal selves, I showed him the butterfly, because it was special. 'Perhaps it can be our emblem or our coat of arms,' I said, and then I finally confessed to having been to the library in the middle of the night. I was starting to realise I needed to be honest with him, for us to build trust.

My story did take us back a step or two.

'You went to the library, alone? Violet—'

'I know,' I said. 'I know. It was a stupid thing. I will not do anything like it again. I was angrier than I have ever been, because… I do not know if you understand what it is like to live in a world where you are constantly told you cannot do things? Does anyone ever refuse you anything?'

'Sometimes a certain lady refuses to listen to me,' he said wryly. 'But mostly, I impose society's rules on myself. I do, for what it's worth, understand it must be frustrating to be hemmed in by others. I will not harp on at you for your behaviour. What did you take?'

'Nothing,' I said. 'I put them all back.'

'I suppose I should be glad I am not marrying a criminal,' Benjamin said. 'But Violet—'

'I know. I feel the shame deeply enough already. I think I learnt something character-building from it, and I do not need your frown too. Let us change the subject. Did you speak to the tanfrocks?'

'I did,' he said. 'They are angry; they think it's just the latest in a long line of manoeuvres to get them off the beach. You'll know there are plenty of business and council men who want them to move to the harbour at Rye, so they can add more attractions to the seafront. All those troubles with the building of the harbour, when they were threatened with the removal of their capstans; thank God in a way the harbour failed, even though they'll be hauling their boats up the beach for centuries.'

The wooden and metal capstans had rested solidly on the beach for years, used for winding the rope to make it easier to bring the boats up the beach. Fishing was a daily slog and a harsh life, dependent on weather and the elements. The tanfrocks often lived on the edge of poverty. This winter, there had been a spate of such severe weather they had not been able to take their boats out for five weeks; but then the previous autumn a glut of herring had kept them working solidly through two days and a night without cease, and they had frequented the inns for weeks afterwards. There had always been distrust between the fishermen and the town officials, stemming from a rich history of smuggling on the part of the fishermen, although it had ended many decades past. The overzealousness of town officials had not helped.

'Did they tell you who had found her?'

'It's a man called Kilpin, coming back from a night out in Lewes; he'd drunk a few and thought he'd sleep it off in his boat rather than disturb his wife. Found Mrs Withers at around three o'clock in the morning. She was lying – forgive me, do you want the details?'

'Of course,' I said. I would handle descriptions of death, the same way if I was ever allowed to attend a funeral, I would not weep at it.

'She was fully dressed, lying face down under a capstan. She had her hat, her shoes on; her reticule over her arm, seemingly untouched – it had money in it. She might have stepped straight out of the ball. She had a large wound on her forehead, which they think is the cause of death.'

'What else was in her reticule?'

Benjamin consulted his notes. 'A handkerchief, one of those fancy silver kits that have nail files and embroidery scissors in them, what do you call it? An *etui*. Twenty pounds, enough to be worth stealing; a small green bottle containing Dr Spencer's Wondrous Water of Life, half empty; a spare pair of gloves; a prescription list of some kind.'

'That might be it,' I said. 'Perhaps she had been taking Water of Life and realised it did not work or was dangerous. What was on the list?'

'Good question, I should have asked them,' Benjamin said. 'Her funeral is tomorrow morning. I'll go there first and then I'll go back to the police. And maybe the day afterwards, we should call on Mr Withers together? Share our condolences, see if he needs any assistance.'

He was so much better at including me than any other man; I felt a warm rush of emotion in my chest. But Dr Spencer's words were still too fresh, so I would excise it all, and become as emotionless and cold as any man, small brain or nay.

'I would like that,' I said.

Chapter Twenty-Six

A woman might not be allowed to attend a funeral for fear of her wailing and fainting, but I could still watch the procession, so the following morning I stood in the street and waited for it to pass. It was a Saturday, but it was early, the streets were not yet full of rowdy day-trippers who might not care for the solemnity of the occasion.

It was a fine procession. Colonel Withers had spared no expense. There were six black horses with plumes of rich ostrich feathers on their foreheads and velvet coverings, pulling a velvet-covered hearse piled with flowers. Behind the hearse were two coaches containing Colonel Withers and other key mourners, pulled by more plumed horses. All the men walked behind, in full top hat and silk gloves, and I spotted most of the significant gentlemen of the town: Lord Brassey, Lord Laxton, the Lord Mayor and even the various members of the Cinque Ports, a historic group that looked after the trade of five of our coastal towns. Benjamin was near the back; he saw me and nodded gravely. I noticed he cut a much finer figure than many of the other men in the cortège. They walked at a slow pace, the long, flat promenade suiting the gravity of the occasion; the musicians and even the candyfloss and ice-cream sellers paused their activity to watch it pass, bringing a rare moment of quiet to the seaside, although the seagulls still screeched overhead, silent for no one.

At the bottom of Old London Road, the procession took a left, heading up towards the steep cemetery of All Saints Church, where many of the inhabitants of the town were laid to rest. I watched them for a while, a mass of black horses and suited men heading solemnly up the hill, and then I turned to go.

The Spencer sisters were at my elbow, the last people I wanted to see, after perhaps their father. They hovered, looking ready to speak, and I did not have the energy for it.

'I do not have the energy for you,' I said, vaguely surprised when the words came out of my mouth, and I turned to head along the seafront towards home.

'Wait,' Mabel said. 'Felicity and I would like a word. It might be… of use to you.'

'I am busy,' I said, but I had never been one to turn down a useful word. 'However, very well, then. Shall we go to the teashop in Rock-a-Nore Road?'

'Too public,' Felicity said. 'We should be overheard. We can go and sit on the Castle Rocks perhaps, near the sea? There are no children there today.'

Beyond the shingle of the beach lay flat sands, embedded with an outcrop of sandstone rocks, called Castle Rocks simply because they sat opposite Hastings Castle, high up on the West Hill. Often covered at high tide, their pools were usually a magnet for little shrimpers, but today the weather was overcast, the rocks likely damp and slippery with seaweed. Were the sisters planning to push me into the sea to protect their father? Well, I would take my chances. I was far fiercer than them. I had done things unbelievable for a genteel lady. I nodded and headed off across the shingle, always a tiring exercise as the stones pulled one backwards with every step, found the best and most comfortable spot on the rock, which was still hard and cold, and sat on it without waiting for them. I was learning to look after myself.

'We understand you have been asking questions about the death of Mrs Withers,' Mabel said, she and her sister perching uncomfortably beside me, at a satisfyingly lower level, adjusting their skirts so they did not dangle in pools. 'And you have been working as a Lady Detective. We have several theories.' Felicity nodded vigorously.

I did not understand why they thought I would believe them, when they had made their dislike of me clear and I was most interested in the activities of their father, but it seemed judicious to listen. I nodded.

'We think it is the fishermen,' Felicity said. 'They are so rough, so… physical. We think one of them spotted Mrs Withers on the beach and was overcome by urges. It happens to men, you know. They have urges they cannot control.'

'Surely her giant hat would have stopped them,' I said, and then shook myself, because it was not a time for levity. 'I apologise. Pray continue.'

'One of them grabbed her, and tried to KISS her,' Mabel said, 'And Mrs Withers fought him off and fell and hit her head. So it was an accident, but it would not have happened if he had been able to control himself. They are so very muscular, the fishermen. It would be difficult to fight them off.'

'Or,' Felicity said. 'It was the man who owns the fortune-telling dog.'

'I'm sorry?'

'Everyone knows he doesn't have a proper home. He is an Itinerant Traveller. He goes about all the seaside towns with his dog, and he has a very rough-looking beard. Sometimes he shouts at people for no reason. He shouted at us, once, when his dog picked a card and then it didn't come true. It said I would meet a man with strong forearms when the daffodils came out, and it didn't happen, so we went back and told him the next time he was here and he *shouted* at us.'

'Or,' Mabel said, and I was beginning to sense a theme here, 'It might be the man who runs the Punch and Judy show. He beats his wife up all day long, doesn't he? Even if it is just through the puppets. Theatrical violence must affect a man's brain. He gave me a funny look once.'

'A funny look?'

'The kind of look a man gives you when he wants more,' Mabel said, in hushed tones. 'And sometimes, he simply stands around, his hands on his hips, looking arrogant.'

'Ladies,' I said, 'These are very fine and colourful theories, but do you have any evidence?'

They frowned at me and each other. Mabel sat up straight and pushed her shoulders back.

'All we are saying,' she said, 'Is you are looking in the wrong places. Gentlemen are called gentle men for a reason. It will be a rough person involved.'

'Do you think it was murder, then?' I asked, mildly.

'We do not know, of course,' Felicity said, with dignity, 'But we suspect countless dark and evil things happen in Hastings and St Leonards.'

'Your father was treating Mrs Withers, wasn't he?' I asked.

'That's immaterial,' Felicity hissed. 'Do not bring him into this. He is our father and a doctor. Leave him alone, or we will... we will ruin you.'

Listening to them, I realised how far I had come in the last year, how meeting Benjamin and working as a detective had allowed my feet to touch the ground. Had I been as foolish as they were, a year ago? Building demons out of thin air? I hoped not. They sounded as if they had been reading too many penny dreadfuls. I wondered how real their defence of their father was, whether they already suspected he was not the fine doctor he pretended to be and were coming to his defence knowing their safe world might crumble.

'Ah, ruination,' I said. 'You have not been immensely supportive of my role in society already. Do you think your father is an honest doctor? What time did you and he leave the Harvest Ball?'

They scrambled off the rocks in haste, almost frothing at the mouth.

'You have always been irrational,' Mabel said. 'Always. My father is right when he says you are not well.'

'At least I am looking for facts and not fiction,' I said. 'Take care with your wild theories. It does not do to tar strangers with a brush on a whim.'

They joined arms and started to march away across the sand, turning only to give a parting shot. 'You should be locked up. You are a danger,' Mabel said.

'Your father tried yesterday,' I said. 'He didn't succeed.'

I was very pleased to have the last word.

Later I met Benjamin and he told me about the funeral.

'There was not much to notice,' he said. 'All the great and the good were there. Colonel Withers gave a surprisingly moving speech, in which he talked about her contribution to society and how much she cared about this town and the people in it. I have said we will call on him tomorrow. Everyone was suitably morose, but I am not sure if was of particular use to attend. It was more helpful to go to the police and look at the list.

'Here, I copied it,' he said, handing it to me. 'It is a letter from a Dr Smythe from the British Medical Association in London, written to Mrs Withers, and it lists the ingredients of a bottle Mrs Withers has sent him. It does not name it, unfortunately, but given she had Wondrous Waters of Life in her reticule, it is possible it may be for that. They have analysed it, and apparently it contains bicarbonate of soda with a solution of glycerine, quinine, liquorice root and alcohol. The doctor who analysed it says it is not in any way efficacious. He warns against the proliferation of so-called medicines of dubious composition, which do not remedy illness and either do nothing or are actively damaging. There is a plan to bring in some kind of official regulation, he says.'

'So there was reason for Mrs Withers to call him a quack!' I said. 'Do you think Dr Spencer followed her along the seafront to prevent her from ever telling anyone else?'

'It certainly seems he had reason. We will need to see if we can find out what time Dr Spencer left the ball. Well done for asking more about the letter. You have shown yourself to be a very sensible detective.'

'I am very sensible generally,' I said, and beamed at him.

Chapter Twenty-Seven

Edith greeted us at the door. Would she and Mrs Withers have got on? Mrs Withers would have been a far more exacting mistress than I. She would have cared about the removal of dust, the arrangement of cutlery at dinner, the starching of shirt collars, the cut of beef, the cleanliness of the coal cellar and all the other endless tasks I pretended did not exist.

I thought Edith looked a little tired and woebegone, but her lip curled in a familiar, disparaging way when she saw me. It was mildly comforting.

'Ma'am,' she said, curtsying, 'Mr Blackthorn. The Colonel is at home. If you will wait in the hall I will announce you.' We did not have to wait long before we were ushered into the front parlour.

Colonel Withers was alone, sitting by the parlour fire, and he rose immediately as we entered. He was smaller than his wife and I had often thought of him as a friendly goblin, appearing at her side to spirit her away after she had shared her opinions too forthrightly. Now he looked very small and there was a frailty about him.

'Miss Hamilton, Mr Blackthorn,' Colonel Withers said. 'It is kind of you to call.'

'We came to offer our condolences,' Benjamin said. 'I did not know your wife, but my fiancé held her in high esteem.'

'She was always very interested in my welfare,' I said.

There was a slight sheen to his eyes, and he took a handkerchief from his upper pocket and briefly coughed into it.

'I will greatly miss her,' he said. 'The house always felt busy, active; and now it is very empty. She had such a strong sense of how the world should be. Without it I find myself a little lost.'

'I am sorry,' I said. 'It must have been a terrible night for you.'

'She admired you, you know,' Colonel Withers said.

'Did she?' I asked. 'I...' did not know what to say.

'She said you had spirit. Gumption. But she worried you had no guidance in life, without your mother. She took a concern about many of the younger ladies in town, with a... maternal view. We had... there were reasons. But look! Now you have a fine gentleman as a fiancé and a profession, so she need not have worried.'

'Do you know yet what happened to her?' Benjamin asked.

'She disappeared from the ball at around one-thirty, I think, although I did not realise until fifteen or so minutes after. We are – were – free to enjoy ourselves and come back together at will. Once I realised she was missing, I searched for her for most of the rest of the night, until she was found. I thought she must have gone home at first, although our coachman was still waiting outside and it would be unusual for her to leave without speaking to me. I called on her friends, went to the police; but we did not look for her on the Stade. We had no reason to think she might go there. She had a head injury, but they do not know how it happened.'

'We should disclose,' Benjamin said, honourably, 'that we are informally looking at matters, in our occupation as detectives.'

The colonel smoothed his whiskers.

'I wondered if you might be. I am glad,' he said. 'The police are inclined to take the easy option, because they have too many drunk navvies to deal with and they do not want to antagonise the fishermen further. But if you happen to find out anything more... I should like at least to understand what happened.'

'Had she been acting differently in recent weeks?' I asked.

'She had... been going through what women of a certain age—' he stopped abruptly. I guessed he might be talking about a change I was dimly aware happened to women in later years, but it was a topic rarely discussed by women, and never by men. 'She had not been entirely happy, so she had been seeing Dr Spencer. I am not sure he had been helping her. She was anxious, not herself.'

I did not judge it kind to tell Colonel Withers about the conversation I had heard between Mrs Withers and Dr Spencer until I had evidence it was important. But it added to my understanding of why she had called Dr Spencer a quack, if his potions were not working.

'What was she like on the night of the ball?' Benjamin asked.

'A little... angry?' he said. 'Her moods shifted, so it could be unpredictable. But there was something righteous about her anger, as if she felt she had to correct some great wrong. She could... sometimes she could interfere in matters not her concern, so I warned her not to meddle. She said if she did not take a stand for others' wellbeing, the town would fester into moral decay, and I should mind my moustache.' He smiled, sadly. 'She always did have a colourful turn of phrase.'

'She had a bottle of Dr Spencer's Wondrous Water of Life in her handbag,' I said. 'Was that the medicine she was taking?'

'Why no, I don't think so,' Colonel Withers said. 'I think they were called Female Pills. Nurse somebody or other's Female Pills. Although Dr Spencer may have provided her with more. So you are a detective? My wife thought there was something up. A... singular profession for a lady. She always thought you were bright.'

He was a kind man and I was impressed with the depth of his feelings for his wife. Was he being kind to me and her, in how she had thought of me? I might never know. But guilt ran up inside again like a fresh burn.

'I am honoured,' I said.

'I feel, as a lady, you may be better at finding out if there was anything else going on. Perhaps you could enquire discreetly among the ladies in her circle? I can give you their names. They would not talk to me, or the police, about many things, but possibly you...'

'Of course,' I said. 'Do you know much about Dr Spencer?'

'Not a great deal. I've occasionally come across him in my role on the council. I sit on the planning committee. We turned him down for a project not so long ago, which he wasn't too pleased about.'

'What was it for?'

'It was for a bigger Hydro, but in the old part of town. A fanciful scheme, ill-thought through. It proposed knocking down half of the old town to do it, which may not be pretty to look at, but it has history back to Roman times, and half the people who keep this town afloat live there. Not the gentry, but the workers. We shot it to the curb, anyway and he came to see me afterwards, all bluster and outrage, but I explained the reasoning. I think he came round.'

'Can we see the application?' Benjamin said. 'Would it have affected the Stade?'

'Yes, I think it would have,' Colonel Withers said. 'The Stade, George Street, All Saints Street, even the West Hill Lift built only a year or so ago. Nonsense. There's entrepreneurialism and there's impracticality. I'll get a copy sent to you.'

'Would you mind if I spoke to Edith? You may know she used to work for me, and she may have... feminine insight,' I said.

'Of course,' Colonel Withers said. Benjamin stayed talking with him, while I went to speak to Edith.

Chapter Twenty-Eight

Edith had begun working for my mother not long after my family moved from London to Hastings, when I was ten. She had loved working for my beautiful, fashionable, exciting, lively mother, admiring her glamour and London sophistry. After she disappeared, my father and I were poor leftovers.

Edith had never been the same after she disappeared, another casualty in my mother's flight to happiness. She had been resentful and disdainful, finally quitting nearly nine months ago now for the allure of Mrs Withers' household. I hoped it had been a better sojourn and I was sorry it had come to such a horrible end. I found her in the small back parlour, darning a large pair of socks, which must have been Colonel Withers'. He clearly had large feet.

'Hello, Edith. Please accept my condolences on your mistress. Can I speak to you for a moment?'

She instinctively shook her head and then gave up. 'Very well, then, miss,' she said, and I took a seat in the wicker armchair opposite her.

'I'm so sorry about Mrs Withers,' I said. 'Did you enjoy working for her? I ask you not in comparison to me, of course. Just... I hope you were happy.'

'She certainly had opinions on it,' Edith said. 'I never met a lady with more opinions. She was forever sharing her opinions with the world, about everything.' She shook her head at herself. 'I didn't say that. I didn't mean it. Don't listen to me. I'm just a bit... at sixes and sevens, now she's gone.'

'I am going to look into it,' I said. 'Edith, I don't know if you know, but I am working as a Lady Detective nowadays.' It was getting easier to tell people, the more I said it. 'Do you remember the day when I asked you to go for a walk with me, and we ended up following a gentleman? It was not because he was my fancy man. I was working on a case.'

Edith sat for a second looking at me, and I remembered how impossible it was to impress her.

'Well,' she said. 'It's an odd calling for a lady. I can't say your mother would have liked it.' Everything with her veered back to my mother, one reason why I was not unhappy Edith had left us.

'What was she like to work for, Mrs Withers?' I asked, changing the subject. 'I would like to try to help to find out what happened to her.'

'It's an awful business. No matter what she was like it's sad, miss, to die alone on the seashore. I always hoped that wasn't what happened to your mother, drowning in the sea alone, with nobody knowing.'

I thought seriously for a second about letting her know my mother was alive and well, but if I did, how outraged would Edith be? She would be furiously upset, to know my mother was living happily in Buxton and had not bothered to let her know she was alive. They had been almost friends, gossiping about clothes, hairstyling, Edith's romances, the people my mother met at social gatherings. Had Edith even had a romance after my mother left? I did not know.

If I told Edith my mother was alive, how long would it be before my father heard? Would Edith find out my mother was living with another woman and judge her for it? Would she, in her hurt, turn towards bitterness and revenge in the form of vicious gossip? I did not know and would not entirely blame her if she did, but it did not seem right for me to open that basket of worms.

'I don't think she did come to harm,' I said. 'I'm hopeful she's happy somewhere.' Edith looked doubtful.

'Mrs Hamilton would never have left us,' she said, and I felt again a sharp kick of hurt, because my mother had done not only exactly that, but failed to tell me she lived, beyond a hastily scribbled letter.

'She was not the angel you think,' I said, but Edith looked so horrified, it was time to change the subject.

'I am concerned about Mrs Withers... and what happened. If there is anything you think I should know, please say. How had she been, in past months?'

She shrugged her shoulders.

'She was going through the change. Made her a bit moody and hot, but she was getting on with it. She got a bit obsessed with Dr Spencer and his water cures for a while, surprised she didn't turn into water, the amount of it she drank and sloshed around in. She said Hastings and St Leonards could be the best hydropathic resort in the world. Tell that to the fishermen who spend all day gutting fish and mending nets.'

'She admired Dr Spencer then?'

'For a while, but then she got uppity about him, said he was a fraud. She had some pills he gave her, and she said they gave her nothing but, begging your pardon, excessive air. She was obsessed with his cures and then she got obsessed with proving he was a charlatan.'

'Was she taking Dr Spencer's Wondrous Water of Life?'

'No,' Edith said. 'It was Widow Welch's Female Pills. Supposed to cure all ills, cured none, she said. Dr Spencer gave them to her, though.'

'Did... did the change make her unstable?' I asked.

'It made her more righteous, I'd say. I've seen her at a distance on and off over the years, and she's always been a besom, excuse my words. But recently she seemed more annoyed with the world and its ways. I feel like women do get more righteous, as they get older. Less willing to put up with nonsense. Infuriated with injustice. That's sanity, not instability, to my mind.'

Edith had always been bright, and perhaps it was because she had never had the chance to use her skills, because I was so uninterested in it all, hair styles, fabrics, jewellery and make-up, that Edith had been so resentful. I had not given her room for more than drudgery. I did not blame her for it. Our town had been brighter for everyone when my mother was in it, and it had taken me a long, hard time to begin carving my own path towards joy.

'Very wise,' I said. 'Do you have any idea what might have happened on the night of the ball?'

'She got a letter that made her very excited,' Edith said. 'She kept saying "I knew it, I knew it," but she wouldn't tell me what it was about. She didn't trust me with her secrets.'

'Thank you, Edith,' I said. 'This has all been most insightful. If you think of anything else, will you let me know?'

'There was… it's a small thing, probably nothing.'

'Please tell me.'

'It's only that… I got given her clothes she wore on the night of the ball. I'm not sure the men knew what to do with them, afterwards. She wasn't buried in them. I dressed her in her favourite dress and hat for the burial, with silk lilacs on it.'

'So you have her clothes here?'

'Not sure what to do with them, so I've wrapped them in tissue paper for now and put them in a drawer. But the hat…'

'The hat?' Edith was slow to reach the point.

'It had three hummingbirds on it, when she went to the ball. I helped her put it on, and because they were all balanced across it, like a picture. They were attached with wire so we could move them about a bit, make sure they were perched right, looking in different directions. Not all clumped together.'

'And?'

'When the hat came back, there were only two.'

'Did the police not notice?' By Edith's expression, I had asked a stupid question.

'Why would they? To them, it's just a hat. But I like millinery, so I keep an eye on them, on fashion. One thing about Mrs Withers, she was fashionable with her hats. But one of the birds had been pulled off, from the back, and the wire had left a tiny tear in the brim, not so as you'd notice unless you knew. But it couldn't have fallen off. It would have to be wrenched. Someone had to have wanted it.'

'How odd,' I said. 'Are they so rare, hummingbirds?'

'No, they catch them by the thousands in Central America. Common as rats. There was an auction in London last year where they sold twelve thousand. But these ones are rarer, fork-tailed hummingbirds, I don't think anyone else has them. An army friend of her husband brought them back as a gift from Peru. She was very proud of them. I expect she told people about them at the party.'

'Can I see them?'

Edith shrugged and went to get the hat.

They were exquisite, when one looked at them closely. Only about five inches in length, their feathers were iridescent green and blue. The tail was extraordinary, two thin purple feathers curving down in a semicircle, crossing each other and widening at the bottom into the shape of a tiny, delicate leaf.

'I saw them at the ball, but I did not notice they were so beautiful,' I said.

'When your hat is always a certain way, people stop noticing,' Edith said. 'She was forever trying to make her hats bigger, more startling, so people would look. "I don't want to be invisible," she said. I wanted to say: "Wear a small hat, then, and everyone will notice," but it wasn't my place.'

It was true. She had worn ebullient hats for a long time and I had stopped registering them, beyond a cursory glance; it was like watching the same play several times, with different actors, or those garish street advertisements one looked at but didn't take in.

'Thank you. That's really helpful, Edith. I'll think on it. If something else occurs to you, please let me know.'

'Of course. It's grim here, now she's gone,' Edith continued. 'Mr Withers is never in, and when he is, he's miserable. There's not enough work to do. If you want me to come back…' but she possibly caught the look on my face, because she rapidly backtracked. 'No, well, never mind then. What's done is done. I'd better be getting on,' and I knew it was time to leave. I went back to the parlour and told Benjamin we could leave.

'We were good together, Edith,' I said on the doorstep, 'But it's better we admit it wasn't working and look to the future.'

By the disdainful grimace on her face, I realised I sounded exactly like a fiancée ending an engagement. 'Goodbye, miss, sir,' she said, shutting the door in our faces, and thankfully, things between us were back to the way they had always been.

Chapter Twenty-Nine

'We have been summoned, you and I,' Benjamin said, the next morning. He was looking particularly magnificent today, tall and masculine, his dark hair wildly curling, a little like an engraving I had seen of the poet Robert Burns, although of course Benjamin was without the wenching, the poetry and the drink.

'Summoned?'

'Lord and Lady Laxton have asked us to call on them at their town house in Lower Park Road. Our reputation as detectives must be growing. Are you free to go now? They are in a hurry to see us.'

It would be fascinating to meet Lady Laxton. She was the freakishly pale and beautiful elf from the ball, who had languished against a pillar with a circle of admirers. Would I feel the need to save her too, as all her admirers had? Would Benjamin? The thought did not fill me with glee.

'Of course. I shall bring a pencil and some notepaper,' I said, importantly, shaking myself into practicality. This could be a proper, important commission, establishing me as a detective in the town. Benjamin was already respected, but I had hitherto merely been tinkering at the edges. This might be the case to make my name as a detective.

We walked along the seafront together, side by side, and I could not help but wonder if bystanders would guess we had an important appointment. It was a blustery day, the parade wet with rain and sea spray, and ahead a lady shrieked as she was hit by the end of a wave gusting over the balustrade. The tide must be full in. The tide times changed so often I could never keep up with them, although the fishermen would know them like the back of their hands.

The Laxtons lived in a newly built mansion overlooking the expanse of Alexandra Park. Palpably more modern than Lord and Lady Brassey's house, it was light and airy, with stained-glass feature windows and wallpaper printed with foliage. The furniture and the decor was of a newer, art-deco style, less beholden to ancestral tradition, and there were colourful stained-glass lamps and delicately carved wood chairs in abundance. Lord and Lady Laxton were sitting in a long conservatory designed in white wrought-iron and filled with ferns, a very appropriate setting for the lady in particular. She was less pale today, but still ethereal, her black hair swept up into a massed halo around her head, swathed in a white dress looked to be made of bandages, resembling the habit of a Greek goddess or perhaps to the less charitable, an Egyptian mummy. Her husband, tall and suave, bade us sit down on somewhat uncomfortable wrought-iron chairs, while she blinked at us as if we had woken her from some otherworldly dream.

'Thank you for coming,' Lord Laxton said. 'We have a conundrum. We were very pleased to hear there is a new husband-and-wife detective team in town, because you may be able to help us with it.'

'We are not quite married yet, sir,' Benjamin said. 'But soon.'

'Nonetheless,' Lord Laxton said. 'We were pleased.'

'Pleased,' his wife said, aiming a very small pleased smile solely at Benjamin. Where was I in her pleasure? I sneaked a look at my fiancé, but he looked exactly as he always did, solid and reassuring. I hoped he would not be lured by her delicate woodland charms.

'My wife has an aunt,' Lord Laxton continued. He put out a spindly hand and rested it on his wife's shoulder. He had very long, thin fingers to go with his long thin frame. 'Mrs Laughton.

She loves to visit us and is coming this very evening for a house party. She will stay overnight as always. Effie is very fond of her.'

'Fond,' Effie said, nodding. She said the ends of her husband's sentences firmly, as if she thought her own brief utterances were whole sentences. Her husband still had his hand on his shoulder and she turned and gave him a smile of exquisite trust and sweetness. She had a narrow gold circlet in her hair and he reached out his hand and adjusted it a millimetre to the left.

'But she steals,' her husband said. His wife's smile faded and she twisted her hands in her lap in distress. 'We have an ante-room with a great deal of ornaments in it... snuff boxes that I collected from all over the world. Eleanora likes to pocket one or two each time she comes. In every other respect she is an exemplary relative, but we don't want to lose any more. And of course, we can never, ever raise it with her. We wondered, as you are a lady—'

'A lady,' Lady Laxton said, still looking between Benjamin and her husband as if I did not exist. I was beginning to find her fey girlishness a little irritating. How old was she? She must be in her early twenties at least, but she behaved as if she had sprung fresh from a dewy field. She did not act like any real woman I knew, but perhaps as a man might expect a woman to behave, if women were an illusion lifted from the pages of a love-sick poet. Her husband seemed to find her charming. Would Benjamin see through her, or would he be beguiled? I took another sideways glimpse at him, but he looked as stoic and business-like as ever. I would interrogate him afterwards.

'So we wondered if you might find a way of preventing her, this evening,' Lord Laxton said. 'It would mean attending our little Tuesday soiree, as a guest, and perhaps just keeping an eye on the room, so she cannot infiltrate it.'

'Infil...' Perhaps realising she was overdoing it, Lady Laxton did not finish the word, but let it trail off artfully into nothing. She blinked, wide-eyed, at Benjamin. 'I am so very fond of her.

And I do not ever wish her to suspect… she would be so mortified if she thought I knew. So upset. Is there a way you can…?'

'I would be delighted to assist,' I said, firmly. 'I am happy to attend your soiree and I will form a plan to keep your snuff boxes safe without offending your aunt. Never fear.'

She looked at me briefly as if surprised I was there. Was there, behind those big innocent eyes, the knowledge I was not fooled by her?

'Oh, but Mr Blackthorn must attend too,' she said. 'We need a proper… we need a man. In case it all goes wrong. I am sure it will not. But if it did!' She looked at Benjamin in horror and then turned wide-eyed to her husband.

'Of course, of course, both of you must attend,' he said. 'So, it is settled then. I also look after several businesses in town, for my sins… the Pavilion Theatre, the Waxwork Museum and suchlike… it may be I could also do with a big strong gentleman to help me settle my accounts from time to time.'

'I don't do debt collection,' Benjamin said. 'My apologies.' I admired him for his confidence in saying no to the peerage, without explanation.

Lady Laxton looked a little wounded, as if he had rejected her, but her husband shrugged it off.

'Well, very well, it's of no consequence,' he said. 'It's tonight we need you for after all. Starts at ten.'

'We shall look forward to assisting you,' Benjamin said, and we took our polite leave. It was not until we were halfway down the hill I stopped walking, dropped his arm and swung around to face him.

'It will be our first case together!' I said.

'Yes,' he said, looking wary.

'The aristocracy have hired us!'

'They have.'

'If that fake forest creature tries to charm you and you let her,' I said, 'I will not answer for my actions.'

'Violet Hamilton,' Benjamin said, 'are you jealous?'

'Indubitably not,' I said and tried to turn to begin walking again, but he took both of my hands in his, preventing me.

'I am flattered,' he said, laughing. 'But pray do not trouble yourself. She is a very faded sort of female, in your company. I fancy I prefer a woman with more verve and vivacity, who could argue me into a cocked hat if they chose. I prefer you, in fact, the very lady I am fortunate enough to be engaged to. If I am to spend several decades seated beside the fire opposite a woman of an evening, I'd prefer one who can form her own sentences.'

He kissed the back of my hands through my gloves before we carried on walking and our little exchange, in a nutshell, was why I should stop prevaricating and marry him immediately.

The event was an evening party, not quite a ball, with some dancing and a light supper, but far more mingling and standing around expected.

Lord and Lady Laxton greeted their guests in the front hall. He looked like a twig in the wind; his wife was pale and interesting again, her hair as loose and as thick as a Pre-Raphaelite model, topped with a crown of ivy dotted with pearls. She might be Ophelia, floating melancholically down a river full of flowers, or the Lady of Shalott. Her hair was thick enough for her to ride down a high street naked any day without immodesty, if it was real.

'Delighted,' she said, pressing my proffered hand, but then she saw Benjamin and dropped it too quickly for politeness. 'Mr Blackthorn,' she said, wide-eyed, breathy. 'I am so *pleased*.'

'Yes, welcome. You must mingle quite as if you are ordinary guests,' Lord Laxton said, which made me feel as if we would not be welcome if we were not working, but perhaps he did not intend it in that way. Then other people arrived in the line and we had to move on, and they had not managed to point out Mrs Laughton. It did not matter. All I needed to do was loiter near the room with the ornaments, which our hosts had shown us earlier, and my suspect would swing by soon enough.

I had a plan, which I had discussed with Benjamin on the way there. His role was less clear, because he could not spend too much time loitering with me. His tall and strong demeanour was a little over the top when our thief was of advanced years and frail. She must not suspect we suspected her. He might have to spend more time mingling with other guests, enjoying the party. Well, so be it. It was our first proper case together and if we were to work as a team we could not always operate as equally as cart horses. Sometimes I would pull the weight more than him. I only hoped our hostess would not attempt to entangle him in her ivy.

We had been one of the first to arrive, but the rooms still filled up fairly quickly. There was a lady playing the piano in one room; a small dance floor in another; a buffet in a third. The conservatory was open to anyone who wanted to admire the ferns and the fig trees. The guests were a mixture of young and old; the young ones were there for Lady Laxton of course, who flitted through the middle of them looking startled; while several older gentlemen and their wives, who must be Lord Laxton's contemporaries, were grouped around the fringes. There was no timetable to the party, or schedule; it was merely a chance for people to perambulate from room to room, mingling in whatever form they chose. At intervals the older gentlemen shot to the smoking room.

My heart stopped briefly when I saw Dr Spencer arrive, but Benjamin was at my side and I took his arm.

He looked down at me. 'What is the matter, Violet?'

'It is only… Dr Spencer,' I said. I felt weak to be so glad my fiancé was with me, but it had not been very long since I was dangling off rooftops and with Benjamin at my side no one would dare to infer I was anything less than healthy of mind and body.

Benjamin's mouth thinned and he looked ready to dive across the ballroom and set Dr Spencer to rights, but I squeezed his arm and he merely stiffened and stood straighter. 'Blackguard,' he said under his breath. 'Do you want me to speak to him? Or more?'

'No, it is all right,' I said. 'He is still a suspect, so giving him a black eye might not help our cause. But I do, truly, appreciate the offer.' I smiled at him and the smile I received in return would warm my cockles for the whole evening. I was almost tempted to lure him into the conservatory to frolic among the ferns, except of course, ladies never did such a wanton thing.

Dr Spencer caught sight of us both and I enjoyed the look in his eyes when he registered the size and breadth of my fiancé. He did not acknowledge us but veered off to the ballroom, an unusual destination when all his contemporaries were in the smoking room. I felt the triumph of it.

His daughters were behind him. I had forgotten about them. What did they think of their father, with his untrustworthy cures and threatening methods? Did they believe his every word? But it was to no account. They headed straight for the cloud of adoration surrounding Lady Laxton, who was perched on the edge of a delicately carved chair, its legs so spindly they might snap at any second, which would put Lady Laxton in a pretty sort of peril and cause at least a dozen gentlemen to rush to catch her.

Then I forgot everyone else, because a small elderly lady with dazed eyes tottered across the room towards me and I knew in the deepest depths of my soul it was the thieving Mrs Laughton.

'You can mingle!' I said to Benjamin. 'She's here!' And I pushed him away with a haste I might regret. He gave me a look of amusement and sauntered off, not, thankfully, towards our hostess. My job had begun.

Chapter Thirty

There was something about Mrs Laughton which reminded me of her niece. Her grey hair was softly shiny and she had an air of innocent, warm frailty. If Lady Laxton was playing a naive woodland sprite, her aunt breathed the vibes of an elderly Hestia, gentle Greek goddess of the hearth and domestic life. She was not heading towards me, of course, but for the room beyond.

I glanced at Lady Laxton, who broke briefly from her sylvan reverie to glance at me anxiously. I tipped my head towards the newcomer, and Lady Laxton nodded. My suspicions were right. Mrs Laughton was active.

There were few other people in the room, because ornaments once admired, were admired, and there were better rooms for mingling. Mrs Laughton must have believed she had a clear field, because she headed straight for a silver snuff box with a little red and gold elephant on top. But when she arrived, I was there.

'Good evening,' I said. 'Isn't it a *wonderful* party? I am so pleased to be here. I have not known Lord and Lady Laxton very long, but my father does a great deal of business with him, and I am so *delighted* to be here. Forgive me introducing myself, but I do not yet know many people here. I am Miss Violet Hamilton, of Matthew's Gardens. How do you know their honourable graces?'

She hid her irritation very well but craned her neck just a little in an attempt to look around me at the snuff box. Then she smiled, tremulously, wringing her hands together in shy pleasure, a gesture not so removed from one her niece might make. I wondered briefly how close they were.

'Delighted,' Mrs Laughton said. 'I am Effie's favourite aunt. Her ladyship, that is. We are very dear to each other, but we do not meet so very often now she is married. Young love, or should I say, old love of the young. Are you here alone?'

'I am with my fiancé. He is off playing billiards. He often leaves me at parties. I can get a little lonely. But now I have found you! Perhaps we shall become bosom acquaintances.'

'Oh my dear, my bosom is too old to get acquainted with anyone,' she said. Was there a sharpness to it? Surely I had not already dented her facade. But she smiled warmly and patted my arm. 'Are you interested in antiquities? This seems a dull room for a young girl.'

'I *love* old objects,' I said. 'Especially shiny ones. This one, here, with a little elephant on it. So sparkly. The elephant looks exactly like a real elephant, except of course, a real one would not fit on such a tiny box. I love boxes too. It is magical that you can open a lid, put things inside, and then not see them again until you want to.'

'Such a perfectly *simple* soul you are,' she said, smiling gently, sliding past me to a display of six snuff boxes, arranged in a semicircle on top of a round mirror, so they reflected each other beautifully in the glass. But somehow, I was there too, and now I was talking about billiards.

'Such a dull game,' I said. 'I cannot understand why men like to hit little balls with long sticks. I tried it once and gouged up the green felt with the tip of my stick and then no one could play all evening and Herbert was very cross with me. He said I was a baize destroyer. Do you play?'

'Not billiards,' Mrs Laughton said. She gave up on the mirrored display and moved eastwards towards a little wooden shelved cabinet full of boxes from top to bottom. 'Is that your Herbert, there?' She pointed far beyond the room, but inexplicably I was admiring the little cabinet and thinking about cheese.

'That box, there,' I said, 'is it made of soapstone? It looks exactly like a miniature wheel of cheddar. I am fond of cheddar cheese. Did you know someone once made a giant cheddar cheese for our great Queen Victoria, and challenged her to eat it all? She could not. I might have managed, because as I may have said, I am very fond of it.'

'Ivory,' Mrs Laughton said. 'It is ivory, and I do not think a craftsman from the Qing dynasty would be thinking of cheese products. The delicate lace effect for a start, is incredibly difficult to achieve in ivory. It is not a pattern usually found on cheese.'

She was beginning to crack, so I moved on to an observation about the electric lighting in the room and thence to the electric lighting installed on Hastings and St Leonards seafront a whole six years before, but which to me remained a perpetual wonder.

Her eyes had glazed over, but I could not forget my other case.

'That bird, there, reminds me of the birds on poor dear Mrs Withers' hat the night of the Harvest Ball,' I said. It was a squat robin, but it would do. 'Did you know her?'

'Pshaw,' she said. 'A more thoroughly unpleasant woman I have never met. Always sticking her nose in business that wasn't her own. Perhaps her sins caught up with her.' She realised she had dropped her pleasant façade and sat down abruptly on a small tapestry-covered bench.

'You must allow me some rest,' she said. 'I am quite unused to company. I will sit here, on this little couch, next to the china display. Pray, will you fetch me some refreshment?'

'But of course!' I said. 'Oh, there is my fiancé!' Benjamin was crossing the hallway and happened to glance over, so I beckoned him our way wildly.

'Darling Herbert, will you fetch us some refreshment?' I said, and he raised an eyebrow at me, but bowed and went.

'A very giving man,' Mrs Laughton said, 'I would not leave him to his billiards too much,' and something about her dry tone made me wonder if she knew exactly what I was up to, but when I glanced at her, her face was smooth of all expression.

After Benjamin brought us each a drink and departed again, my wit and repartee recommenced with vigour and it was a mere ten minutes before she quit the room, claiming a headache. I did not follow.

I congratulated myself instead. It was quite as successful an endeavour as my attempts to rebuff attempts at courtship over the years, which had involved a similar amount of subterfuge and waffle. Although this, of course, was kinder, because Mrs Laughton was a kleptomaniac.

Benjamin caught my eye and wandered over again. He looked extremely fine in his evening dress, with his dark hair and eyes, and I felt the rush of pleasure that came across me every now and again at the knowledge he was temporarily, and possibly permanently, mine.

'Successful, were you?' he said.

'I think so,' I said. 'Although she might come back so I'll need to linger nearby for a while. What have you been up to?'

'This and that,' he said. 'Asked around a bit about Dr Spencer. Seems he is quite well respected, in these circles at least. People think he's full of good ideas to make this town a better place. Ambitious, visionary even. I told one or two of them his activities might merit a closer look, and I might as well have criticised Prince Albert himself. Where did Herbert come from?'

'I'm not sure,' I said. 'Maybe you look like a Herbert. Can you dance?'

'I can,' he said, and we had to wait until Mrs Laughton left the party in high dudgeon an hour later, but after that we danced, and he was excellent indeed.

Chapter Thirty-One

Lord and Lady Laxton were very pleased with us, although Lady Laxton in truth seemed more pleased with Benjamin, staring at him with eyes resembling dark pools full of liquid longing. But it may have been my imagination, because I had had two glasses of fruit punch and was dizzy with success. I decided not to worry. Benjamin did not seem likely to drown in them.

Lord Laxton paid us via a smooth sliding handshake with Benjamin. 'We may have more work for you,' he said. 'Not settling accounts, fair enough, although it could have been lucrative. I'm on the Boards of a great many businesses in town and I like your style. I'm investing in a major project that should come to fruition soon, so I'll be in touch.' I felt a flush of irritation because it was I who had prevented the theft of their precious knick-knacks with my execrable conversation, but it did not matter. I had succeeded, we had been paid, there might be further work, we had enjoyed the evening – there were so many reasons I should not care if Lord and Lady Laxton saw me. And I was glad not to have to take Lord Laxton's skeletal hand.

Benjamin walked me downhill towards home. It was a crisp, clear night, and the sea glowed cerulean blue above the rooftops. He had his arm around me, because no one would see, and we were quiet in a comfortable, companionable way. The mingled scents of the sea carried faintly on the breeze, as well as the occasional sharp sweetness of a magnolia.

'You will take the money for tonight,' he said, shortly before we reached St Matthew's Gardens. 'Apart from my brief shining moment of glory as Herbert, I mostly ate cake and drank wine.'

'We will put most of it towards the business,' I said. 'And I will take a cut. That is only fair.' I was coming to understand how a business was run, which was as important for me to learn as anything else, investment and outlays as well as wages.

We agreed to meet at the shop the next morning at ten o'clock, and he said goodbye to me in our usual fashion under the oak tree growing at the corner of our street, a tree old enough to have been there long before our house was built. Then he walked me to my door and sauntered off into the night whistling, his hands in his pockets.

I think we had both thoroughly enjoyed the evening and I hoped we would have many more cases like that, working together. We brought out the best in one another.

I slept deeply and I rose cheerfully the next morning.

But when I reached the shop, my reverie was rudely interrupted. The door lay ajar, half off its hinges, its two glass panes smashed. A rosewood and marble cabinet lay broken on the cobblestones of the small yard, and I could see a scene of devastation lay within. Someone had broken in.

I recognised the tall form of Benjamin inside the shop already, so I clambered over the little step and went in. He was trying to right a wardrobe, and he looked at me grimly.

Someone had destroyed everything they could lay their hands on. All the furniture was upended, drawers lying everywhere, cupboards askew, lamps smashed, wardrobes with doors swinging open. It looked as if it had been done with anger, as if someone had come in and deliberately caused as much damage as they could.

Benjamin sat down heavily on an upturned crate and put his head in his hands. This was his livelihood, his oeuvre, much more than the detective work; he had used his furniture business to put himself back together after his father died, inch by lovingly polished inch, and I could not bear it for him. I sat next to him and took one of his hands.

'It will be all right,' I said. 'We will put it back together. Maybe some of it can be saved.' Although I had to admit to myself, looking at the level of destruction, it would be hard, if not impossible. Someone had taken an axe and gone wild with it, leaving gashes and dents wherever they could.

'It brings in the money,' he said. 'It's what helps me support Agnes and the children. It was a successful business, and I'm not sure we can resurrect this.'

'Why would anyone be so vicious?' I asked. I spotted my typewriter lying in a corner upside down, and unexpected tears welled up in my eyes. But I would not let them out, because this was worse for Benjamin.

'Someone has a grudge,' he said. 'Or they were searching for something. I cannot envisage...' He did not finish the sentence, just sat quietly contemplating the destruction of his dreams. I rested my head on his shoulder and sat with him.

'Your typewriter,' he said eventually, and got up to right it. It was almost too heavy to pick up, but together we managed to lift it and place it back on the oak desk that had magically stayed upright, although its drawers had been thrown across the shop. The typewriter keys were stuck together, and the wheel that typed the letters had become dislodged. Some of the paint, the delicate black and coloured lettering that made it such a beautiful machine, had chipped off. I gave it an affectionate stroke.

'It is not too badly harmed,' I said. 'There may be other things we can save too,' but my fiancé gave a sigh so deep from within his soul I knew he was not ready for optimism yet.

'Someone will have seen who did this,' he said. 'I will go and ask around. I cannot face... I will deal with all this another day.'

'And I will help,' I said. 'Do not despair.' He gave me a hug, resting his chin on top of my head briefly.

'We'll find the bastards,' I said primly, startling him into laughter. I hoped he would not judge me for it. It was not a word a lady should say, but I had very much envied Hildebrand's ease with it.

'Heavens, you shock me in new ways every day,' he said. 'But you're right. Bastards, the lot of them.'

'Shall I see you tomorrow, then?' I said, because I could see he wanted to shut up shop and start asking around town.

'Yes,' he said. 'Go home and stay safe for today. And tomorrow... meet me at the Old Roar Quarry at one o'clock. It's time I taught you how to shoot.'

The Old Roar Quarry was so called because it was near a twelve-metre waterfall whose roar could be heard for miles in heavy rains. There were many active quarries in the area, with hard Hastings granite, clay and sandstone gathered for road and house building, but this quarry, not far from Silverhill Park, was long abandoned, its dips and valleys filled with water and with banks of grass and ferns set low within its walls, so there was less chance of us disturbing the peace or accidentally shooting anyone. But today it had not been raining, so the waterfall was no more than a gentle swish of background noise.

He had brought me a revolver, small enough to fit in my reticule. 'It is called the Cyclist's Friend,' he said, and I stared at him, startled.

'Why is it called that?'

'So women can take it along with them if they choose to cycle alone, apparently. Though I hope you'd outride someone before you shot them. Still, it might be a good deterrent. Can you ride a bicycle?'

'Not yet, but I am going to learn,' I said. 'Do you think it might be useful for detective work?'

'Definitely,' he said. 'I'm thinking of getting one too. Gets you places in half the time. Well, let's get to it.'

Bit by bit, and taking his time, he showed me the techniques for firing the Cyclist's Friend, how to access the cylinder, pull the hammer back to half-cock and load it with live bullets. He lined up three short logs several feet away and then showed me how to stand and hold the gun, while I set my jaw, determined not to be distracted by the physical proximity. I was a detective. Sensation was not appropriate. I was a hunter, a shooter, focused only on my aim and the trajectory of a bullet.

Benjamin showed me at first, firing with careful precision, the sound ricocheting off the walls of the quarry. Then he put the gun in my hands and helped me into position, standing behind me and holding me quite firmly in his arms. If I had not had a mission, I might have been distracted by it. He held me the first few times I fired, taking the weight of the recoil in his own arms and shoulders, showing me how to balance and adjust, and I was a little forlorn when he stepped back and made me do it alone.

Most of the birds had flown away at the racket, but just as I was about to fire again a small chaffinch flew across my line of sight and I nearly shot it. I lowered the gun and Benjamin laughed at me.

'You'll have to get used to blood,' he said. 'Hold your nerve. Try again, and this time if you see a bird don't stop. We'll make a revolveress of you yet.'

I liked his description. It gave me determination. The hardest part was the recoil. At first, I did not like it, the violence of the movement along my arm and the noise, and I was disappointed with myself. But I persevered, and after a while, I got the basics. It was important to stand loose and free, planting both legs firmly on the ground, and in the act of firing, it helped if I threw my weight forward on the left leg, using the other foot as a pivot, touching only lightly on the ground. I went through a great many bullets aiming at the logs, adjusting my hold on the gun and my stance until I felt secure and in control.

It would be easier to use a rifle and rest it against my shoulder, I realised, as my shoulder would lessen the impact of shooting, which I felt in my hands and arm. I used my non-dominant hand to support the other over the grip, but the hardest part was holding a steady aim as the bullet fired.

'Straighten your elbows! Shoot with both eyes! Anticipate the pull back! Keep breathing and don't tense up when you're about to fire—' Benjamin's advice was comprehensive, and by the end of it my head was buzzing. But I hit a log, and then another, and although my shots were not perfect, I did not feel so intimidated.

'That'll do!' Benjamin said when we ran out of bullets. 'You are not perfect, but you'll get by. Now, to clean it,' and he spent another half an hour showing me how to clean my gun and carry it so I didn't shoot my own leg.

I was learning. I was learning all the things I needed to be a good detective. I could not be dissatisfied with my day, even though half the bullets had bounced off trees, and my wrists ached all the way to my shoulder and neck.

'Thank you, thank you,' I said to Benjamin. 'I owe you so much for today, and other days.'

'That's what a fiancé's for,' he said. 'To teach you how to kill.'

I had asked Hildebrand to make me a picnic, so we sat beside a sycamore tree and drank ginger beer and ate ham sandwiches while peace and the birds came back. I sat in the nook of his arms, warm in the early spring sunshine, and savoured the moment. A wren was chirping its scatter-gun call. A great-crested grebe, as delicate as a ballerina, swam past on the water with five little stripy chicks balanced precariously on her back all fighting each other for room, until she abruptly upended them into the water to dive for a fish.

It was so quiet in the quarry, the destruction of yesterday fading and it was hard to believe what lay in wait for us back at the shop. There were several bees buzzing around a hydrangea bush, busy with contentment.

'What did you do this morning?' I asked him.

'I began to tidy up a little, set things to rights. It won't be easy.' He was not normally a man to give into defeat and he was coming back to himself slowly, I could see, working out solutions. 'Some pieces might be saved. The rest are only good for firewood.'

'We must take on more cases,' I said. 'Advertise. Perhaps we should take on debt collection for Lord Laxton—'

'No,' he said, and I could feel his jaw set where it rested on the top of my head. 'No, I will not overwhelm us with more detective work or become a rough man for hire. It is not my way, Violet. I've lived long enough in the world to know what I want from life, and it's not solely the detective agency or racketing around making poor folk's lives miserable. We'll make the best of the furniture we've got left, and I might purchase more, if I can juggle it. I need to look at the accounts, if I can find them, work it all out.'

'I can help,' I said. 'I can take on more cases and I don't mind collecting debts. I am not as big as you, but I can be fierce.' Truth be told I was terrified at the thought, but sacrifices would need to be made to get us on our feet again. I would take my pistol and learn how to look mean.

I felt his smile on the top of my head and he tightened his arms around me.

'I'll not have it,' he said. 'We'll find a way that doesn't involve you strong-arming half of Hastings into submission. Life has a way of throwing good fortune after bad. Let's wait for a bit and see what happens.'

It was extraordinarily peaceful. He was good company, my fiancé, content with silence if conversation was not needed, restful in himself and with me. Unlike me, he felt no need to rush at life. It was a quality I appreciated in him, his ability to sit and reflect, take life slowly, without needing to be anywhere else. With him, I felt less of my own restlessness, less of my need to throw myself at life headlong.

I realised I still had the little drawing of a brown butterfly in my pocket.

'Do you think it might be by Marianne North?' I asked, and

he did, but when I said it had felt like a message, he laughed at me.

'You are not a little brown butterfly,' he said. 'Didn't she paint hummingbirds too? You are more like a little hummingbird, all vibrant colours, always zooming about, never still. Chasing nectar. That's how I imagine you. Brown butterfly, indeed.'

What was I to do with my exemplary fiancé? It was clear he was too good for me. But for the afternoon, cocooned from the world, I let myself relax. We were together. He was fond of me. I had nothing to prove, nothing to fight for. I had learnt, most satisfactorily, how to shoot. Despite all the destruction and danger we would return to, and although a part of me still longed to move beyond our eternally wholesome innocence, it was a perfect afternoon.

Chapter Thirty-Two

I had not seen my father much these past days since our confrontation, but he was in that evening, sitting in our front parlour reading some Greek mythology, looking, if I knew him at all, a little lost.

'Are you well?' I asked, and I sat down opposite him and picked up my own book.

'As can be expected,' he said, and returned to his book.

We had read opposite each other for years, but it had not always been in happy accord, because neither of us had been content without my mother. She had not been kind to him in their marriage, declining further intimacy after I was conceived, because she had hated marital relations; despite that, they had made a kind of happiness together, off and on, until a few years before she disappeared, when their marriage had declined into spitefulness and arguments.

After she disappeared, I had not had time to spare for sympathy for my father, I realised, nor the strength to lift up his emotions when mine were so jangled. He likely felt the same, so we had existed but not communicated, not supported each other, spiralling around each other in coldness and rules for too long. He had tried to offload me onto suitors, and I had fought back, perhaps not ready to abandon my last family connection. The insight was a new one to arrive and I blinked at it, startled.

I was going to speak again, but before I could, he cleared his throat and lowered his book.

'I have been thinking,' he said. 'About your profession. And while I cannot approve of it – cannot see it as a safe and appropriate occupation for any lady – it seems times are changing and I must move with them. Your fiancé seems like a sensible man and you are... you are happy. So I will not object, or disown you. And if you want to continue living here, you may. But I must ask you to take proper care of yourself. This world is not a gentle place for women.'

It was a long speech for him and the most genuine care he had shown for my wellbeing in years.

'Thank you,' I said. 'I know being a detective will not be easy. But I think I will be better for it, for being out in the world and learning to fight its battles.'

'You are a very modern young woman,' he said. 'I have spoken to Dr Spencer and reprimanded him most seriously for suggesting risky and experimental cures. I told him you are perfectly sane. I have never had any doubt you are. I simply – and unfortunately it was exactly the same with your mother – I simply do not comprehend you.'

He was churning up too many emotions by saying things he had never said, so I decided to change the subject.

'Maybe it does not matter I am incomprehensible,' I said. 'I have not seen Tilda... Mrs Beeton recently. Has she been unwell?'

Two spots of red appeared high on his cheekbones.

'We have had a falling out,' he said. I had never seen him look more miserable.

'With Mrs Beeton? Surely she is impossible to fall out with?'

'She does not know. She thinks I am just busy. It was... the ball. Someone said... someone said she was common.'

'Common? She is never that. Who said it?'

'A gentleman who holds several accounts at our bank. Lord Laxton. He is very influential, has brought us a lot of other clients. He said she was not a good reflection on me,' my father said.

'So, you are not seeing her because of him?'

'Because of him,' he said, heavily. 'He said it was not wise for me to sport with a lady who milks cows.'

'Mrs Beeton is splendid,' I said. 'She was the most splendidly lovely person at the ball. She enjoyed herself immensely, and she lit up the room. Working on a farm does not make her common.'

'I did not think it,' he said. 'But the viscount is our biggest client.'

'Who is he?' I said. 'A man you smoke cigars with twice a year? I have met him, he is very spindly, and his wife has the personality of a cigarette card. Mrs Beeton is worth ten of him. She is bountiful and generous, and she has made you happier than you have been for years. Do not let her go. Without her, you will desiccate.'

'Desiccate?'

'Yes. You need her warmth to keep you alive. Do not give her up for Lord Laxton, I beg of you.'

'She is so very different from your mother,' he said, running a hand wearily down his face, 'Your mother was admired and respected wherever she went. Tilda is different. She is easier to love. She embraces life without self-consciousness, without sophistry, and she is the warmest, most giving person I have ever known. I am surprised by it, delighted by it, constantly. I already know I have been a fool. But I suspect your mother is still alive, Violet, so there are very few options for us.'

I nearly told him my mother was alive. But I did not want to ruin our rapprochement, and I still wanted my mother to take responsibility for telling him, to take on the burden of allowing us to heal from the damage she had wrought. It should not be my load to carry. I resolved instead to write her a very stern letter.

'If she is still alive,' I said, 'She has been away so long, no one will expect her to be living. I see no reason why you could not find an amenable vicar and quietly marry Mrs Beeton.' The Reverend Bartle would not do, because he had known her to be living all this time and kept her confidence, and we could not test his principles even further. Or perhaps because of his deception, we could.

'It is against God,' my father said, but he was not especially religious at heart, so it was a comfortingly weak excuse.

'Can you not forget the silly words of an unimportant man, and make it up with her?' I asked.

'I have left it too long,' he said. 'I have neglected her and now I do not know if she will forgive me.' He had the face of a soldier facing a firing squad who believed he deserved the bullets.

'Think on it,' I said. 'And if all seems lost, there is a lot an enormous bunch of flowers will achieve.'

I wrote my mother a letter and posted it the very next day. It was not long. It just said that I was tired of the secret, and that I and my father deserved better treatment. If she chose to cut all contact with me and disappear again, well, this time at least I knew we could survive it.

Chapter Thirty-Three

When I went to our detective agency the next day, there was a large pile of broken furniture outside. Benjamin was slowly setting order back with his usual focused dedication; throwing out items that could not be rescued, setting aside the pieces that could be saved, or reused, or remade into something else. He was a self-taught carpenter as well as everything else, so where there was life in a chest of drawers or use for a piece of wood to mend a bookshelf, he would puzzle it out and make order from the chaos, creating new life.

Some of the items were not too damaged at all, others had angry wounds or gashes across them that could be sanded down, filled in and varnished, others were splintered to pieces.

'Whoever did this was bent on damage,' Benjamin said. 'It doesn't feel like a common or garden burglary. Nothing much has been taken, as far as I can see – it's all destruction, as if they were searching for something and then got angry when they couldn't find it.' He ran his large hand over his face wearily. He had had two tough years; the purposeless murder of his father, killed by smugglers with a grudge, and now this, but always he seemed to patiently accept life was hard and carry on, rather than rail against injustice, feathers up, as I did.

'Let me help,' I said, so we spent the day sorting out what could be mended and what could not. Our investigation into Mrs Withers' death and whether or not it was linked to the destruction could wait. The silver coffee pot was dented, but still working, so he made us coffee on the little stove in the backroom and we sat for a rest on an upturned blanket chest, its lid wrenched off rudely. It might be mended. It was not so difficult to put new hinges on a lid.

'It is as if we had offended the Greek gods,' I said, 'and they have blown a great storm inside the shop to punish us. It must have taken a lot of concentration to wreak so much havoc.'

'Who have we offended?' Benjamin asked. 'Is it you, stealing from libraries and escaping from asylums? Or even liberating goats?'

'It might be you, rescuing damsels from their evil husbands or standing around looking handsome but engaged at evening parties,' I said.

He looked pleased.

'So you think I'm handsome, do you? I must admit it's a while since I wore the full regalia. I'm inclined to agree. Perhaps I should wear it more often, day to day. I could be the Gorgeous Gentleman and you the Luscious Lady Detective in a ballgown, and we'll cut a swash around town, helping only the richest and most discerning clients. The Sophisticated Sleuths. The Aristocratic Investigators.'

I swatted him on the arm.

'There is a danger your enormous head will not fit through doorways,' I said. 'Yes, I find you handsome, but I think being celebrity sleuths might lose us more cases than we solve. If you can rein in your good looks for a short while, I would like you to look at my typewriter and tell me if it will still work.'

He swung off the blanket box immediately and began to look at my typewriter, proclaiming it chipped and damaged but very much still in working order.

But our conversation had helped lift our moods a little, and at one point, I heard even him whistle a tune. The repair, after all, was what he loved best about working with his hands. He definitely loved this job more than being a detective; the slow restoration of purpose to furniture forgotten and neglected. I did not like to think too closely about whether he was doing the same for me.

Chapter Thirty-Four

As I headed home along the seafront at around five o'clock, I had the distinct sensation of being followed. It was the feeling of eyes on my back, perhaps, or that when I turned around quickly, a man disappeared abruptly behind a pergola not tall enough to hide the top of his hat. A brown hat.

I was good at following people myself, having followed Miss Turton's former fiancé for several days. My new gun was holstered to my thigh, accessible through the cut pocket of my skirt, so I took a firm grip on it and when I reached the weather station, a small booth-like building listing the day's weather and the tides, I slipped back around the sides of it until I estimated he was ahead of me, so I was following my pursuer instead.

It was Mr Gallop, the librarian. He turned around to look for me when I was not ahead and jumped.

'Miss Hamilton,' he said, and then, surprisingly, tipped his hat and bared his teeth at me. It took me a few seconds to realise it must be his attempt at a smile.

'I was hoping I might run into you,' he said. 'May I have a word? Perhaps on this bench?' It was a prettyish sort of bench in green-painted wrought iron, overlooking the sea. I was not keen to speak to him, still mortified from my night-time adventure at the library, but curiosity won. I sat down. The sun would set in an hour or so, but there would be no glorious vista of reds and oranges tonight, as oppressive grey clouds covered the whole sky. A seaside town always felt a little bleaker than other towns when it was not holiday weather, as if a blessing had been withheld; the promenade was still busy, but people's enjoyment seemed muted and more desperate.

Mr Gallop harrumphed for a bit, his moustache twitching, staring out to sea.

'Miss Hamilton, you were at the library the other night,' he said. So, he knew. Was he going to threaten me, blackmail me? Stand up in church and denounce me? I would handle it and tell the world he was a book despot. And if he was particularly nasty, I would shoot his foot off. Mr Gallop had crossed a line and need only to breathe to incense me beyond reason.

'And if I was?' I asked.

'We got off on the wrong foot,' he said, turning to look at me and baring his teeth again in an unsettling, fawning way. 'We should let bygones be bygones. Whatever happened all that time ago... you were entitled to know your own mind about marriage. And even though you could have shown better judgement, more... but it is the past. The past. I am quite willing, to let you take out any books you choose. Going forward,' and he threw his arms out wide, startling a sparrow, 'The Brassey Institute Library can be your second home.'

What on earth had made him do such a volte-face? Had Benjamin threatened his person? It would be so unlike Benjamin.

'Thank you?' I said.

'And so perhaps,' Mr Gallop said, 'You can give it back.'

'Give what back?'

He laughed, in a knowing way, a long laugh, as if I was very clever.

'Ahaha, Miss Hamilton, well played. You have always been a lady of... verve. Give back what you found, the night you broke into the library. Or visited, shall we say, as you didn't take any *books*, did you? No, not the books. Give it back and we can both move on, and the whole episode can be forgotten. I can even order in some books you like, if you wish. Detective novels, was it?' He attempted a smile again, but his lips were very tight over his teeth and his moustache quivered with the effort.

'I didn't take anything,' I said. 'I put them all back through the letterbox, and the constable watched me do it. I was wrong to consider taking anything. What have you lost?'

'It is nothing,' he said, 'Nothing,' staring at me with wild hope in his eyes. But then his shoulders slumped. 'But you must have it. What is it you want? Is it money? If it is books, I have already said you can have whatever ones you want. We could even extend the loans for two months instead of six weeks. Or three. Three months.'

'Mr Gallop,' I said. 'I am afraid whatever it is, I do not have it.' His behaviour was so bewildering that my anger dissipated. I did not have the cruelty to play games with him. He looked a little… haunted.

He looked out to sea again, as if he might find answers in the waves or on the empty shingle. There was no one sitting on this part of the beach today, apart from the odd seagull and a brown-and-white-feathered turnstone or two, scuttering back and forth looking for insects.

'You must disregard it,' he said, and was there even a break in his voice? 'Burn it, destroy it, however you wish. None of it was meant, I was simply… as head librarian, I like to be *organised*. But it is all fiction, of course. Please… lives can be ruined. Destroy it.'

'Mr Gallop, I honestly do not have whatever it is you are looking for. Please do not distress yourself further. If you need my help in looking for it, as a lady detective, I may be able to help.'

He looked at me and gave a long laugh again, that began hopeless, turned nasty halfway through and then ended on a note of almost a hiccup. Had he been drinking? Mr Gallop? Surely not. I could not smell anything on him, and he got up abruptly from the bench and stood poker straight.

'Very well,' he said. 'Well played, well played. We are at an impasse. I will leave it for now. But know, Miss Hamilton, you are the source of my sleepless nights and my endless torment.'

He headed off along the seafront and I stared after him, bewildered. Whatever was on that piece of paper had turned Mr Gallop into a man entirely unlike himself.

Chapter Thirty-Five

Further along the street, I felt I was being followed again, so I turned around and saw the Spencer sisters again, dogging my steps.

'Oh, for goodness' sake,' I said. 'What?' It was the furthest from politeness I had ever been, and there was something liberating about it. Maybe I would become addicted to rudeness and run about town, committing effronteries.

'We are sorry for last time,' Mabel said. 'Please stop walking. We were upset. We did not mean to offend. Can we sit here on this bench for a short time, and talk?'

'Very well,' I said, but I sat on the very edge of the bench, because I had more important things to do.

'It is only we have been thinking,' Felicity said. 'And we remembered the charcoal burner was in town that weekend.'

'I beg your pardon?'

'The charcoal burner. He travels around creating charcoal, for use in iron-making and hop-drying. He is very dirty-looking because of the charcoal, and he leads a very solitary existence because he has to live in a tent beside the fire to make sure the fire does not burn too fiercely. We saw him, in his tent, up East Hill.'

'And?'

'And he must get lonely. He is a very big man,' Felicity said in a rush. 'Strong. The kind who could overpower a woman quite easily. We thought—'

'Stop,' I said. 'I do not want to hear any more theories.' Theories – or fantasies? I remembered again I thought I had seen them when Mrs Monk had taken me up East Hill to watch naked men bathing. 'Did you even care about Mrs Withers?'

'No,' Mabel said defiantly, 'we did not.'

I looked at them both, so prim and trapped by their gentility, their naivety allowing a certain kind of shallow cruelty, like children who hurt small animals. I was fiercely glad to know more about life and its realities.

'Why not?' I asked.

'She ruined my chances,' Felicity said. 'I was almost engaged, and I was at an evening supper, and she came up to me and the gentleman and said, in front of him, that he was a quite unsuitable match. Dr Patmore—'

'Dr Patmore? Dr Septimus Patmore?'

'Oh yes,' Felicity said, 'we know you liked him too.' I had not liked him at all. He was an ophthalmic surgeon, who last year had obtained some mildly naughty pictures of my mother purely to ogle, and who had attempted to blackmail me into indecent relations because of it. He was handsome, a little devil-may-care, but also an out-and-out-bounder.

'You are far better off without him,' I said. 'He is a blackguard.'

'The point is,' Felicity said, breathing heavily as if tears were starting, 'The point is he was coming to the point and she ruined it all. Afterwards, he walked away and never spoke to me again. I did not get to choose, because she took the choice away from me. She was evil, and she deserved...'

'No, Felicity,' Mabel said. 'Don't say it. She didn't deserve that. But she was not a nice woman.'

Were they angry enough to have taken revenge? I did not think they had it in them, but it added an extra puzzle to the mystery. Perhaps their father had gone to their rescue, to right the wrong against them as well as himself? It bore further thinking about.

'I am sorry to hear it,' I said. 'But really, Dr Patmore is the last man you should ever marry. He is quite unsuitable.'

'We are not debutantes,' Mabel said. 'We do not possess the mystery and elan to swan about town flicking our fingers at gentlemen and still securing a fiancé. We need to make the most of every opportunity, and Mrs Withers denied Felicity hers. We are getting old.'

They were not old, of course, younger than me, maybe twenty-six and twenty-seven, but in the society we lived in, marriage did generally become harder once you topped twenty-one. I had been immensely lucky, I knew. I felt a twinge of sympathy for them.

'Any discerning gentleman will not care about age,' I said. 'And you should not want one who does. Have you thought about going fox hunting?' It sounded a little bizarre, but I was trying to think of the places they could meet gentlemen who were more... physically active than the average pampered man of their class. I sensed they were not women for soft hands.

'I don't know what you are on about,' Mabel said, which was fair enough. 'We have to go now. But we must ask you to leave our father alone.'

'I certainly will do,' I said, 'If his actions merit it.'

'Must you? Must you always have the last word?' Felicity said. 'Gah!' And she and her sister stomped off along the Marine Parade. As last words went, it was not very good.

Chapter Thirty-Six

At six in the morning, I rose and put on my brown velveteen Turkish trousers.

I crept out of the back door and along the alleyway running at the back of our garden, and then took a right down the hill. The birds were up early, but there were few people about. A gentleman staggering uphill after his night's adventures, raised his top hat and pointed at my legs, sniggering.

'Ha! A lady in trouuuusers!' he said and weaving to the left he fell over a small hedge, landing face-first in someone's front garden. 'What the blazes...' I left him to it. I had to. It was a long, steep walk and nearly half-past six by the time I made it to Miss Turton's mansion, breathless. The ladies were already outside, and Miss Turton had brought the bicycle.

'Miss Turton, Mrs Monk,' I said, feeling very formal, because this was an important moment. There was nobody about, apart from a few early morning delivery boys.

'This is a load of nonsense and I'm too old for it,' Maria Monk said, her expression glacial, but she was wearing a very practical-looking divided skirt and she already had one hand on the handlebars. Miss Turton looked flushed and delighted.

'We must take it in turns,' Miss Turton said. 'And perhaps the two who are not on the bicycle can help to keep it upright until we have gained a sense of balance. When I tried it alone, I fell off very quickly. I have brought a manual, with illustrations.' She was the most daring of us all, wearing a rational dress in the form of a skirt that stopped at her knees, her woollen-clad legs showing below. 'It is a Columbia model, made in Boston, and it has brakes to help make it stop!'

We studied the manual for a while, but Mrs Monk was getting impatient, so we let her ride it first. It was a beautiful machine with pneumatic tyres and a little bell you could ring to warn people you were coming.

At first it was impossible. We discovered it was better to have just one person supporting the bicycle, as two led to a confusion of direction, but it did mean we had to run very fast, which soon got tiring. As soon as we cycled alone, we keeled over, and I acquired several scuffs on my knees, which was sad for the beauty of my Turkish trousers. I should have worn something more practical, like the other two. But we persevered, and eventually mastered the art of staying upright for more than a few yards, and after a while, the euphoria kicked in.

'It's magic!' Miss Turton cried. She had mastered it on her own, and was spinning up and down the parade, even managing to turn around without stopping. Maria Monk and I sat on a bench, drank tea, and ate the very fine sandwiches and cake Miss Turton had brought.

'Have you spent time with your mother?' Maria said.

'Not yet,' I said, and she looked at me without saying anything.

'Mine died of the drink when I was seven,' she said, briefly, and I put my hand on her arm quite spontaneously, expecting her to shrug it off, but she didn't.

A farmer clattered past on a hay cart, and the moment passed. Miss Turton, with uncharacteristic cheekiness, waved at him. He didn't wave back. His face took on an expression of horror and he pointed at her and said 'Legs!', before twitching his horse to move faster to escape us, the hay cart swaying wildly from side to side. We laughed a lot, and Mrs Monk made us laugh more by shouting 'Legs!' in a scandalised fashion at Miss Turton.

It was an exciting morning and at the end of it I felt a certain certainty that I could stay upright on a bicycle, even though I was not entirely sure I would not fall off.

★

When I returned home, there was no sign of my father. And when he staggered in drunk at nine o'clock in the evening, I knew he had not yet attempted a rapprochement with Mrs Beeton.

The coachman had helped him up the steps through the front door, because my father was a little unsteady on his feet.

'He seems very sad, ma'am,' the coachman said, removing his arm from under my father's armpit.

'It's the drink,' I said, and I propped my father against the wall, in between the hat stand and the hall table, so the coachman could leave.

My father was very docile, so he didn't protest. He stood there, swaying slightly, while I removed his hat and struggled him out of his coat. His shoes could wait.

'I feel sad,' he said, sadly. 'That painting. Who put such a brown and glooooooomy painting in our hall? Is it religious? Are they wearing togas?'

'Come and sit down in the parlour,' I said. 'You always get sad when you drink whisky. That's why you don't drink much, remember?' I manoeuvred him into the room and dropped him into a chair. 'It was your grandmother's painting. You said she liked to be reminded life was most likely better after death.'

'Miserable old bint,' he said, more cheerful for a second, and I realised he was truly in his cups, because he had never, in all the years I had known him, insulted his grandmother.

'Shall I get you a glass of water?' I said, but he was staring into the distance again, silent and lachrymose, so I went and got him one.

'Mother always said you should never drink beyond two glasses of whisky, do you remember?' I said on my return, while he stared miserably into his glass. 'It always makes you sad, after two. It's been years since you drank so much.'

'Ha, your mother,' he said. 'I can't marry her. I'm married already. Nothing to offer. Offended her now,' and after some untangling of his words I realised he wasn't talking about my mother.

'Are you missing Mrs Beeton?' I asked, and he harrumphed.

'Don't need any woman,' he said. 'All of them, nothing but trouble. Shouldn't have listened to Laxton, though. He wouldn't warm my sheets.' He sniggered a little and then stared hard at the mantelpiece. 'Why do we have a statue of a cupid? Fat little boy, ugly. No good at love, at all. Slings and arrows of outrageous fortune... I don't want a winged infant in my drawing room. Who put it there?'

'Your grandmother,' I said. 'She said it reminded her that God is always watching us. Do you think perhaps it's time you went to bed?'

'Pah,' he said. 'I do miss her, though. So warm. So full of life and joy. So much... so much... abundance. I've never wanted to *be* with anyone so much, just to *be*,' and now he was definitely talking about Mrs Beeton, because his words bore no resemblance to the thin angry woman in our family portraits.

'It's not too late to get her back,' I said, and he looked at me properly for the first time as if realising I was there.

'You're a good daughter,' he said. 'I just don't *understand*. In-com-prehensible. Like your mother. Lord Laxative. Pah.'

I took off his shoes, put on his slippers, made him a hot cocoa and left him there, mumbling to himself. It was clear he was not coping without his lady love and I would have to do something about it.

Chapter Thirty-Seven

I did what I often did when life confused me and went for a swim very early the next morning, just before six o'clock. It took me twenty minutes to walk to the seafront at a fast pace, and as I headed down the hill the sun rose in front of me, a theatrical display of orange with streaks of red across the endless expanse of the horizon, turning the sea golden-blue. The bathing attendant had only just unhitched the horse from the last bathing hut, after bringing them down to the water's edge from their night-time berth on the shingle, and now he was unfolding the little ladders at either end of the huts. His horse shook its mane and stamped its feet, impatient for the day to begin.

Last year the council had refused a proposal for mixed sea bathing because it might encourage 'excursionists of all classes, who might get up to their "capers" in the water.' As always, language was vague; I wondered if capers were less or more innocent than Benjamin and mine. But capers or no, the status quo held, and ladies bathed some distance along the shore from gentlemen.

I gave the attendant a shilling, chose a hut in the middle of the row and climbed in to get changed. My outfit was old but serviceable – a blouse, knickerbockers and skirt in navy blue mohair, and a matching cotton cap with a frill around the bottom. They were not comfortable when wet, but such was the lot of women. I piled my clothes neatly on a little stool and had just opened the far door to step down into the sea, when I heard a kerfuffle outside.

'This is the ladies' bathing area!' the attendant said. 'You can't go into a bathing hut while a lady is changing!'

'I am a doctor,' I heard a smooth voice say, 'I can go anywhere. I am treating her.' A thin piece of cardboard came through the crack in the door and was pushed sharply upwards, lifting the latch, and Dr Spencer opened the door and stepped inside, closing the door behind him.

'Miss Hamilton,' he said. 'Going for a swim?'

'You can't come in here,' I said. I had not thought to bring my pistol, and my outfit, while respectable, still showed my bare legs below the knees. Even my fiancé had not seen those, yet.

Dr Spencer's beard looked more exuberant than usual. I wondered whether he had not had time to brush it.

He shrugged and sat down on the narrow wooden bench running along the left-hand side of the hut, adjusting the knees of his trousers. His eyes looked tired and he passed his hand over his face, rubbing away sleep.

'I am concerned about you, Miss Hamilton. You left in the middle of the night and now you are running around town spreading wild rumours about me. How did you escape, by the way? The window was ajar, but I cannot believe you scrambled across rooftops.'

'I left,' I said. 'It does not matter how.' I crossed my arms in front of me, to bolster my courage.

He smiled, wearily. There were open slats near the top of the hut to let the light in, and as shaft of sunlight fell sharply across his face, I could not quite see his expression.

'You must be a sore trial to your father.'

'My father has already told you I am quite well. Did you send men to break into our detective agency?' I asked.

He shook his head. 'Miss Hamilton, enough. You are a silly, silly girl. It has to stop.'

'I am a Lady Detective and I am twenty-nine,' I said. 'It is not a game.'

'No, no,' he said. 'You and I both know you have no

qualifications and no possibility of such a role. Your fiancé is deluding you. A pampered, sheltered girl, with no knowledge of the real world, no aptitude, no sense, running around playing childish games? Smearing the reputations of serious men? This town is not your playground.'

'Dr Spencer, my business is as serious as yours,' I said.

'I have dealt with men, bleeding and bloodied from war,' he said. 'Women dying in childbirth. Gangrene, pus-soaked wounds, amputation, tumours, syphilis sores, all of it. I have seen the horrors of this world. I heal. I have ambitions to make your town a centre of health and wellness respected across the world. And you, barely more than a child, a nobody, think you can have any wisdom, any authority? Think you have the right to meddle, when foolishness is all you know?'

'I heard you. At the Spring Harvest Ball, on the night of Mrs Withers' death,' I said, trying to save myself from drowning under his words. Because he was right; I had not witnessed anything close to the worst of life, had been ignorant for so long, and was only now struggling uphill to change it. 'She accused you of being a quack. Are you? Is that why she died, because she threatened to tell the truth about you?'

Even that accusation could not garner respect. He looked disappointed rather than angry.

'I was not at the ball when she died. I was with my daughters. This is what I mean about you. You cannot even look clearly at basic facts, because you are too full of emotion, of exaggeration. There is no ability in you to be dispassionate or logical.'

I took a deep breath, because his words were crushingly effective.

'I am no different from your daughters,' I said. 'Would you dismiss them as easily?'

'Their mother died,' he said. 'She died when they were barely fifteen, and they do not run around wearing the wound of it like a badge. Yours is likely still alive, living a life as stupid as your own somewhere else. But my daughters were bereaved, and still they know how they fit into the universe, where they belong. They do not try to be something a woman cannot ever, ever be.'

'I am sorry,' I said. 'I did not know. How did it happen?' Had I been so self-absorbed at school I had not noticed their grief? It was, I was ashamed to admit, possible.

'This is not relevant,' he said, angrily. 'She is the reason I am working to better the lot of women in this world and the reason I cannot allow you to run free with your nonsense. Sit down.'

'No, thank you,' I said. It was still only March and my feet were cold. Had I been wrong about him? I could no longer tell if he was bad or good, or something in-between. Surely somebody who cared so much about women's welfare must be honourable at heart? My head felt muddled and the bathing hut claustrophobic and dank, even with the weak sunshine coming through the slats.

'Come here,' he said, gently. 'Sit down. I have here a cure for all sorts of ills, that will make you feel a great deal better. A little laudanum, some essence of rosemary, it will help you not to care about the emptiness. Because this is what lies at the heart of all this frantic running about, isn't it? A way to fill the emptiness, that might be best filled by a husband, by children. By following a more natural path in life. Here.' He took out a small bottle and offered it to me, kindly, without threat, as if he knew he had won the battle by exposing all the weakness in me.

I stood shivering for a second or two, looking at him, allowing the humiliation, the uselessness and hopelessness, wash over me to their fullest strength, shrivelling me to nothing. Because the feelings had always been there, hadn't they? Even before my beautiful mother disappeared, when I had compared myself to her and found myself wanting, and then in the ten lonely years where I racketed around trying to find a purpose without her. He was right. I amounted to nothing, would never hold his importance or as much entitlement as him to take up space in the world.

I hugged myself a little to warm myself, and then I shook my head.

'I came for a swim,' I said. I ran towards the far end of the hut, took a leap and dived into the sea.

Chapter Thirty-Eight

The water was shallow near the bathing hut, but my dive took me out into deep water. I was lucky I did not land on rocks. The water was ice-cold after the cool night, and the shock of it almost froze me into immobility. But it was sharply refreshing too, and freeing; impossible to think about whether I was good enough or not; a fool or not a fool, in such deep water.

I had realised in the last second in the hut, these feelings of inadequacy might always be with me, like chains around my ankles. I could either allow them to drag me down or ignore them and do what I wanted to do anyway. And I had always had a slight grain of perversity alongside the insecurity too; a refusal to do what was expected of me. Dr Spencer wanted me to deflate; I would swim instead. But goodness, it was cold.

My mother, always in fashion, had taught me the trudgen kick when I was small; a sideways stroke, faster than any other, with a scissor kick every second stroke, but it required my head to be underwater most of the time and I wanted most desperately to see where I was going as well as watch out for the danger behind. Dr Spencer was unlikely to swim after me, in his tweed suit, but would he somehow find a boat and come up behind me? Was he any threat to my physical wellbeing, or just my mind? The thought of being unaware of danger behind me was mind-numbing, so my swimming was a mixture of trudgen kick and the breaststroke; too ladylike to feel I was making any progress.

I headed parallel to the shore towards the Stade. I was fit from walking, but not so strong in my arms, and there were seaweed and jellyfish in the water brushing gently against me as I swam. I was warming up a little, but the water was still icy. Had I really come here to swim for fun? Had I a choice, I would have splashed around for seconds and got dressed again.

Where would Dr Spencer go, left alone in the hut with my day clothes? A wave hit me at the same time I realised it would be much quicker for him to keep up with me on land, a gentle stroll along the shingle. I swallowed a lungful of salt water, emerging spluttering.

I was exhausted by the time I came parallel with the men's bathing area, just before the half-built harbour arm. My muscles were cramping with tiredness, and I knew I would have to get out before I did not have the energy to swim ashore. My brave escape would be less brave if I drowned, even if there was the prospect of Dr Spencer lurking at my destination. Perhaps I could fight him, or recruit others to fight for me, if I could convince them I was sane.

A few of the bathing gentlemen looked shocked as I staggered through the waves to the shore. Others were delighted.

'What ho!' one cried. 'It's a filly! Come this way, my bathing beauty!'

'A Nyad!' his friend said. 'A siren, fresh from seabed.' His knowledge of Greek myths was poor. 'Come hither and sport with us amid the waves.'

I waved an arm at them weakly, and carried on towards the shore, scanning it frantically. I could not see any danger.

The bathing attendant, a different one, came running towards me as my knees gave way and I dropped face down on the shingle. It was a painful landing.

'This is the men's bathing area!' he said. 'The women's is further down, that way. You can't bathe here.'

I looked up at him, unable to move. 'Do I look as if I am here for pleasure?' I said.

'No,' he said, 'but rules are rules. It's mostly for your safety as a lady. Pick yourself up and move along to the ladies' section.'

I ignored him, and lay prostrate for a few seconds, my head

on my arms, catching my breath. I could hear the two excited men behind me shouting about mermaids and sea goddesses.

'Madam,' the evil bathing attendant said, 'if you're not deceased, you have to move.'

I ignored him, because he would have to lay his hands on me to get me to move, and propriety would hopefully deter him. I tuned out his voice to concentrate on regaining my breath.

As soon as I could feel my limbs starting to recover enough to stir, I raised myself to my elbows, and then finally, to a sitting position.

The two gentlemen were wading towards me, concerned at last, now talking about drowned damsels. The bathing attendant looked conflicted; a man unable to enforce the rules of his job. It was time to go.

I pushed myself up onto my hands and knees and finally, my unsteady feet.

'Good day, gentlemen,' I said, and then walked with as much dignity as I could with wobbling knees and bare feet, across the shingle to the promenade.

Where I went from there, I was not sure. I was attracting attention. The smooth paving stones of the promenade were easier to walk on than the shingle, but several people were already looking askance at my lower limbs.

I could go home, but it would mean passing the bathing hut again or taking a winding uphill route, and Dr Spencer's words currently placed more fear in me than a threat of violence. I could go to my friend Maria Monk, who had a useful understanding that life was not straightforward and might offer me a change of clothing and some advice.

I decided to go to Maria Monk, the most open-minded person I knew. I crossed my arms over my chest in case the damp wool was too shaped against my skin and began to walk through the town towards West Hill, confidently, hoping to fool people into thinking it was perfectly normal.

Chapter Thirty-Nine

By the time I reached the narrow, steep path leading up the side of West Hill, I had been laughed at by three separate shopkeepers and a newspaper delivery boy, and the soles of my feet were filthy and sore. I had pulled the frill of my bathing cap as flat around my face as I could in the hope no one would recognise me, but it was possible everyone had.

The challenge of climbing the hill was not a small one, for someone who had swum a marathon. There was a very smart lift that would take me up in minutes, but I would be surrounded by exquisitely dressed ladies and gentlemen and had no money for the fare. Instead, I began the climb, knees quivering. After a while I heard some baa-ing behind me and then a man's voice. 'Miss Hamilton!'

I had been recognised, but thankfully it did not sound like Dr Spencer. I turned with reluctance and dread and there was Farmer Wicken, with a herd of sheep and an overexcited Welsh sheepdog.

'Good mornin',' he said, and tipped his hat at me, to his credit making no mention of my déshabillé.

'Good morning,' I said, and attempted to walk on, but we were going in the same direction and I did not have the energy to overtake. If he wanted to shut me in his oast house again, at least I could rest among the chickens.

'Bin to the market,' he said after a while. 'Got some sheep, though my wife will say we have plenty already. But these were a bit – forlorn-looking. Farmer Haddon's, and he no more knows how to look after sheep than his wife can starch his collars.' The ten or so sheep behind him looked exactly the same as any sheep, startled and dim, and I wondered how he would face it when the time came to make them into mutton. The sheepdog circled them quick and sharp, more alert and efficient than an army general.

'They are lucky sheep,' I said. 'I apologise for my... dress. I am investigating a case and it went a bit awry.' Perhaps I could rest across a few of his sheep, while they carried me up the hill.

'No offence,' he said, red in the face again, but then he reached into the knapsack over his shoulder and pulled out a blanket. 'Want this? 'Tis only a horse blanket, but it might cover...'

'Thank you,' I said, and wrapped it around me. It smelt of animals, was covered in bits of hay, rough but comforting.

'I'm due to go off that way,' he said, pointing right. 'But I'll walk you a bit of the way. Doesn't seem right to let a lady walk alone.'

I smiled at him.

'Mrs Withers,' he said after a while. 'Seeing as you're a detective...' and then he went silent, ambling along until I could bear no more.

'Yes?' I asked.

'The night she died. I can't sleep some nights. I worry. It's the animals. The cows, the horses... they're like family. Whether the pigs are getting on with each other, whether the horse that's foaling is eating enough. If the hens aren't laying. Some nights I can't switch off and the animals don't want me wandering in checking on them at all hours and me wife doesn't want me tossing and turning so I take Barney – that's me dog – or Marjory – that's me horse – and we goes for a walk. Just for an hour or so, and then when I get home I can sleep fine.'

'And?'

'The night she died I was out for a walk along the seafront. There's something about the waves that calms me. They change their moods so often, some nights they're wild, some nights—'

'And this night?'

'This night was mild enough, a bit of a chill. So, I'm walking along the seafront and I see Mrs Withers being pushed along in a bath chair. That's odd, because the bath chairs are only operated in the daytime, and they get parked up by the train station at night. But she is being pushed along, and the chair-man who's pushing her, he's running. Fast, as if he's in a tearing hurry. Usually, the people in bath chairs want to be pushed very slow, as they're invalids. But this was fast. And she looked…' here he paused again, torturously slow, 'She looked like Boudicca.'

'Boudicca?'

'Yes, fierce. Like a warrior queen, ready to fight a battle. She didn't even notice me. She was looking straight ahead, leaning forward in the chair, pointing ahead, and she was like the prow of a ship or Boudicca, ready to go to war. Hard to say why, but she did.'

'That is a wondrous observation, Farmer Wicken,' I said. 'Thank you.'

'I don't know what happened later,' he said. 'That keeps me awake at night too, what happened. It was nowt to do with me,' he added, looking horrified, as if he'd suddenly realised I might draw conclusions. 'She shot past me near Pelham Crescent 'tis all. I might have took 'em goats, but I've never harmed a living creature.'

'I believe you. What time did you see her?'

'Around half past two of the clock, I reckon,' he said. 'Haven't told the police, because they don't like folk wandering around at night without good reason. But I'd like someone to know, when she was in the bath chair, she was right fierce.'

'Would you recognise the chair-man?'

'Heavens to betsy, no. There are so many of them hanging around these days. He was bigger than most his age – mebbe fourteen or fifteen. Shock of brown hair. But I was looking at her, most of the time. Figure you can let the people know who need to know, without mentioning my name?'

'Yes, I can. Thank you, Farmer Wicken,' I said. 'This might be very useful. I am sorry you have trouble sleeping. Have you tried any herbs?'

'I tried Dr Spencer's Sleep Elixir,' he said, 'But it gave me terrible dreams. Terrible. Threw the bottle out of the window one night, and when I got up in the mornin' my Barnaby here had lapped it up and judgin' by the way his ears twitched, he had nightmares too.' Barnaby came to his heel upon hearing his name and he stroked his head with a mournful hand. 'Poor boy. I'm going to head off here. Will you get home all right? You can keep the blanket.'

'I'm sure I will,' I said. 'And thank you again. If anything else comes to mind, please let me know.'

'I will,' he said, and he raised a hand in farewell and ambled off, his sheepdog keeping the sheep in neat formation behind him.

I had a lead. I had to get to Maria Monk's, and then once I was respectably dressed and had my energy back, I would go to see Benjamin and find the right chair-man to see if he could tell us anything about where Mrs Withers had been going and why. I was glad to know she had been a woman on a mission, even though it had ended badly. Now I needed to find out what it was.

The news gave me the energy I needed to make it to the top of the hill and the sanctuary of Mrs Monk's neat conservatory.

Chapter Forty

Mrs Monk's maid, Rose, knew me and invited me in straight away, but I asked to remain outside until I had washed my feet.

She brought me a bowl and some warm water and soap, and I sat on the back step and washed them, taking my time, trying to muster my strength again and not let everything that needed to be worked out overwhelm me.

'You are a little far from the sea for a swim,' I heard the voice of Maria Monk and she came out from behind me into the garden. She looked pristine and elegant and I wondered why she never looked the same as the first day I had seen her, when she had appeared to have no teeth, and I had thought her old and hag-ridden. She must have a pair of false teeth made by the best dentists in London. She was in her later years, but she held herself so well, dressed so beautifully, it was easy to believe she could still have any man at her feet, should she wish. But she had had her great love affair and seemed content without one.

'Forgive my appearance,' I said, and the wonderful Rose brought me a soft towel to dry my feet on.

'I predict you have a story to tell,' Maria said. 'Are you cold? Do you want a dressing gown?'

'Yes, please, thank you,' I said. 'I apologise for calling on you without warning.'

'Apologies are for people with no spine,' she said. 'Come inside to the warmth. Rose, would you mind fetching a dressing gown? The ruby velvet one, I think. And a glass of brandy, perhaps. Cake?'

'Yes, please.' I would have kissed Maria except she was not the demonstrative sort.

'All the cake, then, Rose,' Maria said, and we settled in her conservatory, which had a small fire going, even though it was March. I warmed my hands on it and felt my bones relax.

The cake when it came was a rich sultana variety, luscious and delicious, and I ate two pieces.

'So?' Maria said.

Where to start?

'You know I am a Lady Detective,' I said. 'Well, I am looking into Mrs Withers' murder, and people seem to be getting quite threatening. I had to flee the Hydro across the rooftops, and someone smashed up our shop, and Dr Spencer came into my bathing hut, and threatened me.'

'Deep breath,' Maria said. 'And tell me something that makes sense. I can't knit a jumper from a bird's nest.'

I took a breath, and took my time, and told her the stories about Mrs Withers and Dr Spencer, and all I had learnt so far. She listened and sipped her tea delicately, while I gulped three cups to recover from the saltiness of the seawater. She listened without giving any advice or interrupting.

'If I am to reconstruct the evening,' I said, 'Then Mrs Withers got a letter which contained the ingredients of Dr Spencer's Wondrous Water of Life, or possibly Widow Welch's Female Pills. She went to the ball, knowing she had uncovered Dr Spencer was a quack. She confronted him in the garden, and told him so, and he threatened her in turn. At around one-thirty, she left the ball and caught a bath chair pushed by an unknown young chair-man, still looking determined, and not as if she was going to give in to blackmail. Shortly before three in the morning, she was killed.

'But there are other things bubbling in the ether. There was the break-in at the shop, and...'

My words were getting slurred and I was feeling very sleepy, in the warmth of the room and with a surfeit of cake. She took my cup from me and put it on the tray.

'Sleep for a bit, if you want,' she said. 'It will be all that swimming. We can talk when you wake up. I'm all for rest when you need it.'

Maria picked up a book and began reading it in silence, and I felt safe and grateful, because this was the second time she had helped me. She was a wonderful woman to know, asperity and all. I fell into a very deep sleep in the armchair in her front parlour, the fire burning in the grate.

It was only a half-hour nap. When I awoke, I felt ready to face the challenges ahead, although my muscles ached and I was thirsty again. There were clothes laid out for me, a dress a little long and tight and slippers a little soft for outside but would be perfect to see me home.

'Thank you, so much,' I said to Maria. 'I am eternally grateful for your friendship.' She began to frown, as she didn't like compliments, so I changed the topic. 'What do you think I should do?'

She put down her book, and stretched out her arms and her back, and suggested I do the same.

'You will be stiff,' she said.

'No, I mean… about all that is going on?'

'You're the detective,' she said. 'It's best if you solve your cases yourself.'

I looked at her in disappointment.

'I hoped…'

'Talking out loud and sleeping might have helped you sort out your thoughts. I only know about men,' she said. 'I built my life on them. Often, their troubles are about desire, anger, power, humiliation and revenge. Which of those are linked to Mrs Withers?'

'I don't know yet,' I said. 'Although she made Dr Spencer angry, I think. And was mildly annoying to a lot of people.' I could be honest with Mrs Monk.

'What holds you back from solving this case yourself?' she asked.

'Mostly the feeling I am not strong enough to be a detective,' I said. 'I am gently-bred, perennially foolish, stupidly naive, blindingly ignorant and wholeheartedly an idiot. That I should give it all up and have babies.'

'Ah,' she said. 'Mere feelings then. How do you think I felt when I had no power over men who used my body as and how they wished? As if I was a book to be opened and read at will, my words thrown aside when they had read enough?'

'I cannot imagine it. I am full of admiration for you always. Your experience of life is vastly different from mine.'

'Those feelings would not have allowed me to survive. I turned them into anger and made myself instead into a woman whom men begged for. I see emotions like mountains – they can be climbed over, and after a while the paths across them become smoother. The biggest strength a woman can have, I believe, is to judge herself solely by her own guiding principles. To not compare, to not be diminished by the views of others, to hold firm – always hold firm – against anyone and everyone who judges you, because only you can know who you are.'

'Your wisdom hurts my head a little,' I said, because I understood, almost, but it would require further reflection.

'Any woman who breaks a mould, who is a pioneer for a new way of being a woman, will be more subject to censure than most. Don't add your own voice to the melee. Be your own fiercest champion so that you can face your worst critics. And if you believe in yourself, in who you are and what you do, and follow through, you will find most people take you at your own accounting.'

'Thank you,' I said. 'I don't suppose you would write this

down in a letter or on a piece of paper? It is exceedingly sensible, and I should like to carry it around with me for weak moments.'

She laughed. Perhaps it was one of my womanly powers, to make people laugh.

'I will send it to you. More importantly,' she said, 'How do you feel about this man of yours? I do not think you know yet. Think about whether you want to spend your life with him. Whether you want to be with him through everything life will throw at you – the dullness, the craziness, the despair, the struggles and occasionally, the joy. Life is short. If you want to be with him more than anything in the world and it's only fear stopping you, marry him.'

'I don't want to give up my career,' I said.

She picked up her book and started reading again.

'So, don't,' she said. 'You want to be a detective; you want to be a New Woman. Tell him that. And then if he agrees to it and you love him, for God's sake marry him. It won't kill you. And forgive your mother. She was a fool, but life's too short for grudges. They eat you up inside.'

'You are, as always, immensely wise,' I said. 'How can I thank you for being such a friend?'

'Stop the piffle,' she said. 'I have not grown to be the age I am without gaining some experience along the way. The credit is to you as a young person for listening. Oh, and my last piece of advice – learn to fight. Learn to fight when your back is against the wall and fighting is your last hope to stay alive. Viciously and without fairness, I mean. Go for the jugular, between the legs, the eyes, the nose, anywhere he or she is most vulnerable. Gouge out his eyes, spit in his face, anything that throws him off guard so you can run. Marquess of Queensberry rules don't work for women.

'Now I need to go and change for dinner. Have I put you back together again? Humpty Dumpty could have done with my help. Mackenzie has arranged the carriage for you.'

'You have,' I said. 'And if ever I can return the favour, let me know.'

'Pah,' she said, and walked splendidly upright from the room, leaving me alone. I thought about the difference between her sharp, clever words, Lady Laxton's empty vacuousness and my mother's warm vivacity, and how all approaches seemed to attract men like moths to a flame. Perhaps there was space for my own quirkiness in the mix too, even though the only moth I wanted was very large and called Benjamin Blackthorn.

I pulled my weary self to my feet and went to find Mackenzie and his carriage. It was time to go home.

Chapter Forty-One

It was nice to see Mackenzie again, a Scot who had once lent me his clothing to steal from Hastings Museum and who talked volubly all the way home about the things his mistress was fond of. I suspected he might be fond of his mistress.

I made it home in record time, shot round to the back door as fast as my aching legs would let me and met Hildebrand in the kitchen. She was making a hat, weaving a brim from straw, and I wondered what other skills she had, and whether she might prefer to be a milliner. Would she want to come with me, if I got married?

'Would you mind sending a boy to the seafront, and collecting some items from one of the bathing huts?' I asked her. 'I had to leave... abruptly, and I don't want to lose my clothing.'

'Of course,' she said. 'Was it work?' And I wanted to hug her, for treating me with such nonchalance and respect when others would have imagined all sorts about a woman turning up in the back kitchen in an ill-fitting dress.

'Yes, it was,' I said. 'Hildebrand... Dr Spencer. Do you know anything about him? Did he visit you in the— in your last home?'

'No,' she said, 'but I'll ask around if you like. I have a few friends who might know things. If you don't mind my seeing them.'

'Of course I don't mind,' I said. 'Thank you.'

I ran up to my bedroom, washed, got changed into my detective dress, and headed out to the agency to see Benjamin. I had a lead. And this time, a pistol. If I ran into any Dr Spencers, I would shoot them without hesitation.

HANNAH DOLBY

As I reached the small square, a man came out, flanked by two constables. A tall man, handsome, the kind of man who stood out in a crowd. He was wearing handcuffs. It was Benjamin.

He saw me and stopped still.

'Ah, yes,' he said.

'We need to get going,' one of the constables said, taking his arm, but Benjamin shrugged one of his magnificent shoulders and the constable dropped his arm immediately. Even under arrest, he exuded authority.

'I will come with you,' Benjamin said to the constable. 'I need a short word with the lady, that's all.'

'What is happening?' I asked. 'Why are you in handcuffs?' I stepped towards him again, the pull greater than any notion of proper conduct, but he put up one hand again.

'Stop,' he said. 'Will you write Mrs Ellen Fraser, and get her to send proof she is alive? I am in a spot of difficulty.'

The lady he had helped escape from her evil husband, the husband who had lured him on a wasted mission to Scotland?

'Of course,' I said. 'But her address—'

'It is with Mr Remington,' he said. 'I'm under arrest for her murder. I'll be in jail for a bit. Hopefully we can get this sorted out quickly as Mrs Fraser's very much alive. It might be best to steer clear of me for now, for your reputation. But when you hear—'

'Of course,' I said. 'But—'

'I have to go,' he said. 'Listen, look after yourself. Stay safe, keep an eye out for trouble.' He nodded at the constables, who looked embarrassed at the necessity of manhandling him. He was very well respected in town. 'Wilberforce, Smith, we can go now.'

The constables put him in a covered coach and took him away and I was left in the street, staring after him as it clattered away over the cobbles.

*

The Remington. Of course, my typewriter. I went straight into the shop.

Benjamin also took up a significant space, I realised, remembering what Mr Withers had said about his wife. It was not only the physicality of him. It was his steady, stoic presence. There was a stillness to him that could not be true, because he was so often moving; lifting furniture, woodworking, sanding down surfaces, bringing order to chaos; but there was something in his essential approach to life, a slowness and a focused dedication to whatever he set his mind to, bringing calm to the room. Give me time, he seemed to say, and I will make everything well. I had felt the power of that slow, patient attention, and suddenly longed for it.

In the corner of the room, where I had always sat, he had righted my little desk, reattached a leg that had been snapped off and set my typewriter back upon it and when I got closer, I saw he had repainted some of the lettering that had chipped off when it fell. 'Re–ingto' it had said last week, and now it said 'Remington' again, some of the letters a different shade, the 'n' perhaps a little wobbly, but he had mended my typewriter and made it whole again. I found Ellen Fraser's address, wedged neatly in the cavity at the bottom. He must have hidden it there when the police came. Had he known, then, someone might come for him?

I walked at a fast pace to the post office, still aware of the danger to my person and not wanting to encounter any impediments I might have to shoot.

I sent Mrs Fraser a telegram:

NEED PROOF OF LIFE YOUR HUSBAND CLAIMS
MR BLACKTHORN

KILLED YOU WRITE 9 MATTHEW'S GARDENS
HASTINGS VIOLET

HAMILTON DETECTIVE

What else could I say, beyond ensuring she knew my address? Hopefully the words were enough to make her trust me. Should I have said I was Mr Blackthorn's fiancée? I did not know what was more effective. The postmistress was looking at me, eyes agog, and I knew there was a risk the contents of the telegram might be disseminated across town within the hour. I only hoped it would bring me the evidence I needed.

With Benjamin away, it was up to me to find out which chair-man had pushed Mrs Withers along the promenade on the night of the ball. From the post office, I headed to the Provincial Hotel, which had a row of bath chairs outside, lined up in the street.

The infirm came in their droves from London and other towns from spring onwards in search of cures, to rest and recuperate, to be faced with a plethora of sharply ascending hills. They often looked to a method of transport cheaper and easier than a carriage. The boys who ran them were strong by necessity, as many of the roads were still poorly surfaced and it was often required to take a longer route to avoid the many flights of stairs and twittens. Most chair-men were aged between eleven and sixteen, graduating from poor houses and orphanages to a job which required mostly brute strength and the patience to wait around in the street. There were several of them hanging around today, playing dice and other games on the pavement.

The chairs themselves were like rather large perambulators, with two big wheels at the back and a smaller wheel or two at the front, and a hood that could be pulled over the passenger in the advent of rain. There would be no such protection for the chair-men, but like the fishermen, they looked as if they were used to an outdoor life. I felt a twinge of trepidation about speaking to them after my failed excursion to the fishermen but squared my shoulders and went in for the kill.

'That'll be Big George,' a lanky, red-haired one said immediately. 'He hangs out across the hill. I'll give you a lift.'

'No, if you just tell me where, I can walk,' I said.

'S'awright, I'll give you a lift,' he said. Another boy looked as if he might pipe up, but the red-head gave him a look so severe it would fry a fish. 'Not far. I'm not doing anything else. I'm Lobster, by the way. Not by choice, but it's how everyone knows me.'

'I don't mind just paying for the information,' I said, somewhat helplessly, but the look of horror on his face was enough to make me climb meekly into his carriage without another word.

I was pushed at great, rough speed up a street, down another, round a corner, through a small square with a garden and across a public park, hoping against hope I would not have to face the indignity of being seen.

'Going a bit faster than normal,' Lobster shouted, 'because you're not sick.'

By the time we reached our destination I was feeling very sick, and enormously relieved when Lobster proudly dropped me off in front of a boy sitting on the kerb of a hotel in Cambridge Gardens.

'Big George! Lady here wants you,' he said, and then waited, grinning, until I had paid him my fare. I did not begrudge him it. He pushed his chair away at speed, weaving it playfully across the road, and I turned to Big George.

He was reading a book, which surprised me, but he put it carefully on the pavement beside him and stood up to greet me, tipping a non-existent cap.

'Ma'am,' he said. He was bigger than the other boys, and his brown hair was very wild, shooting up from his forehead like a wave.

'I am wondering if you are the boy who took a lady along the seafront on the night of the seventh of March,' I said. 'Mrs Withers.'

He looked panicked and bent to pick up his book to flee, so I put my foot over it, gently, so as not to mark the cover. I judged he was not the sort to fight me for it.

'I am not going to identify you,' I said, 'or drag you into anything. I am just investigating her death, which you must have heard about. I only want you to tell me anything you can tell me about the night – how she was, what she said. It is a great mystery I am trying to solve.' His book, I had noticed, was about the detective Sherlock Holmes.

He looked at his book and back at me, torn.

'I ran across her outside the Royal Victoria,' he said. 'I'm not normally out so late but I'd been asked to make a special trip for a nob – for a guest who'd arrived late – paid double for it. I'd just dropped them off at the hotel and I saw her standing in the street, waving at me. It was not long before two o'clock in the morning. Ten to, or so. She was hard to miss, with that hat.'

'Thank you.' I kept my foot fractionally above his book. 'And then?'

'I'm not one to turn down a job. She gets in, and she says: "Follow him!" And sure enough, there's a carriage going along the seafront, pretty fast, quite far ahead, so I get going after it as quick as I can. It's not as bad along the parade, the road is all right and it's flat, but we lost the carriage pretty quick, I'm not a horse.'

'What happened?'

'She told me to keep going, she could see the carriage parked up ahead, and then when we reached the Queen's Hotel, she told me to stop and let her off. I was fair puggled, I tell you. But she paid me what I was due, and I went and parked the chair and went home.'

'Did she tell you anything about who was in the carriage or why she was going there?'

He thought for a second, scrunching up his face.

'Nooo… she did say she was going to let him know. "I'm going to let him know," she said. "She needs protecting," but I didn't ask her about it, I was tired. Sometimes you get tipped more if you listen, but it was too late. She was all afire, though. Determined about summat.'

'Thank you,' I said, and removed my foot. He sank down onto the pavement and retrieved his book, dusting it off and clutching it.

'I don't want any trouble,' he said. 'I only dropped her off. I don't know what happened afterwards, I didn't know that was going to happen. Are you going to tell the police?'

'No,' I said. 'This is between you and me, unless at some point in the future, I desperately need your evidence, and if so I will come and ask you first. Can I pay you for your time?'

'No,' he said. 'It worried me so I'm glad if what I've said can be of use. It's a nasty business and I feel bad for her. I hope you find out what happened.'

'You like books?'

His whole face opened up, wreathed in a smile. 'Love 'em. Detective novels, mostly. There's a whole lot of 'em out there. Nothing wrong with a penny dreadful either. I spend too much on 'em, but then what do I need to eat for?'

'Do you go to the library much?'

'Naw. Mr Gallop's not keen on people like me. I'm not the right sort. Might scuff the carpet.'

'If it's any comfort,' I said, 'I'm not the right sort either. I haven't been allowed to take out books since 1891. But I'll see if there is anything I can do.' It was a grand statement backed up by nothing, but I felt he deserved better. Books should be available to everyone.

'All right then, miss,' he said. 'Need a lift anywhere?' But sadly, I had to decline. Although I had to go to the police station, it would be preferable to walk.

Chapter Forty-Two

I had to go to the police and try to convince them of my... credibility. It was the right word to encapsulate a whole other group of words, including sanity, respectability, authority, intelligence, and honesty. It was a tall order, so I was glad I was wearing my detective dress. I took a twisty route to the police station and saw no one I need worry about.

I swept into the front entrance with the assurance of an elderly dowager. It was Constable Carruthers at the front desk, of course. He looked at me with a weary surprise.

'I have come to be honest with you,' I said. 'I was borrowing the books from the library because I am working as a Lady Detective, and they were intrinsic to my training.'

'Theft is intrinsic to your training?' he asked.

'Not theft, but books,' I said.

'Well then, Miss Hamilton,' Constable Carruthers said, 'Since we didn't charge you, have you come to clear your reputation?'

'Not entirely,' I said. 'I mean only partly. Mr Benjamin Blackthorn is my fiancé and I want to know what evidence you have to arrest him. It is an outrage.'

His expression was not easy to read, so I added an extra dimension. 'I am also employed to assist Colonel Withers with investigating the reason for his wife's death, unless you have solved it already. I believe I may have useful information.'

He looked at me over the big wooden desk and there was, for a second, a look that edged towards respect. Or at least a willingness to hear what I had to say.

'Please sit down then, Miss Hamilton,' he said, and he took

a big important notebook and a folder of information from his desk drawer.

This. This was what I wanted to be. A woman who said things interesting enough to make men listen.

'Mr Blackthorn has been arrested because the Scottish police believe he may be implicated in the murder of a Mrs Ellen Fraser,' Constable Carruthers said. 'Her husband, Mr Daniel Fraser, has provided evidence to show Mrs Fraser came to stay in Hastings in summer 1895. Mr Benjamin Blackthorn and his father, Mr Bernard Blackthorn, were hired to watch Mrs Fraser and report back to her husband, as he had concerns for her wellbeing. After several weeks of sending reports, they reported they had lost contact with her and severed the account with Mr Fraser. Mr Fraser has stated he believes his wife was vulnerable, that Mr Benjamin Blackthorn may have pressed his attentions on her, and when she rejected him, acted maliciously.'

'I have never heard such nonsense,' I said. 'As Mr Blackthorn's fiancée I can say categorically he would never behave like that. Has he not explained he was concerned for Mrs Fraser's safety at the hands of her husband? That in fact, he helped her to escape?'

'Yes, but as he is unable to tell us where she is, this presents a difficulty. Miss Hamilton, I like your fiancé. I respect him. His father was a good detective and we worked with him regularly. Benjamin is of the same cloth and it's shameful we have had to lock him up. But we're dealing with Scots law and a very angry advocate, and worse, they claim to have evidence a lock of her hair and her hair ribbon, stained with blood, was found in Mr Blackthorn's premises. At the moment I can't see a way out for him and if we can't find Mrs Fraser soon, things look very serious for him indeed.'

'A ribbon? It might be mine,' I said. 'But in any case, it must have been planted. When did they find this in his shop? Was it when they smashed it up?'

'Smashed it up?' Constable Carruthers said, and I explained what had happened to it and when. 'You should have reported it,' he said. I didn't tell him it had never crossed our minds to do so. It seemed odd to ask someone else to solve a break-in at a detective agency.

'Will I be able to visit him?' I asked.

'Unlikely. He's in the cells for those accused of serious crimes. Not many are allowed in or out of there.'

I would have to go to the jail and see what it looked like, work out whether I could break in, or he could break out, or if I could pretend to be a fishwife delivering fish and swap clothes with him. Benjamin would make a good tall fishwife. But I needed time to think about it all and make a plan.

Next was Mrs Withers.

'As I said, Benjamin and I have been asked to look into Mrs Withers' death, by her husband, Colonel James Withers,' I said.

'Likely an accident,' Constable Carruthers said confidently. 'No cause to interfere in police business. We're investigating the matter. I've already spoken to Mr Blackthorn.' But when I pushed him on it, the investigations were all apparently leading nowhere.

'How did she die?' I asked.

'Are the details what a lady wants to hear?'

'Yes, this lady does,' I said. It was wearying, the constant expectation I might fall apart.

'She hit her forehead. Significant head injury from falling on the capstan. A lot of blood. We had to chuck buckets of water over the shingle, to get rid of it before the sun rose. Don't want to scandalise the day-trippers.' He was watching me closely, waiting for me to have a fit of the vapours, forgetting no woman would be unused to the existence of blood. I was determined not to show, even by a twitch, I was affected.

'And were there any clues to how she got there?'

'No. She left the ball at around one-thirty, we think, although no one saw her leave. It should have taken her about an hour to get to the Stade, if she walked.'

'Was there anything that happened at the ball to make her leave?'

'Not that anyone is telling us. She was a bit of a besom – sorry, she had a lot of opinions she shared freely, which might have rubbed a few folk up the wrong way in general. But really, we can't find anyone who might have a grudge. The navvies and the fishermen are forever getting drunk and causing trouble, so it's possible she fell afoul of one of them, except she still had money in her purse and wasn't… interfered with.'

'Interfered with?'

The policeman coughed into his hand and flushed a dark red.

'Nobody had touched her. The injury on her forehead was the only sign of anything wrong.'

'What do you think happened?'

He cleared his throat. 'Here's the thing,' he said. 'She was at a time of life when women do odd things. It's a difficult age for a woman, and sometimes… it's possible she went to the Stade for some fresh air after drinking too much and tripped.'

There it was again, dark hints of unstable behaviour. Mrs Withers had only ever struck me as perfectly certain and sane of her place in the world.

'She could have got fresh sea air ten minutes from the ball,' I said. 'There was no need for her to travel so far along the seafront so early in the morning.'

'Dr Spencer said she'd been having troubles,' the constable said, and I had been planning to tell him some of my discoveries, but I instantly changed my mind.

'You have spoken to Dr Spencer?'

'Of course, as her doctor. There is patient confidentiality, of course, but he hinted… the cessation of… it's a difficult time for a woman.'

'You have said that already,' I said, feeling furiously angry all of a sudden. 'I have spoken to her several times in recent months, and I did not notice any material change in her personality. I do not think she would travel alone along the seafront, without informing her husband, purely for a fleeting moment of instability. There will be a reason. You just have not found it yet.'

'You overstep, Miss Hamilton. Dr Spencer has his concerns about you too. He said—'

'I do not care what he said. You should be very careful about how you interpret his words. I have reason to believe he may be a charlatan, and if so, you are very unwise to align yourself with him or place any credence on his words whatsoever.' I stood up. If I was jeopardising our future working relationship, I did not care.

'Miss Hamilton, I would warn—' Constable Carruthers said, but I had had enough.

'Good day, Constable. I trust you will carry on investigating this incident with a balanced view, driven by evidence and not speculation. I will do the same. I will let you know if I reach a satisfactory conclusion. Meanwhile, I would be grateful if you could see sense regarding my fiancé, before I am forced to embarrass the entire Sussex constabulary over this travesty of justice.'

I spun about on my heel and left him scratching his head.

My nerves were thoroughly jangled, although I was not sure I could have explained exactly why. It was linked to a feeling that the actions of all women were, eventually, attributed to some inherent instability of character, when by and large, it was men who beat their wives, committed murders and generally caused havoc in society. There was something in me calling me to a fierce defence of Mrs Withers, whatever her faults. It was not right her death should be dismissed as an accident resulting from a fleeting mood. I did not believe for a second that Dr Spencer, with his crackpot cures and mad corsetry, had not had something to do with it.

It had been too busy a day, perhaps. I had been accosted by

Dr Spencer, swum miles along the coast, met Farmer Wicken, seen Maria Monk, found Big George, seen my fiancé arrested and visited the police station in the space of ten hours. It was quite enough to warrant exhaustion. I went home, ate dinner and without a postprandial pause, collapsed into bed to sleep.

Chapter Forty-Three

My father was late for breakfast, but before he arrived, I received a strange letter from my mother, in which she waffled extravagantly about her day, the male neighbour who had taken a fancy to her, her invitation to judge floral arrangements at the county show, and then at the end the following lines:

'I do appreciate life has not always been easy for you, and perhaps I have not helped. The Reverend tells me there is a Pierrot show on the seafront on Saturday morning that is much anticipated by everyone – some kind of new silent theatre? Perhaps you and your father should go and enjoy yourselves for once. Everyone who is anyone will be there, I hear.'

Well, of course, a Pierrot show, which as far as I was aware was clowns in white outfits making sad faces, would solve everything. Mrs Withers' death, Benjamin in jail, my father's romantic difficulties, would all be solved by my mother's suggestion of a Pierrot show. How delightful and entirely typically typical of her.

It was perfectly obvious she had some kind of plot afoot, the machinations of which I could not discern. Perhaps she planned to matchmake me with a Pierrot, even though she knew perfectly well about Benjamin and had met him. Part of me was tempted to go, just to find out what she was up to, and as a distraction from the intensity of all that was going on around Mrs Withers and Benjamin. There had as yet been no correspondence from Mrs Ellen Fraser.

'There is a Pierrot show on the pier on Saturday,' I said when my father arrived, hiding the letter in my skirt pocket. His face was permanently woebegone these days but at my words it brightened.

'Capital,' he said. 'Let's go. I could do with some fresh air,' and I realised he hoped Mrs Beeton might be there and he could attempt a rapprochement. It was set that my father and I would go in two days' time, our first daytime outing together in many, many years, the oddity of which I was not unaware. But perhaps Dr Spencer might be there and see me with my father, perfectly well, and stop insinuating I was otherwise. And perhaps I would be able to use it as a chance to observe the audience, the great and the good of Hastings and St Leonards, and see if I could spot any clues. I could not be in danger, surely, on a seafront with half of the town attending.

But before any Pierrot show, I had to rescue my fiancé. I felt singularly unprepared, even though I had been a detective for six months. But there had been no letter from France, so jail-breaking seemed the best option.

I went prepared for all eventualities. I wore my oldest corset, the one easiest to move around in, my detective dress, my strongest boots and my hat with a half-veil. I took my lock-picking tools and a small hand-held telescope from my father's study because it might be useful. I was lucky my new dress had voluminous pockets, so some of these things could be hidden. I had enough money to bribe the jailer and hire a hackney carriage for the return journey, if I could find one.

There had been a small jail in Hastings until forty years or so ago, when the jail keeper had been murdered by two inmates and it was converted into the police station. Nowadays prisoners were kept in Lewes Jail, an hour's train away. I did not know much about it, although a woman had been hung there several years before for feeding her husband a poisoned onion pie.

There were only five trains a day, and I caught the first one, at ten o'clock in the morning. It took twenty minutes to walk to the prison, a huge imposing building covered in grey flint, which must house many hundreds of men. I wandered around the outside several times, but it was a fortress, its windows small, arched at the top, high up from the ground. Some of the walls were embedded with shards of flint, which would make it painful to climb. I looked through the telescope at all the individual windows, but they were dark and barred and I could not see inside.

I knew from newspaper articles I had read that prisons were being reformed. A government committee had recently sought to improve conditions, with solitary confinement and pointless tasks, such as treadwheels and picking out oakum from old rope, no longer recommended. But his condition would still be bleak; he might be sleeping on a plank bed, eating sparse meals and sharing with rough people in a cell less than clean. Because he was who he was, he would handle it all with the same stoic calmness he handled everything, even if he was miserable and despairing. I ached for him.

I spent some time watching ins and outs to the jail. There were a few carts of provisions that went in and I thought about flinging myself into the back of one of them, but really, would I be better able to help inside than out? I might get locked in a cell too. Miss Cately came to mind again. She would probably inveigle her way in with charm, browbeat everyone into behaving, and march out again arm in arm with Benjamin. Maybe he would like her better. Even though she was fictional, I was starting to dislike her.

At lunchtime, a man with a covered basket and three teeth sidled up to me.

'You watching the jail?' he asked. 'Lookin' for a loved one? Want me to get a message in? I'm in and out all the time, delivering nuts to the Governor. Can go anywhere I like, no problem. Three shillings.'

What was I to do? I tore out a page from my notepad and quickly wrote a note to Benjamin, letting him know I was thinking of him and would come to his aid as soon as I could, folded it up and gave it and the money to the man, and he pocketed both and then disappeared around the corner.

I assumed he must be going in by a back entrance, but a woman selling lemonade who had overheard our exchange eventually took pity and came over.

'Never give any money to Joe,' she said. 'You'll not see it again. He's got no more access to the prison than you or I. Best go home and get on with your life.'

Eventually I had to admit it would be impossible for me to break into Lewes Jail in broad daylight and even if I succeeded, I would not know what to do once inside. How would I find Benjamin in such a cavernous building?

I caught the train home, conscious that I was both hopeless and stupid. All in all, it had been a wasted and woeful day.

The day of the Pierrot show began with rain but brightened slowly in time for the performance. It was late March but there was still a slight chill in the air, so I wore a woollen shawl over my dress and my father sported a smart scarf, newly knitted by Hildebrand. He had come to appreciate her household skills enough to forget her dubious antecedents.

When we arrived it was clear the Pierrot show was a day out for more people than us, and I recognised many familiar faces from the ball as well as from around town. There were two tranches of wooden benches arranged in tiered rows on the beach near Hastings pier, on either side of a little high stage, with two tall boxes on either side of the stage to act as the wings. There was a little piano to the right-hand side of it, and I guessed the whole theatre set must pack up into the boxes, so it was easy to move it about from town to town.

The benches were already crowded with ladies and gentlemen in straw boaters and parasols, as in fine weather it could get burning hot when the sun reflected off the shingle. As well as the paying customers on the benches, a large crowd was also gathering on the promenade to lean over the railings, and there was a buzz of anticipation in the air.

We managed to find a small space at the end of the fifth row, near the back, and squeezed in. The Spencer sisters arrived and sat in front of us, but not before both of them shot me a look so full of hate I flinched in my seat.

'Those young ladies seem out of countenance with you. Have you offended them?' my father asked in a low voice in my ear. He was unusually observant, perhaps because he was looking out for his light o'love.

'No, I have that effect on most people,' I said, not wanting to discuss it, and he harrumphed in annoyance and settled down on his seat. The rows filled up fairly quickly. Mrs Beeton arrived, and my father shot to standing, tipping his hat at her. She gave him a small quiet nod and went to sit on the first row of seats on the other side of the stage, and he dropped heavily back onto the bench.

'Do not despair, all will be well,' I said, perhaps a little too loudly, because Mabel turned around immediately.

'All will be well?' she said. 'Will it? That's a fine thing for you to say, isn't it, when you've set the police on one of the best human beings in this town, when you have everything in your behaviour to be ashamed of, prancing around the streets with goats in a bathing suit.' Had Constable Carruthers believed me then, and seen fit to investigate Dr Spencer too? Was there any way I could separate out the two offences I was accused of?

'Excuse me, young lady,' my father said, for once spurred into speech, but she turned her back on us both because the Pierrots bounced onto stage, all eight of them, in white costumes with giant frilly white collars and pom-poms down the middle of their tops and the sides of their legs, with silver conical hats and white-painted faces, capering about and playing banjos. It was a great cacophony of sound, but Mabel had not finished, because she turned around and yelled at me over the music.

'And don't think we don't know you tried to burgle a library.'

A sad looking man with a banjo appeared at her shoulder, strumming a little tune at her, because she really was disturbing the whole show, and she pushed him over with the flat of her hand. He fell on the shingle, and all the other Pierrots dropped their instruments and ran over to help him.

She stood up and turned properly to face me, and Felicity stood up too. 'And now you are pretending to be a detective too, a ridiculous profession for a lady,' she said.

I opened my mouth to defend myself, but one of the Pierrots hit Mabel quite hard around the back of the head with a giant sunflower, and she turned around and shrieked. The Pierrots had formed a semicircle around us and quite a lot of the audience stood up too, craning their necks to watch us.

I looked around the crowd and realised this might be the last time I would be welcome among them, if I ever had been. I had made a choice, for good or bad. The Spencer sisters had been right in saying that lady detective was not a calling anyone in society would accept. To give them their due, they had warned me they would ruin me.

'It's true, I am a Lady Detective,' I said to everyone, standing up. 'A real one.' Everyone might as well know the truth. 'If my actions around town have upset you, I am sorry, but it is my profession. My services are available at quite reasonable rates.' My father looked ready to speak, but I shook my head at him and he subsided. It was my battle to fight.

Lord Laxton saved the day, briefly rising from his seat and making a gesture to encourage us to sit down. 'Ladies, ladies, this is a parlour room squabble. Calm down. We are here for a Pierrot show. Let's watch it.' His wife was sitting beside him, her little hands clasped in front of her face, eyes huge, as if we were murdering each other.

'Yes, let's carry on,' Mrs Beeton said, as always so kind she brought tears to my eyes. 'Leave poor Miss Hamilton alone.'

Everyone settled back into their seats slowly, and the Pierrots picked up their instruments again, but I could feel fifty pairs of eyes still staring at me. It was fair to say my reputation was well and truly in the dirt.

I was confused. I should have felt devastated to know I would never be welcome in polite society again, could never attend balls and evening suppers, could expect to be regularly cut in the street. The humiliation was there, but underneath it all there was a sense of… liberation. There was no turning back now. I would have to go forward, to be who I wanted to be. I was a Lady Detective or nothing.

My father's back was as stiff as if he had been nailed to a plank. 'Should we go?' I whispered in his ear, but he shook his head. 'Brazen it out,' he responded, unusually calm.

I realised he was still eyeing Mrs Beeton, longingly, and she was staring determinedly at the performers and ignoring him altogether.

We settled down to watch the performers, who returned to the stage. It was a funny show, and the Pierrots were very comical, even though they had sad upside-down smiles and tears painted on their faces. The one who had hit Mabel with a sunflower caught my attention.

I thought it was a woman, even though her outfit was so baggy it was hard to tell. It was something about the way she moved. She was the most exuberant, the most confident; she played the piano and leapt on to the stage to dance; she leapt off again and did a somersault before picking up a banjo. It was familiar, that expressive, boundless energy, full of gracefulness even amid the comedy, and it drew everybody's eyes. She was the star of the show, without a doubt.

It did not take very much longer to realise she was my mother.

Chapter Forty-Four

My father did not recognise her. Why would anybody, after eleven years? It was only because I knew she was alive, had seen her so recently and had had the letter from her; also, she had hit Mabel very hard with the sunflower. Some of the petals still lay on seats and hats around us. My mother was mesmerising, as always, with an easy charisma and an unselfconsciousness not entirely real, because she had always known how to play an audience.

It was watching her capering joyfully around the stage that made me realise how selfish she had been, all those years ago, not so much for leaving, but for not telling us. She had seized happiness so freely and left us behind so lightly; injuring not just me and my father but everyone who knew and loved her, like Edith and the Reverend Bartle. A lot of people had cared for her, as she was immensely loveable. She had charmed us all effortlessly and left without thought, or at least it seemed so to me. If she had lain awake at night tormented, as I had been, it did not show in her behaviour now.

The realisation she had been selfish helped me. Not to forgive, but to understand that someone who cared less for other people could not be blamed so much for hurting them; it was a defect in her character, not mine.

The show came to an end and the Pierrots bounced off the stage at high speed, returning only briefly for an encore. The audience began to disperse, and the Spencer sisters marched away without looking at me. I was not sure their little scene had reflected well on them either.

I thought my mother might come over to us, but instead all the Pierrots were packing up the stage, the piano, the instruments; all of it disappeared into those two boxes within minutes, and then they wheeled them up a ramp to a cart on the promenade, and not long after, were gone. Was that it, then? Had my mother just come to caper briefly onstage? I did not think so, and I waited uneasily for her next move.

The crowd dispersed slowly, some flocking onto the pier and the promenade in search of new entertainment. Mrs Beeton left quite quickly, and I saw despondency in my father's shoulders. No one looked at us or acknowledged us as they were leaving, and I hoped it was solely due to me; I would not want the taint of my behaviour to affect my father. We made our way to the promenade and headed for home.

My father was focused on the loss of Mrs Beeton, silently chewing it over as we walked, but he was surprisingly comforting about the scene the Spencer sisters had caused.

'A pair of silly girls,' he said. 'Do not pay them any account. If you are to be a detective, the town might as well know now. Well done for mentioning your reasonable prices.'

We walked home up Old London Road quietly, the sun at our backs, but when we came into the front hall together, I heard laughter from the kitchen, and I knew.

'Wait,' I said to my father, but he knew her laughter, remembered it even from eleven long years ago, and he froze stock-still, halfway in removing his coat.

'I think she was one of the Pierrots,' I said, miserably, which wasn't entirely helpful. He completed the removal of his coat, slowly and carefully, and then went down the small flight of steps leading to our kitchen.

My mother was having tea with Hildebrand. She had no make-up on, and she was wearing a normal dress, in dark forest green. She had already charmed Hildebrand, apparently, because they were eating biscuits and giggling. I disliked my mother more in that minute than I ever had, because she had won over Hildebrand so easily, so quickly, dispensing with barriers as if they did not exist, casting my lumpen efforts into shame.

'You were such a long time!' she said to my father and me, as if we had only seen her yesterday. 'I wondered if you were ever coming.'

'Lily,' my father said. He stood in the centre of the kitchen like a man lost. 'A word in private.'

'It is lovely to see you too,' she said. 'Although I saw you at the Pierrot show, I don't think you recognised me. Did you, Violet?' She was a little nervous. I saw her hands were clenched in her lap. But no one would guess, if they only looked at her face.

'Yes,' I said. 'Thank you for hitting Mabel with the sunflower. I think she deserved it.'

My father started at my words, putting the picture together in his mind. 'Lily,' he said again, 'A word.'

'I am not doing it the same way, Lucas,' she said. 'I am not going to the study so you can shout and I can throw things at you. We have changed, I hope.'

He sat down at the end of the oval pine kitchen table, heavily. 'Where have you been?' he asked.

'In Buxton,' my mother said. It was hard to believe she was here, in our kitchen, back again. Hildebrand was looking worried.

'Hildebrand, would you mind going upstairs for a while?' I asked, and my mother looked as if she was going to ask her to stay, a friendly bulwark against her fractured family, but I shook my head at her, and Hildebrand left us.

'And you are well?' My father looked exhausted suddenly, as if he felt the full weight of eleven years of worry.

'Yes, I am well.' She was wringing her hands now, in her lap. 'Violet, will you not sit?'

I sat at the side, my mother and father at each end, and spread my hands out flat on the smooth wood, fingers wide, to sustain me.

'I am sorry,' my mother said. 'I know it can never be enough. But I am, Lucas. I have apologised to Violet, and I know she does not forgive me, but—'

'Violet knows?'

'Only since a few months ago,' I said. It was over six, but it sounded a lot. 'I found her when you gave me her letter,' and he had the grace to look briefly ashamed.

'I am sorry,' my mother said. 'I did not mean to leave it so long, without telling you. It was difficult, building a new life and I… was confused. But we did not have a good marriage at the end, Lucas.'

It was too soon to be making excuses. My father looked at me. He was a private man, and he must hate that I was witnessing this, but he did not bid me leave.

'It was marriage, Lily,' he said. 'It was marriage, made before God, in sickness and in health. One does not leave a marriage. Especially, Christ, especially without telling your family where you are. When they long for you, worry about you, think you are dead, murdered, drowned – that cannot be forgiven.'

My mother was crying beautifully, tears running in neat tracks down her face, but she did not brush them away.

'I know, I know,' she said. 'I thought you would hate me. Lucas, I have made my home with a woman. I am with a woman. It has been hard. So hard. But I think that is why… I am sorry for that, too.'

He put his head in his hands briefly, and we both waited to see how he would take it. He might be disgusted or disbelieving, angry or anguished; a whole raft of emotions was possible. Life with a woman was simply something I had never dreamt of; as unlikely as cheese growing on trees, but now I knew about it, had seen my mother and Evelina together, it did not seem so very strange. But my father must have suffered far more than I because of it; must have questioned himself and his marriage many times over. However, when he raised his head, he simply looked sad and perhaps a little relieved.

'Well,' he said, 'Well, stranger things have happened at sea,' and they almost smiled at each other, although for both it was more of a grimace.

'And you have come back now, why?' he asked.

She gave a small, self-deprecating shrug. 'It is a little too late,' she said, 'but I think our Violet needs me.'

'I don't need anyone,' I said, not even sure why I said it, and I got up, left them both in the kitchen, and went for a walk.

Chapter Forty-Five

I went back to Hastings Pier and paid my entry fee to sit on a bench at the end and stare out to sea. It was the pier from whence my mother had blithely stepped on a boat and left me. I realised belatedly I had forgotten danger and was unarmed if Dr Spencer decided to impose on me with his tinctures. But perhaps I would acquiesce. It would be nice to be cocooned in the glow of an experimental potion.

The hordes were out in full, but nobody tried to join me on my bench, and there was something infinitely calming about sitting there and staring out across the water, even with boats and swimmers breaking its calm. The sea was a vast expanse, its passengers mere specks on the surface, and I could almost understand, looking at the beautiful, hopeful horizon, why she had chosen to escape our small, overcrowded town.

If Benjamin... I could not go there in my imagination, but if I did not manage to rescue Benjamin, perhaps I would leave this small town, too. I definitely did not belong in high society anymore, if I ever had.

My mother found me there, an hour later, wearing a half-veil so she would not be recognised. The pier was full of day-trippers, so there was anonymity in the crowd. She stood hovering at the end of the bench as if hesitant to sit and then sat down beside me, in a silence that lasted a good five minutes. It was not like her, but it was peaceful to look out across the stillness of the sea, while emotions churned like a storm inside.

'You were hard to find,' she said eventually, and I laughed sharply at the woman who had taken ten years to track down.

'All the apologies in the world will not do it, will they?' she said. I shrugged my shoulders and looked out to sea again, knowing I was behaving like a child.

'Your hair is escaping its pins,' she said as she sat. 'You have always had such beautiful curly hair, haven't you? I used to braid it for you, when you were little. Do you remember?'

We had always been more like friends than mother and daughter, and I had helped style her hair as much as she had mine, when our maid Edith would let me. My mother had loved the process of getting ready for a social occasion; the jewellery, the make-up, lightly applied; the hair, sleek and obedient to styling; and the accessories, carefully chosen and matched. As a child I had often sat on her bed watching her as she got ready, telling me stories about people she had met, bringing them to life with a vibrancy more entertaining than a theatre show. Her stories were perhaps why I had been so excited to join the adult world, before she left.

'Yes,' I said. 'It was kind of you.'

'I know you hate me,' she said. 'I know I abandoned you cruelly, and you cannot forgive me. I am sorry, even though it will never be enough. Please know I will do anything to make it up to you. Or if you will not forgive me, to help you. Let me be a mother again.'

'I cannot write to you every five minutes, when I have not seen you for ten years,' I said. 'I am not in the habit of it. I am happy you are content in life with your lady friend. Is that not enough?'

'It has never been enough,' she said. 'You are part of my bones, my soul. I missed you every moment.'

'Well, that's nice,' I said. 'And where does ruining my reputation come into it?'

'Your reputation?'

'The last ten years, when people gossiped and scandal-mongered about me because you had vanished. People stopped inviting me to anything and avoided me in the street because it was so shocking. For years I thought men courted me only because they presumed I would be easy prey.'

'Well, that was foolish,' she said. 'Men do not court publicly if they are just chasing a fleeting passion,' and I huffed and looked out to sea, because she was partly right, though some had tried to take advantage in private. It was tiring to explain. I was tired of being told I was foolish. There were seagulls perching on the iron balustrade and I wished I could fly away with them.

'You are so much stronger now,' she said. 'Such a fragile little thing when I left. I am too full of noise and drama. Perhaps when I left it allowed you to grow into who you are.'

'Please think anything you like, if it eases your conscience,' I said, instantly ashamed for throwing pointless daggers. I took a long breath. 'I do not know who I would have been if you had stayed. But I am glad to be who I am now.'

'Always, always, even when I did not write to you, I wanted you to be happy. I asked the Reverend to keep an eye on you. He always told me you were doing well. I am sorry you were not.'

'The Reverend was sparing your feelings because he is a kind man,' I said. 'You should not have put that burden on him.'

A hawker came past and tried to sell us paper cones full of cockles, but my mother waved him away.

'I have helped your father today,' she said. 'We managed not to shout at each other, much. I always cared for him, you know, even though we were not... I told him to marry his Mrs Beetle, legally or not, that he should seize happiness as I have. She sounds a warm-hearted widow. He needs a bit of heat.'

It was too easy to forgive my mother in her company. She had always charmed her way out of every casual offence. I knew it was only when she had gone hurt would return and I would remember the magnitude of what she had done.

'Beeton. You were splendidly over the top as a Pierrot,' I said.

'It suits me. You have grown very wise,' she said, giving me a sidelong glance. 'Your father tells me you stood up to him and made him see you need your independence, and if he admits it, you must have performed a miracle. Tell me about your fiancé.'

'He is in jail,' I said. 'For a crime he did not commit, of course. I cannot work out how to break him out.' I would not talk about feelings with her.

'I find the best way is always to start at the top and work down,' she said.

Had she become a criminal? 'You mean break in through the roof?'

She laughed. 'I mean find the highest-ranking person around and get them to put a word in for you. Lord Brassey or another man who is lofty in the instep. Are there any who might owe him or you a favour?'

'Yes, but do not think I am welcome in society anymore,' I said. 'The Spencer sisters…'

'Pah,' she said. 'Silly girls.' Unconsciously, she echoed my father. 'You are a Lady Detective. That gives you the right to speak to anyone. Soon you will know enough about this town's private business to have a fair bit of power, I imagine.'

'I may do that,' I said. 'Thank you. How is Evelina?'

'She is all the missing bits of me,' my mother said. 'Patient, kind, sensible, practical… I worried about her for a while, after she saved us from Mr Knight, but she does not hold onto drama as I do. She deals with life's difficulties and moves on. Which is strange, because she is the actress. What I am trying to say is… she is fine. We are. Thank you. Does it shock you, she and I? That two women can be happy?'

'I was… surprised, but I see you get along very well together,' I said. 'And I can see an ease in loving another woman. You can share clothes, for a start.'

She laughed at me.

'Oh, Violet, please never let go of your beautiful naivety. It delights my soul.'

'I am letting go of it,' I said, frowning. 'I strive to be worldly-wise and knowledgeable about the universe and everything in it. That's why I am in the profession I am. To find out.'

'Fair enough,' my mother said, 'but don't lose your essential self in it, or allow yourself to be bruised by it. It is what I fear for you most.'

'I have the spirit to bounce back from most things,' I said. 'Desertion included. But right now, I need to rescue Benjamin. Nothing else matters.'

'Then rise to the top,' she said.

She headed off to the train station not long afterwards, and I allowed her to give me a hug, even though I was stiff within it. It was not quite forgiveness, but I did not feel the hurt quite as deeply as I had. In time I expected it would ease, and I could accept her back as the froth in my life. Meanwhile, perhaps I would write to her a little more often.

Chapter Forty-Six

My father was quiet when I got home. He was sitting in the parlour on a winged armchair, his legs outstretched and crossed at the ankle in a way most informal for him, arms crossed, staring into the empty grate of the fireplace.

'Are you well?' I asked. 'I am sorry I did not tell you sooner. I felt... it was not my place.'

'Let us not allow her to create any more division between us,' he said. 'Six months is not eleven years.'

'What will you do now?' I said, hovering in the doorway. I could not discern his emotions.

'Living with your mother was like sitting too close to a hot fire,' he said. 'Seeing her reminded me how different she is from Tilda, and how lonely I was for a long, long time. More lonely when your mother was here, perhaps. Especially towards the end.'

This level of confession was unprecedented, and I was not sure what to say.

'I am sorry for it,' I said.

'There was never anything for you to be sorry for,' he said. 'I have been a father with little energy to promote your happiness. I thought it would be best for you to leave, to make a fresh start with a husband to look after you, rather than live with my doldrums. Your mother told me off for it, a bit late. But you set me right, didn't you? From the first, pushing spotty Ernest Webb into the lake in Alexandra Park.'

I was surprised he remembered that episode, a long, long time ago, when Mr Webb had tried to fondle me under a willow tree on our first outing and had joined the ducks for a swim. 'I have been a bit too set against marriage,' I said. 'But I think, if I am finally to be married, Benjamin will be a far better husband than the rest.' I said it without thinking and then realised it was true, and it hit me that Benjamin likely was the best. It was revelatory. 'Will you reconcile with Tilda – Mrs Beeton?'

'I lack courage,' he said, another startling admission from a man who had not discussed his emotions for a decade. 'I wish I had not listened to Laxton.'

'Why did you listen to him?'

My father shrugged. 'I manage his bank accounts. I am in the habit of it. He has a very persuasive way of talking, of making whatever scheme he is planning sound magnificent, of making you believe he manages the world and understands its machinations far better than the average man. When he said my fiancée might affect my standing in the business world, might tarnish my future prospects, I listened as if I was a green girl. I acted too quickly.'

A green girl. Such a pejorative phrase, for qualities all respectable young girls were expected to possess.

'And I should know better,' my father said ruminatively, 'because not all his business ventures succeed. Some of them fail resoundingly, in fact, but to hear him, failure is no more than a pebble skimmed on a lake, to be forgotten.'

'What kind of businesses failed?'

'Building projects, mostly. Most men at his level of society want to build great edifices which will outlast them, but his are ill-thought through. He often expects to build Rome in a day and is disappointed.'

Something about business ventures failing chimed in my mind, but I could not put a finger on it. I would have to think about it later.

'If you would like me to take a message to Mrs Beeton for you, I am happy to,' I said, and for some reason that made my father root around desperately in his breast pocket, bring out a handkerchief and blow his nose.

'Well,' he said, and there was a slight sheen in his eyes, 'I think I should saddle my own stallion for an apology but thank you. Thank you, Violet.'

I left him alone, because there was too much pent-up emotion eddying around a room that was usually quite chilly.

Chapter Forty-Seven

Hildebrand came to find me in the front parlour the next morning.

'There's a boy here to see you,' she said. 'Hair like an upended sweeping brush. Calls himself Big George?'

'Oh yes, please show him in,' I said, and Big George the chairman bounced into the room, looking nervous.

'Please take a seat,' I said.

'Oh no, ma'am,' he said, but when I insisted he perched on the edge of the chair opposite me.

'You know the books I read,' he said, and when I nodded, 'it's all about observation, isn't it?'

'Yes,' I said.

'Well… it's only… will you keep it confidential? I don't want my name getting out.'

'Of course.'

'Chair-man's not the only job I do,' he said in a rush. 'Sometimes I help build houses, sometimes I work on the railways, any heavy lifting really, it depends on the work going. Anyway, last week I did a few days lifting bricks to build a wall outside the Queen's Hotel, with a man called Ed. He's a nutter, Crazy Ed, but we get on all right. Older than me. He has aspirations.'

'What kind of aspirations?'

'Mostly to blow things up. He had a job dealing with a lot of the explosives to make railway tunnels, and I think he misses it. So… I don't like him all that much, but he likes me. Happens a lot. I'm no good at telling people I don't like 'em. Anyways, I let him talk on about himself and he thinks I'm interested. Mostly, I'm thinking about books.'

'I can understand,' I said.

'We were chatting as we worked last week, passes the time of day. He said he'd been given a real job a while ago, under the cuff like, to blow summat up. Said he had a stash of what was needed, had it all set it up, that the town was going to light up better than fireworks. There was good money in it, but then the whole thing got cancelled, called off because summat happened which made it impossible. He's a bit crazy, as I say, so I didn't ask him too much about it. He was angry his fun had been spoilt.'

'What was it, do you think?'

'Well, he mentioned the seafront and night-time and he said it had happened on a Saturday. Which was the night of the ball, wasn't it? The night Mrs Withers died. I just wondered… if it might have anything to do with it.'

'Do you think he killed her?'

'No, he's not violent in that way. He just likes blowing up rocks and towns. He didn't seem guilty about anything, didn't mention Mrs Withers… not sure he even clocked she'd died the same evening. I just… it's odd isn't it? Anyhow, he's gone to Scarborough for work now. Don't miss him. It's a coincidence, though, isn't it?'

'It's very strange and very interesting,' I said. 'Thank you. It might be important. Was there anything else?'

'He mentioned a toff. That a toff had been behind it. No name or anything else, just a toff.'

Who would that be? Not Lord Brassey, surely. Lord Laxton? Any of the other top-hatted aristocrats who had attended the ball? I could not believe any of them would be involved in such a dangerous enterprise. It was all very puzzling.

'Thank you,' I said again, and then I noticed Big George was staring at my bookshelves. 'Are there any books you would like to take away with you, as thanks?'

'Oh no, miss,' he said. 'Not looking for payment,' but his eyes were still snagged on the bookcase, so I remembered the bound copies of The Strand magazine I had left there and pulled out a couple of volumes. 'What about *The Adventures of Miss Cately*?' I said.

'Ooh, yes!' he said.

'She is a very brave woman. Would you like them? I am quite done with them.' They were my father's copies, but I was sure he would not miss them, and nor would I. I had devoured them from cover to cover and learnt a lot from her chutzpah and bravado, but her stories did not feel quite like real life. My adventures were far more real.

'Yes, please,' he said and he went away delighted, with a promise to return at some point in the future for more.

Chapter Forty-Eight

I t was the first of April and the sun was bright, the hedgerows bursting with birdsong and flowers, the day I went to see Lord and Lady Laxton.

I dressed in one of my new dresses and put my hair up as tightly as possible so it would not spring loose. I wanted to look business-like and remind them of my success in foiling snuff-box theft.

Their butler's importance was revealed by the mobility of his eyebrows, which shot to his hairline when I asked to see both Lord and Lady Laxton at once. We established I was indeed not just calling on Lady Laxton, but he remained standing stiffly in front of me holding out a silver tray for several seconds before I surmised he was waiting for a calling card.

'I beg your pardon,' I said, hitting the flat of my gloved hand against my forehead, 'I forgot. I have just brought my person.' And in case he started looking round the room for a servant: 'I mean, myself.' His eyebrows lowered almost to the tip of his nose before he departed.

Lady Laxton received me alone in a room called the De Vore Room. It was very grand. It had a giant mirror above the marble fireplace and the ceiling was painted extravagantly with luscious fruit, birds and muscled men in togas, presumably a biblical scene. There were lacquered cabinets, their surfaces full of Japanese pottery and silver ornaments and the walls were covered in frames of rare coins, weapons, oil paintings and silk embroidered hangings and portieres. One whole wall was taken up by a mahogany bookshelf, its shelves full of gilt-edged, leather-bound books. But most spectacular was a large circular glass case with a domed top, standing around five feet tall in the centre of the room. It was full of hundreds of tiny exotic birds which must once have flitted around various countries of the world, now clinging in frozen perpetuity to the branches of a real tree.

Lady Laxton looked at me without quite looking at me, as if I was behind gauze.

'Miss... Hamilton,' she said. 'You are lucky to catch me.' She gestured to a high-backed ebony chair and I perched on the edge of it.

'And what can I do for you?' she said, with a note of mild weariness.

I tried to frame my words. 'Your avian display is very beautiful,' I said.

'It is. My husband gave it to me.' She raised her eyebrows as meaningfully as her butler, urging me to the point.

'I am here to plead my case for my fiancé,' I said. 'You of course know him from when we helped you with the situation regarding your aunt. He has been mistakenly implicated in the disappearance of a lady who he simply saved from harm. The police are planning to send him to Scotland, purely because his accuser lives there, and he will have fewer friends to advocate for him and prove his innocence. I would like to keep him here until this matter is resolved. Can you or your husband help me, please?'

'Mr Blackthorn?' she asked. 'The tall, handsome detective?' She smiled as if there was a special understanding between them, and I restrained my wish to inflict bodily harm. 'Well, we must save him. I of course... can do nothing. But my husband never lets anything in life defeat him – will you ring the bell?' She pointed a languid hand to a bell on the wall, and I got up and pulled the handle, which brought the butler within seconds, and shortly afterwards Lord Laxton appeared.

'My dear,' he said to her. 'It must be nearly time for you to have your morning rest. Miss Hamilton, I understand you are looking for assistance?' and I explained the problem again.

'Such a *helpful* man, Mr Blackthorn,' Lady Laxton said, her voice as warm as if Benjamin had fed her pineapple ice-cream from a gold spoon. I tried to dismiss the vision.

'We must act,' Lord Laxton said. He was not a man I could entirely take to, but he was quick and decisive. 'I'll send a note to the prison governor. Ask him to hold fire on the transfer. There need be no rush. What's being done to prove his innocence?'

I explained about sending a telegram to Mrs Ellen Fraser in France, and he suggested sending a telegram to the police in her province in France, to see if they could ensure the news reached her. It made perfect sense, of course. I wished I had thought of it myself.

'If you give me the address, I will organise it,' Lord Laxton said, and I began to take it out of my pocket and then something about Lady Laxton's beautiful bland face, or perhaps the butler stiff and proper in the far corner of the room, made me hesitate. It would not do to share her address too freely.

'I do not have it with me,' I said. 'I am happy to send the message to France, if you will be so kind as to contact the prison governor,' and Lord Laxton shrugged, as uninterested as when Benjamin said he would not collect debts for him.

'As you will. My dear, should you like a tisane, or similar? You look a little fragile this afternoon,' and his wife did look pleasingly wan, but I sensed his words were merely a signal to me my audience with them was over.

'Thank you,' I said, and they bade me good day entirely politely, but with a detachment that signalled they would forget me the second I left, if not before. It did not matter – if they would help.

But when I got home, Hildebrand brought me a telegram and a letter.

'RETURN TO SCOTLAND TWO O'CLOCK TRAIN,' the telegram said. 'CAN YOU STOP B'

The letter was, finally, correspondence from Mrs Ellen Fraser, including a photograph, that showed her looking very well and happily alive next to a flower-bedecked cottage in Brittany, holding a copy of *Le Monde* from three days ago. I stowed it all in one of my skirt pockets and flew out of the door again without stopping.

Chapter Forty-Nine

I stood in the street for a second irresolute and then realised there had never been a more perfect time for a bicycle, so I went indoors again to change. I had my Turkish trousers, at least. I knew the train to Lewes was not for another two hours; the train would take another hour, and by then he would be well on his way to London, where he would change trains to Edinburgh. A horse would not last the distance at speed and unfortunately, I had never learnt to ride one.

I ran to Miss Turton's mansion on the seafront, arriving breathless and exhausted.

'Can I borrow your bicycle?'

'Of course!' she said. 'Is it for a case? How thrilling! My footman pumped up the tyres only yesterday so it should be ready to go. Can I offer you a picnic for the trip? Some lemon cake?'

'No, no thank you, only the bicycle,' I said. 'Maybe a glass of water. And a quick look at a map?'

She brought a map and I worked out my route. In theory it looked straightforward, although there were a lot of hills. I drank the water, thanked her, wheeled the bicycle out onto the promenade and jumped on it.

Fictional Miss Cately had ridden a bicycle in a race. I was riding a bicycle to rescue my fiancé, which was vastly more important. She was no longer my rival. I cycled the long flat road along the seafront as long as I was able. It was a wonderful feeling. Although it was a hot day, a breeze whistled past my ears and kept me cool. I had to overtake a horse or two and a group of barrow boys threw an apple at my front wheel, which thankfully I managed to dodge, but otherwise it was a beautiful straight run.

Before Pevensey Bay I took an inland road past the castle and then the hills began. I had not experienced cycling upwards before and it was exceedingly hard. I was not unfit, because I walked a lot, but my legs were not used to the effort and I fought with myself several times not to get off the bicycle and push it. Downhill by contrast was wonderful again and only the fear of never stopping and going headfirst into a hedge or a wall made me occasionally touch my brakes to slow myself down.

When I was not puffing, it was a glorious landscape of farms and reservoirs, forests and rolling fields. There were few people about; a farm cart or two, a few riders on horseback. A pheasant startled out of a hedgerow as I passed and flew off. Some of the roads had potholes and rutted surfaces, and the part of me in contact with the saddle began to get a little sore.

I passed through a village called Arlington, which I knew meant I was still on the right track, passed another reservoir and a mediaeval-looking priory. The clock in the square said it was one-thirty. Outside the village I hit a rut and fell off, skinning my knees and my trousers, and not long after that I swallowed a fly and had to stop to cough it up. But these small tragedies could not dim my feeling this was what living was for; the reason I had been put on this earth. I could not enjoy it freely, because my fiancé was in danger, but bicycling was yet another aspect of being a detective to bring me satisfaction. Joy for me was all about achievement.

As I was coming into Lewes a trio of boys chased me along the road laughing and one of them tried to put a stick in my wheels. I swore at him in a very unladylike way, hit him very hard across the face with the reticule dangling from my wrist and swerved across the road.

'I don't have time, idiots,' I shouted sharply, and they subsided, falling back until they were specks in the distance.

The main street of Lewes was cobbled, which hampered me greatly, but I was beginning to feel if I got off the bicycle, I might never get on again. My legs felt very peculiar.

I reached the station minutes before the train was due to leave. I had been cycling for nearly two-and-a-half hours. It was likely he was on the train already. I climbed off my bicycle and my knees buckled instantly. I had to stand for a precious second to get the movement back in my legs. I did not want to abandon my bicycle, so I opened the door to the compartment and lifted it in with me, on legs still trembling. I panicked it would be a train with separate compartments and I would have to keep leaping on and off at stations until I found the right carriage, but luckily it proved to be the kind with a connecting corridor.

My fellow passengers were not happy. A portly man was outraged when my handlebars dented his newspaper.

'You can't bring a bicycle on here! That's outrageous! I'll tell the inspector!' A lady joined in when my bicycle wheel accidentally ran over the hem of her skirt. I left them to it, navigating my bicycle into the corridor where it promptly got wedged. This never happened in the detective serials I had read. After some time, I managed to free it and half lifted, half wheeled it along the corridor, peering into compartments.

I was starting to fear I had got on the wrong train or Benjamin was not on it, before I finally spotted him in a carriage near the front.

Chapter Fifty

He was sitting, with handcuffs on, opposite two policemen, and he looked rough and weary, starting out the window as if he didn't care about life or anything in it. It was possible someone had hit him in the eye, as it was black and swollen. My heart took a great surge of its own volition and I opened the compartment door, before realising I couldn't get in the compartment because my bicycle was in the way.

'Blackthorn,' I said, and tried to navigate around it, but there was a big roar from behind me and the ticket inspector had arrived.

'Madam! You cannot bring a bicycle into a passenger carriage! You must move it and get off at the next station. Perhaps in the luggage compartment, for an extra fee, but Madam—'

'Hamilton,' Benjamin said, and he smiled at me, and all the noise and nonsense going on about us didn't matter.

'I have the letter,' I said, 'From Mrs Fraser.' I took it out of my pocket and threw it to him and he caught it beautifully with both hands.

'This letter proves his innocence,' I said to the policemen, 'so you must let him go. And Lord Laxton has written to the prison governor too, to say he should not be taken to Scotland until this matter is sorted out, so you must all get off the train now and go back.' I beamed at Benjamin and he grinned back.

'Madam,' the train inspector said from behind me, 'I must ask you to move. Your bicycle is blocking the corridor,' and he started to put his hand on my shoulder, so I turned to face him.

'Do not dare touch me, sir,' I said. 'We will be getting off the train at the next station. I know you are doing your job, but I am sorting out a grievous police error and for these next ten minutes, this bicycle does not matter. Go away.' And very surprisingly, he blustered a bit, but went. 'Ten minutes and then you're off this train,' but he went.

'This letter,' Benjamin said to the policemen, who were looking a little bewildered, 'Proves Mrs Ellen Fraser is alive and well, but does not want to return to her husband. My business partner has brought it to you. Surely you can agree this means I do not need to travel to Scotland? Here, read it.'

The policemen read the letter, carefully and scrutinised the photograph of Mrs Fraser, a recent one, signed and dated by herself and the photographer on the back.

'I am sorry my husband has caused you such difficulty,' her letter said, I found out later. 'When you have been all that is good and honourable and saved me from a life of misery. I will not go back to him. But if there is anything I can ever do for you, please know I would drop everything and do it. I owe you and your father so much.'

'We had our instructions,' one policeman said, reading it. 'But this does seem to change matters. Best we go back and speak to the superintendent.'

'Naw, ah've got a job tae dae,' the other policemen said. He must have come from Scotland to do it. 'Unless ah'm given special dispensashun, I'll be taking him where ah've been told tae.'

'Your superiors will not take kindly to you taking me all the way to Edinburgh for nothing,' Benjamin said. 'Violet, can you hop over the bike and come and sit down? You look tired.'

I manoeuvred myself around the bicycle and inside the compartment, leaving it propped outside. 'I have bicycled for over two-and-a-half hours and I only fell off once,' I said, sitting down next to Benjamin.

'That is exceptional,' he said. 'I apologise for my disreputable state. There hasn't been much opportunity for ablutions in recent days. You look glowing.'

'That's quite all right,' I said. 'I hope you are unharmed. I have been exerting myself too. I will be very glad when we can go home and have a bath.' I blushed a little because it sounded as if I thought we would be in the same bath. 'I mean... two baths. Each. In our houses in separate parts of town.'

'It hasn't been decided what we should do,' the English constable said. The train drew in at a station, but the Scottish constable put a hand on the door in case we decided to leave. I thought about fighting him and leaping off, but really, my legs were too sore and I was with Benjamin now so everything would be all right, even if we ended up in a Scottish jail surrounded by bearded savages in kilts. Shortly afterwards the train drew off again.

'I have missed you,' Benjamin said. 'Have you been well? In any danger? I could not get messages in or out, until you sent Joe in. He agreed to send the telegram for me. Thank you for him and for your note. He gave me some peanuts too. Odd man, useful.'

My faith in Joe and humanity restored, I found I was smiling again at Benjamin, so widely my cheeks ached.

'We need ta discuss oor course o' action,' the Scottish constable said, looking fierce.

'You two can discuss it between you,' I said. 'It is your decision after all. But if you take my fiancé to Scotland, I am coming too, with my bicycle, and I warn you I am an extremely difficult character.'

'She is,' Benjamin said, his smile wide, 'She is terrible in a train carriage,' and I remembered the last time we had travelled, when he had proposed for the second time and kissed me for the first, and by the look in his eyes he remembered it too.

The constables read the letter again, and conferred between themselves, and the train inspector came back and gave a wail of dismay to find the bicycle still in the corridor.

'I cannot run a train like this!' he said, and it helped the constables make the decision we would all get off at the next stop, Plumpton, and catch the train back.

'My bicycle stays with me,' I said, so we all had to travel back to Lewes in the luggage compartment of the train, but I didn't mind, because Benjamin was back and safe and nothing else really mattered.

They let him go once we arrived back in Lewes, of course, because he was entirely innocent and they only had to look at him properly to know he was overflowing with splendidness and unlikely to kill anybody. Benjamin and I travelled back to Hastings together. I stowed my bicycle in the luggage compartment again and then we shared a compartment with other people, who looked at us suspiciously as we were both a little worse for wear. My hair was coming loose from its pins and Benjamin looked as if he had fought several wars without changing his clothes.

We could not talk about his trials in company, but it was enough to know he was at my side. He was exhausted, bruised and he had more than a day's worth of stubble. I elbowed him gently in the side to let him know I was thinking of him, and he gave me a wry smile.

'I'm in good health, underneath,' he said. 'Don't worry. It's been a tough few days, but a good night's sleep and I'll be a new man.'

'I'm happy with the old one,' I said.

He leant down under my hat and whispered in my ear, 'I'd be happy with one bath.' I blushed, disappointed I could not be sophisticated and louche, but momentarily thrown off-guard. 'We would need a lot of hot water,' I said, lamely, but Benjamin did not laugh at me, although I felt him smile.

'Does your riding on your bicycle all these miles to rescue me mean you finally admit a fondness for my person?' he asked instead. I could feel the warmth of his breath on my ear.

'I admit you are pleasing on the eye,' I whispered back.

'But my heart,' he said. 'Am I pleasing to your heart? Have I managed in these last weeks and months to charm and beguile you on the inside, as well as the out? Have I caught your heart as you have caught mine?'

'You have impressed me,' I whispered. 'But I would not wish you to think I so easily hand over my heart fully unwrapped, like a parcel delivered to your doorstep. A heart should be slowly unwrapped over years, the more to appreciate the gift.' It was a poor analogy, perhaps, but his presence had a tendency to scramble my wit.

He did not seem disappointed. 'I look forward to unwrapping you slowly,' he said, and he kissed my ear under the safety of my hat, before returning to his upright position. He took my arm and wound it under his, clasping my hand in his large warm one, and although it was perfectly respectable, the woman opposite us tutted loudly. 'Fie, Madam, she's my fiancée,' Benjamin said, and he smiled down at me, rakish and disreputable and also, although I kept it to myself, immensely loveable. I liked this side to him, his piratical, daring side, which I had not witnessed since we last shared a train carriage on the way back from Buxton. It … aroused sensations. I would have to encourage it.

When we got back to Hastings, we went our separate ways, because Benjamin needed to bathe and sleep, and I definitely needed to bathe, and take the bicycle back on wobbly legs to Miss Turton. But we agreed to meet the following day at our detective agency.

Chapter Fifty-One

The next morning Benjamin looked refreshed and vital again, even with his eye a fine shade of yellow and purple, and was back at it already, scraping down and mending a Chippendale chair. Its wooden back was carved delicately as to look like intertwined ribbons and the intruder had thankfully slashed only one clean break through the middle; perhaps even his anger and capacity for destruction had been muted by the beauty of a Chippendale. Benjamin was examining the damage carefully and working out what wood infill might be needed to knit it together again.

'It'll need a master craftsman,' he said. 'I'm not of the skill to carve ribbons yet. I'll need to ask around, find a good carver.'

'How are you?' I said. 'Have you survived your ordeal?' I unpinned my hat and carefully hung it on the handle of a wardrobe door.

He let the chair drop and stood up to give me a hug of bear-like proportions, burying his face in my hair.

'Violet, Violet,' he said. 'I am well. All through it, the idea of you was like warm sunshine burning through the clouds. I am glad to be back, to be here in this place with you. You have the scent of home. I have missed you.'

'It is only lavender water,' I said, extricating myself. 'I have missed you too. But how was it? How was prison? Was it horrid?'

'Dreadful,' he said, laughing at me. 'I had to share a cell with a few rough men, there might have been a rat or two. The food was atrocious. But all through it, I knew you would not be content to leave me mouldering in there, and I was right. You sent toothless

Joe, and you cycled all the way to save me. That makes you, I think, well worth having.' He tried to embrace me again but I dodged him and stood a few steps back.

'Please excuse me, I am not avoiding you because I do not want your affections. It is only that I find them... distracting. I want to discuss a few unromantic things first, so I do not get muddled,' I said. I had things to say, and my brain had decided now was the time to say them.

He regarded me quizzically for a second. 'Very well. But if we are to avoid romance, I will make us coffee. Coffee is profoundly grounded in realism and practicality.'

'Do,' I said, hearing the primness in my voice, which might have been due to nerves.

Once he had made coffee, we sat in a couple of easy chairs that had been rudely slashed down the middle so the stuffing was spilling out, but were not too uncomfortable now he had covered them with a blanket.

'What does marriage mean to you?' I asked him. It would be better to start with him, so I did not have to talk about myself.

'It means that the person I esteem most in the world is by my side and we are building a life together,' he said, watching me cautiously over the top of his cup.

'Yes, but what do you expect from it? Do you want a wife who will have scores of babies and juggle the house and all the babies?'

'Not quite scores,' he said. 'One or two would be nice, if the subject of my adoration is amenable. But juggling babies might be dangerous for them. What are you getting at, my Violet?'

'I don't want to give up my career as a detective,' I said. 'And I am not sure about popping out children immediately. I might want to wait a while until I have lived a bit more. A few years. And even when I have children I would want to work. And...' I bit my lip, because this might be the part that finally drove him away, 'I want to live on my own, just for a little bit, while I am engaged. To prove that I can. To find out what it is like, and not move in with you and Agnes and the children immediately. Miss Turton has a suite of rooms available in her apartment.'

He, as always, did not seem in any hurry, taking his time to think about what I had said, drinking his coffee and looking far across the shop, considering.

'An answer before next Tuesday would be nice,' I said, and he laughed at me.

'These are serious considerations, and I will not treat them lightly,' he said. 'I think what you mean, in life order, is that you want to stay engaged a bit longer and live alone; carry on working as a detective when we are married and not have children immediately but wait a few years. And perhaps not have scores of them. Am I right?'

'Yes. I know I am twenty-nine, so I know I should be looking to procreate with urgency. But I have only just started living life properly, and I love... us. I love what we do here, the furniture and the detective agency and this life, now. I do not want that to change too quickly.'

'How long?' he said. 'How long do you want to live alone? If it is twelve years, I may be worried.'

'Four months,' I said. 'Four months engaged and living alone, and then we can be married and I do not give up work for another two at least.'

'If this means you will marry me, I will agree easily,' he said. 'The living alone for a while does not concern me, especially if you are living with the eminently respectable Miss Turton. And of course, you can carry on working, as we have a business to rebuild together if we can. I am not agitating for more children in a hurry, as I have sufficient in my life with my brothers and sisters for now. As long as that does not mean I will be banned from your boudoir. There are ways... not perfect ways... but there are ways to postpone eventualities.'

'I can ask my friend Mrs Monk,' I said. 'She will have lots of ideas,' and he groaned a little.

'I can handle it,' he said. 'But I should say, I do not expect you to live behind our shop. I see us finding a house, with two bedrooms upstairs perhaps, a cosy kitchen and a front parlour with a hearth, and making our own home, our own future, not too far away from Agnes and the children perhaps, as they still need me, and Maud is only five, but far enough away they cannot put frogs in our bed of a morning.'

'You are everything that is generous and perfect in a fiancé,' I said.

'I am not, Violet,' he said, and he leant forward with his elbows on his knees, looking determined and… guilty? 'I am not perfect. I have… lied to you by omission. I am not well-off. I am not poor either; I have some savings, some investments, but if you choose to ally with me, life might not be as comfortable as you are used to. I confess, I may have overstated matters to your father. There may be times we have to scrabble farthings together, that we need to actively seek out business to survive. You should know this.'

'Why did you overstate matters to my father?'

He ran his hands down the outside of his thighs to his knees in one sweeping motion. 'Because I want to be with you. Because I want you in my life, and I did not think your father would accept a man who is only half a furniture salesman and half a detective. I may have exaggerated my achievements in the navy and my regular income. I have not lied to you, but only by omission, because you have not asked. I do not want to offer you a life less than you are used to. I should not have lied and I am sorry. I will not hold you to our bargain, if you change your mind.'

Now it was my turn for silence.

'Well. So, you are not as all out honourable and unimpeachable as you seem, Mr Blackthorn?'

'No,' he said.

'In fact, you are able to lie if it suits you?'

'Yes, but Violet—'

'And you dissembled to my father because you wanted to marry me, above all else?'

'Above all else,' he said. He flexed his hands out wide over his knees in a way that unexpectedly sent a spark of sensation to a most surprising part of my body. It was confounding, how my body reacted to his, and I was fairly certain now I would have no objections to physical proximity in the bedroom.

'Well thank goodness,' I said. 'I was concerned you were too perfect a gentleman generally, and too honourable for a profession that requires a little ducking and diving, but I see I need not have worried. I have no fear of jostling for business, or making ends meet, and in fact I should like to see if I'm any good at it. I have never wanted to be pampered and cared for. I only ask to be allowed to live life as I choose, and you have a talent for allowing it. Shall we do this adventure, then?' I put out my hands, palm up, and he took them in his own large, strong ones and pulled me straight over into his lap, for kissing that said everything he had not said before, and more.

'There is only one thing,' he said, later. 'I have been circumspect with you, because... I did not want to cross any lines that might make it impossible for you to leave me if you changed your mind. But I confess, I want to cross them more than I want the food on my plate or air to breathe. I want to unlace the front of your corset, and slide my hand up to your knee, like this, and clamber up the wisteria at night to your bedroom at Miss Turton's and let you experiment on me every which way you please. But... I will not impeach Miss Turton's household, or overstep until we are married, if there is any uncertainty in you. Any doubt.'

'I am not sure if Miss Turton has any wisteria,' I said. 'But I can check if she has a ladder,' and then I was not allowed to speak for some time, until the shop doorbell clanged and he deposited me on my feet, quite far across the shop, in under ten seconds. He would always be careful of the proprieties and I was glad of it.

I had quashed my doubts. He would not lay down rules within marriage to make me smaller, or if he tried, I would fight him and he would let me win, because he had more willingness than any man I knew to let a woman live life the way she wanted. He was large, generous and all mine and my shrivelled heart was unfurling most beautifully again.

But after a while we halted romance, because we still had a murder to solve.

Chapter Fifty-Two

I told Benjamin all my adventures in detail, and then I tried to make sense of it. 'It's a conundrum. Mrs Withers received a letter listing the ingredients of one of Dr Spencer's medicines, so she accused him of being a quack and in return he tried to blackmail her. At around one-thirty, she left the ball and caught a bath chair, looking determined, and shortly before three, she was killed. Sometime that night, someone took a hummingbird from her hat. On the same night, Crazy Ed was commissioned to blow up an area of the seafront, but it was cancelled.'

'We need to add into the mix the fact our agency was broken into and ransacked and also that I was sent up to Scotland and then arrested for a case I worked on with my father well over two years ago now. I have not been able to understand why Mr Fraser decided to rake all this up now when he took no real action at the time,' Benjamin said.

'Do you have any thoughts about why?'

'I feel the emphasis is on keeping me occupied, away or too busy to notice what might be going on under my own nose. Part of me wonders if it is because I know Hastings and the fishermen so well, I'm dangerous to somebody's larger plan. You, they think they can handle with threats of ruining your reputation and locking you up; me they need out of the picture. I've asked my contacts to look into any business or other connections that Mr Fraser has with anyone else in Hastings who might want me gone.'

'The planning application,' I said. 'The planning application that Colonel Withers mentioned, from Dr Spencer and others, for a hydro on the seafront. It was rejected, wasn't it? Did the colonel send you a copy?' The conversation I had with my father about Lord Laxton's failed enterprises had come back to me.

'He did,' Benjamin said. 'It took him a while and I meant to take a look but I got distracted by the damage to the shop and getting arrested. Here, it's still in our filing cabinet. No one stole it, or any of our notes on cases. Their minds seemed fixed on destruction and distraction rather than theft.'

I opened it up. It was a folder of around five loose pages, so I spread them out across the blanket box so we could both read them together.

Benjamin was a faster reader than I.

'Christ,' he said. 'They would have destroyed the Stade and that part of the beach altogether. Rock-a-Nore Road, the lifeboat house, All Saints Street, Tackleway, The Bourne, George Street – the heart of the old town. Even, God forbid, our agency. To build a hydro, when they already exist in their hundreds across the country, when there are already three in this area alone. What were they thinking?'

'It was Lord Laxton who put in the application,' I said. 'With Dr Spencer... a couple of names I don't recognise, a Mr Smithers and a Mr Topping. And Mr Gallop!' Why did he keep coming back into my world? I mentioned my bizarre conversation with Mr Gallop on the seafront, where he had accused me of taking a piece of paper, and Benjamin listened and nodded and filed it away in his detective brain for consideration.

'Let's keep it in the mix,' he said.

'There's no real thought to the application,' I said, still reading, 'No planning, it's just grand theories. Here: "It will be the finest hydrotherapy resort in the world, attracting over fifty thousand visitors a year to partake of Hastings & St Leonards life-giving, life-enriching water."'

'Twelve swimming baths, four steam baths of varying temperatures, five Turkish Baths, six salt baths, three sitz baths... the whole of Hastings would be a bath,' Benjamin said. 'A bit like the sea, which might be easier than building thirty-five new ones.'

'"Combined with the world-renowned medicines of Dr Spencer, it would make Hastings and St Leonards a health and wellness destination for visitors from all four corners of the globe,"' I read. "The world's most efficacious medicines; Dr Spencer's Wondrous Water of Life; Widow Welch's Female Pills; Dr Nibblets Vital Renewer and others would be part of the core treatment, effecting miracle cures for the ill and unhealthy. Arriving pale and unwell, they would leave revitalised and reborn.' Does it say anywhere why the application was rejected?'

'Here,' Benjamin pointed, 'at the end. "Rejected. The planning committee decided unanimously the application possessed little feasibility, especially given the site proposed is unsuitable for development or the scale of building work required. It would displace communities, destroy an entire area including many existing buildings which are irreplaceable (some only recently built, e.g. the West Hill Lift) and require a severe level of demolition and disruption to Hastings Old Town. The proposal is sadly lacking in detail, with no feasibility studies or architectural plans, and is unlikely to benefit Hastings and St Leonards to any significant degree. The committee is unlikely to consider a resubmission." Ouch. That's harsh. It must have angered them.'

'This is important,' I said. 'Really important. I think it means... do you think they were angry enough to consider destroying the whole area? So they could rebuild it, build their spa, and be seen as saviours rather than destroyers?'

'It's possible,' Benjamin said. 'I'm going to speak to the fishermen to see if there was anything they noticed that might point to it.' He stared at me in sudden revelation. 'What about the wire?'

'The wire?'

'The one stretched across the beach that cut Maud's foot. It could have been a fuse... if the dates add up. They kept the wire

I think, might have used it around the house. I'll speak to them too.'

'I'll go and find Big George,' I said. 'See if we can track down Crazy Ed.'

'Do you have your gun?' Benjamin asked and when I nodded: 'Be careful. I don't like this.'

Tracking down Big George proved, in the end, impossible. He was not working the chairs today. Lobster thought he might be working on the new railway, and another chair-man called Chuff thought he might be working over the other side of town on the building of a new hotel. In the end, after some running around, I left word with Lobster and one or two others that I wanted to speak to him and headed back towards the shop.

Could such a wild idea be true? And if so, who would be involved? Lord Laxton could surely not be a candidate, even though Big George had said a toff was involved. I could perhaps believe it of Dr Spencer, but Mr Gallop? He was perfectly capable of small plots of bitter animosity, but surely not one on such a scale.

In our great country of endeavour and innovation, there were so many accidents. In February there had been a huge disaster at the building of a viaduct in Cornwall, when a platform had broken away, throwing twelve men to their deaths, and last year a gas explosion at Peckfield Colliery in Yorkshire had killed over sixty men and boys as well as pit ponies. How deeply would anyone question an explosion in a town where new railways, bridges, quarries and hotels sprung up all the time, and where the elements themselves often seemed intent on destruction?

Chapter Fifty-Three

I had given up searching and was heading back through Alexandra Park, the long landscape stretching across the upper slopes of Hastings and St Leonards, when a man leapt off a bench and came running towards me.

'Miss Hamilton,' Mr Gallop said, lifting his hat. There was a sheen of sweat on his forehead, his moustache limp and stragglier than I had seen it. 'I have been meaning to call on you. Have you reflected on our conversation?'

'The one about a piece of paper?' I asked. 'I have been unable to make any sense of it.' I did not feel like stopping, so I carried on walking and he skittered by my side, his body half-turned towards me.

'Very well,' he said, 'you have me trapped. Is it money you want?'

'Always,' I said. 'But not from you. What is on this paper, and why is it so important to you?'

He darted in front, spun to face me and stopped in his tracks, blocking my path. 'You can have forty pounds. That is all. I cannot afford more.'

How much could I question him without revealing I was considering him a candidate for an explosion on the seafront?

'Is it related to the spa you want to open on the seafront?' I asked. 'The one that was declined planning permission?'

Mr Gallop went an odd shade of puce.

'I am a man of God,' he said. 'Of course, there is no connection. The note was merely a creative exercise. A novelistic endeavour.'

'I did not have you down as a writer,' I said. I walked around him and took a path to the right, across a pretty bridge.

'Yes, yes. Fifty, then,' he said. 'Since you are a lady of honour and good breeding. Perhaps you will indulge a gentleman who wants only the safe return of his idle scribblings.'

'I do not have them, however poetic,' I said. I stopped on the bridge and leant against the wrought-iron railing. 'Mr Gallop, please stop harassing me. I am not keeping anything from you for revenge, personal benefit or any other reason. You must look elsewhere.'

He straightened and looked about him, and I saw we were alone on the bridge and the path, shielded by overhanging trees and bushes.

'You are nothing but a foolish, foolish girl,' he started, but I had had enough of that pejorative.

'And you are nothing but a tremendously foolish man,' I said. 'To write whatever you wrote, and leave it lying about. Do not make me the focus of your idiocy.'

He drew himself up to his full height, which was not greatly taller than me, but he radiated anger with a kind of desperate despair, and I wondered how often I would be in these situations, alone with angry men, and how I could best learn to defend myself. The disparity in my physical strength was unavoidable, but I did not always want to be pulling out a gun.

'Do you know how easily I could snap your neck?' he said.

'And if you lay a single finger on me, do you know how easily I can ruin you?' I asked, standing straight and upright myself. 'Because even if you did try, I'd crawl on my hands and knees half-dead to turn you in. I am not scared of you. Do not underestimate me.'

'I did not mean it. Forgive me. I would never do any harm. I am overcome, that is all. Please do not... please do... I have a standing in the community, *a profession*. You must understand.'

'I understand nothing, until you explain it to me. And if you are not inclined to, I must bid you good day.' I stood as tall as

I could and looked him straight in the eye, unflinching, and he havered a little but eventually tipped his hat at me in a miserable farewell and took himself off.

I watched his retreat along the path, allowing myself a small moment of triumph. I had won a battle with words. It was a significant success, for a small woman hampered by perceptions of her own foolishness, and it meant I had another ready weapon at my disposal, because wouldn't it be wonderful if I could win wars on wit alone?

Chapter Fifty-Four

As I came out the other side of the gardens, I realised I was on Lower Park Road, where Lord and Lady Laxton lived. I was not ready to run into Lord Laxton in particular, as there was too much new information to process; too much to think about. I thought perhaps Benjamin and I should visit Constable Carruthers and share what we knew, or even Lord Brassey. The theories were too wild, too unlikely, and even though it was a betrayal of my sex, I felt the facts needed the cool, calm scrutiny of gentlemen to help reach the truth.

As I came towards their house, on the opposite side of the street, a butler opened the door and a woman came down the steps. It was Lady Laxton, of course, wearing a fitted brocade coat in forest green and a very beautiful hat, large, although not like Mrs Withers' hats with too many feathers and flutterings; her hat was white, with a large purple sash looped around the brim, simple and elegant. She was, unusually, alone. She saw me, I was sure of it, but looked straight through me in the special expressionless way people who are practised at it do, and then turned right to walk along the street, ahead of me, on the opposite side of the road. Ignoring me so expertly was not necessarily the act of a fragile woman, but I was already wondering about that.

I slowed my pace, not wanting to come even with her although I was on the other side of the road, and then I saw the back of her hat. Perched on the edge of the brim was a single hummingbird. A hummingbird with a beautifully curved forked tail, quivering in the breeze. The bird missing from Mrs Withers' hat.

*

What did it mean? What should I do? I stood irresolute for a second, and then followed her. What stalking her would achieve I did not know. Could there be more fork-tailed hummingbirds in Hastings than Edith thought? Lady Laxton or her husband might have friends who travelled from the Andes as well. I could not accuse the aristocracy of stealing a dead bird from a dead woman's hat.

I could not think of any other course of action to take. If she turned downhill she would be going in the same direction I had already planned. She already knew I was behind her, so possibly she would think we were simply heading in the same direction, unless she took too many twists and turns. I dropped back a little, so we were not too close, and dawdled along after her, admiring the view in the park on my left-hand side, keeping a vague eye on her. She turned into Queen's Road again and downhill towards the seafront, and so our paths coincided, and I was hardly following her at all.

It took around twenty minutes and I was so unimportant she had forgotten me completely, not once turning or stopping. She managed not to run into any of her acolytes. Perhaps the young people were all frolicking in the sea. On the promenade she turned abruptly right, towards the pier, and I knew I would have to think of an excuse if she asked me why I was behind her, because I had intended to turn left towards our detective agency. But she had still forgotten I existed. Along this stretch she met more people she knew but did not seem inclined to stop, nodding her head briefly, the bird's tail quivering with the movement like the lure on a fishing line, walking onwards with neat, quick steps.

She came level with the tollgate at Hastings Pier and took a left to go through the gates. The toll keeper did not try to charge her but waved her through. I followed but had to pay, like all of the less exalted classes, and by the time I made it through, I had lost her in the crowds. The pier was hectic. People were crowding around the strength, electric-shock, phrenology, fortune-telling and gambling machines, the candyfloss stalls, seafood and popcorn stands; sitting, lying and perching on the seats lined either side of the wooden promenade; gathered around a scattering of acrobats and entertainers. The pier band was in full swing with music hall songs and ditties, but they were competing with a couple of organ grinders, a barking dog and the shrieks, laughter and shouts of day-trippers young and old, the whole melding into a cacophony of sound that presented a mild assault on the ear.

The pier was nearly a thousand feet long, so I thought I would have little chance of spotting Lady Laxton again. But as I came near the seaward end, where the exotic pavilion sat with its onion domes and tall finials, like some building out of a mystic tale from Arabian Nights, the crowds lessened a little and I saw her sitting in on a little stool, staring out to sea, completely still. She was having her portrait created by a silhouette artist. Some artists were so speedy they could cut a portrait straight from observation with a pair of scissors, but this gentleman was painting her image onto paper first, to cut out once he was satisfied. She would make a beautiful silhouette, with her delicate features and elegant hat. Would the bird make it in? The tail feathers were perhaps too tiny.

I could hardly ask her questions when she was posing for a portrait. Instead, I was assailed with the smell of fried fish and chips and if I had been hungry before, now it was tenfold. I found the stall with the smallest queue and bought a small parcel wrapped in newspaper, hot, smothered in salt and vinegar. I decided to abandon Lady Laxton, for now; little could be achieved by accosting or watching her. It would be better if I had lunch and went to see Benjamin to discuss all I had learnt and we decided on a plan.

I found myself a small gap on the steps of the pavilion, among others who had the same idea, and ate my lunch, enjoying it with a relish I had not felt in a while. I had been too busy running about to take the time to enjoy such pleasures, to savour a treat that reminded me of days out with my mother, when she had taught me to swim and tumble in the waves, swallowing water and laughing with the joy of it. She had been a good mother, when she was here, the kind of mother every child must secretly long for, who seized all the fun and ignored the rules, a sister rather than a parent, sparing on chastisement and discipline. It had made her desertion harder. But the pain was not quite so sharp since her recent visit.

Then Lord Laxton was running up the steps and surprisingly, he saw me and did not look straight through me. Instead he clicked his fingers.

'Ah, Miss Hamilton,' he said. 'Yes, I have some business for you and your gentleman. Come inside for a moment.' He said it with such complete certainty and authority, and I was so surprised to have been noticed, I stood up to throw the remnants of my fish and chip wrappers in the wastepaper bin and followed him into the front hall of the pavilion before I had a chance to think about whether it was wise.

Chapter Fifty-Five

'It's shut for a week, in between concerts,' he said, opening one of the four front doors with a key and waving me in, before walking rapidly across the parquet hall, 'I might as well show you the next big attraction to hit Hastings and St Leonards.' He threw open the two double doors at the back of the entrance hall leading to the ballroom, and I nearly shrieked, because the curtains were drawn and in the dimness was a group of people, standing entirely still.

'Waxworks,' Lord Laxton said. 'Hired from Madame Tussaud's, of the finest quality. Expensive. Just been delivered. Come and see them.' He ushered me into the room but did not open the curtains covering windows running the length of the ballroom on either side, parallel to the sides of the pier.

'The sun is too strong,' he explained, and instead lit the gas on a few of the lamps, casting pools of quavering light across the ballroom. It was the largest venue for entertainment for miles around, taking two thousand people at a stretch, but there were only around thirty waxworks, looking a little forlorn in the centre of the room like guests too early for a party.

'I am honoured to see them,' I said. They were all wrapped up in dust cloths like mummies, though, so I was, now I thought about it, more worried than honoured. 'What business did you have to discuss?'

He swept back towards the double doors and kicked aside the shingle stone keeping the left door open, so that the stone spun wildly across the room. Then he closed both doors, turned the key with a flourish and pocketed it, and I knew I had made a mistake.

'Simply the business of giving a warning,' he said. 'Do you want to see one of the waxworks? Look, here's one of our great Queen,' and he began unwrapping one speedily, in a way that was a little intrusive and disrespectful of the person underneath it, even if they were made of wax. Underneath there was indeed a vague likeness to Queen Victoria, although her face was a little uneven; the eyes set too deeply within her head like raisins in dough.

'How... interesting,' I said. It was still too dark in the room, despite the watery pool of light. 'What do you mean by a warning? I must depart, I have an appointment,' but Lord Laxton was showing me another figure, this time of the art critic John Ruskin, who looked intellectual but morose.

'I haven't seen them myself yet. It is a warning,' he said. 'To you and your lumbering beast of a fiancé to forget Mrs Withers. To stop meddling in town matters, stop interfering and spreading empty rumours and for you, particularly, to stop sticking your nose into men's business, or you will find out very soon why it's unwise.'

'My fiancé is not lumbering,' I said. I was aiming for mild distraction while trying to control my mounting panic, slithering inside me like an escaped snake.

'I do not...' Lord Laxton said, holding his hands up in the air briefly in a claw shape, as if he was strangling someone invisible. 'I do not care. What you think, who you are, why you have chosen to run around town. You are a woman, and you are a nobody. Nothing. Not important. Less than the dust on my shoe. I want you to shut up and go away, back to whatever it is women do,' he made a shooing motion with his hands, 'and let me do the things that matter. Just shut up and go away.'

I was in for a penny and my gun was warm and heavy against my leg, but I would try words first.

'Mrs Withers had a forked-tail hummingbird in her hat the night she was murdered,' I said. 'They are extremely rare, and one was removed from her hat that night. Today your wife wears the very same one. Is it connected?'

There might have been a flicker of surprise in his gaze, but he masked it, turning his back on me and beginning to unwrap another waxwork, with short sharp motions as if it was the only thing to stop him from throttling me.

'Mrs Withers interfered in business not her own and paid for it. You would be wise to do the same. Florence Nightingale!' he said, and indeed it was, in a nursing cap and uniform, holding a night lamp and looking a little grim. They were not happy waxworks.

'Did you hurt her, because you planned to blow up the Stade?' I said. 'Did she find out about it and try to stop you?'

'Of course not,' he said, dropping the dust cloth and spinning around. 'Of course, it was nothing so intelligent. She came to tell me about Dr Spencer's quack medicines, claimed they were hurting my wife. It was a *trivial* matter, in the midst of important business. She chased along the seafront to bother me about nothing and ruined an entire fortnight's worth of planning.'

'So, it is true? You were planning to destroy the Stade?'

He took out a box of matches from his upper pocket. 'Are. I have never yet failed in something I set out to do. I am so tired of women,' he said. 'Moaning, arguing, complaining.' His voice went high and squeaky. 'Dr Spencer is a quack! You should care more about your wife!' He flicked his fingers. 'I want to build the world's biggest hydrotherapy spa. I want to recreate the glory of the baths in the Roman Empire and I am surrounded by women who *fuss*.' He lit the match and held it near Queen Victoria's face. '*Fuss*.'

'What about your wife?'

'What about her? She is my exquisite distraction. That's all. Nothing more. Everyone flutters around her; I get on with what's important. She is one of my paintings, a precious vase. Beautiful, empty. I took the bird, because she likes birds. An ornament for an ornament. Look, our great Queen is melting!'

It was true, her smile was drooping. She looked as if she was crying.

'Didn't you say your waxworks were very expensive?'

'I do not think women deserve a place in this exhibition after all,' he said. His attention was not fully on me, so I did not argue with him, but I felt the anger in him, a more self-righteous anger than Mr Gallop's and therefore more dangerous.

I looked about the small room, but I could not see a way out. I could dodge around dummies, but it would be a nightmare chase he would win. He was such a spindly man I could not bear to think of those long fingers reaching out and catching me.

'I tried to do it the boring way, fill in the paperwork, sit in on meetings, God, the meetings,' he said, 'But it did no good, did it? Nobody cares about old buildings or the halfwits living in them. Some are no better than slums. We need to clean it all away and build anew and if that bitch hadn't *fussed*, we'd already have done it.' He left Queen Victoria, her face a lump of molten wax, her hair beginning to smoulder too. 'Florence next. I don't think we'll miss the women.'

'How did Mrs Withers die?' I asked.

He shrugged. 'I pushed her. Her head hit the capstan. It was an accident. But the boatman saw it and left us to it and then we didn't have time to light the fuse and get away, and Gallop was gabbling like a freak, and then the blasted fisherman came by.'

I slid my hand in my skirt pocket to take hold of my gun.

'You would have killed so many people,' I said. 'What about them?'

'They are no better than animals,' he said. 'Grubbing about in the dirt, scratching a living. They have no intellectual merit or vision beyond the food on their plate. They will never build great monuments or change the world. I matter. My *plans* matter. I will not be stopped.'

'It is surely foolish,' I began, but the word had a strong impact on him too, because he reached out and punched Queen Victoria in the face with a roar and she clattered to the floor, her face dented and melted beyond repair.

'Do not use that word on me,' he said, turning to face me. 'Do not dare use that word on me,' and suddenly I glimpsed his incongruence, the disparity between the great lord and the little boy who still lurked within him. I had a vision of a stern tutor or governess, shrivelling him down to size so much he felt he had to live the rest of his life proving he was important.

I did not think words would work. I drew out my gun, cocked it, and pointed it at him.

'You need to give me the key and let me go,' I said.

Lord Laxton laughed.

'Ha! Put it away, stupid girl. I am a viscount. Do you know how much trouble you would be in for shooting me?'

'Stay where you are or I will have no hesitation,' I said, and started to edge through the shrouded figures to the door. Perhaps I could shoot the lock open.

'Can you handle the blood? Can you really handle blood and gore? I don't think so. I can.' He charged through the waxworks, pushing them aside abruptly, crashing them to the floor, and I panicked, raised my gun, cocked it and shot him.

It wasn't a perfect shot. I had only had a day's practice after all. But it hit the edge of his shoulder and spun him backwards, bellowing, and it gave me enough precious few seconds to run for the door. But it was locked, and I didn't have the key, and then his hand came from behind me and slammed against the door and his breath was heavy on my neck, and he wrenched my gun from my other hand. A drop of blood splashed on the front of my dress.

'Now I'm angry,' he said.

Chapter Fifty-Six

For a second fear overtook me and I couldn't move or breathe. Was this to be it then? The end of my small life? Then my sense of self-preservation came back, and I twisted myself free and darted under his arm towards the far wall, where I had spotted a half-unwrapped waxwork of Boudicca, the third and last female waxwork, holding a sword I prayed was real. It was as if for a second, Mrs Withers had spoken to me. I grabbed the sword, and it was real, or real enough to cause damage, but as I wrenched it free, Lord Laxton landed on top of me, a dead weight, and as I crashed to the stone floor his thin fingers landed over mine to pry the sword from my grasp. His heaviness stole my breath, his knees and elbows hard and sharp, driving into my back and legs and he grabbed the back of my neck, pushing my face into the floor. I gasped out a breath and tried to bite the thumb nearest my mouth.

He moved it away and swore at me, a litany of violent words. He was still relentlessly unpeeling my fingers from the hilt of the sword with his other hand and he slammed my wrist down hard onto the floor and my hand went numb, my fingers slack.

And then he froze, and I froze too, because one of the waxworks moved.

It was one I had not noticed, nearer the far wall, and it was beautiful, already unwrapped, in a giant white hat and a dark green coat, gliding towards us, its skin pale and ethereal in the half-darkness.

It was Lady Laxton.

'Really, Freddie?' she said, all trembling and hurt, tears glistening. 'I am only a distraction?'

'Effie,' Lord Laxton said, scrambling to his feet. She was not so unimportant after all. 'I did not know... I thought you were outside. Having your portrait...' He was momentarily stunned, but I saw him pull himself together to his usual assured self, reasserting the balance between them. 'Of course, I did not mean it, my little flower. This woman... is a filthy liar. Mad and unstable. I am just protecting you. Do not distress yourself. I will deal with her and then I will take you home.'

He bent down to brush the knees of his trousers, and for what felt like the first time, Lady Laxton looked at me. It was a hard glance, full of import, as if she was telling me something. But then Lord Laxton looked up at her and I wondered if I had imagined it, because she was frightened and childlike again.

It was enough. I had the sword and he had forgotten me for a second. I rose to my knees and then my feet and hit him around the back of the knees with the flat of it, as hard as I could. I was lucky. It caught him off balance, and he crashed quite easily onto the floor, onto his backside, but he was only down for a second and he gave a roar that shook the room.

He spun round onto his knees to push himself to standing again, and I started to dart to the door in search of the gun, when Lady Laxton kicked over the stone that had held the door open, smoothly, with the side of her foot, so it spun past me. I picked it up and before any feminine hesitation or rational thought could come into play, I hit him hard over the back of the head, and he collapsed again on the floor, heavily, and did not move again. There was a brief silence.

'I hope I have not killed him,' I said.

Lady Laxton looked down at his sprawled, skeletal figure, and a shoulder might have moved in the briefest of shrugs. 'He would have killed you,' she said. 'You need to learn self-preservation,' and I looked at her and laughed weakly.

'Why would you help me?' I asked, and she pursed her mouth.

'I did not want him to kill you. I was not aware he hurt Mrs Withers. He brought the bird to me as a present, and I did not think twice about it, because he knows I like birds, although he has never troubled to ask if I prefer them dead or alive. I did not know there might be blood on it.'

'Mrs Withers was trying to save you,' I said.

Her nose wrinkled. 'She tried to talk to me on the night of the ball, and I would not listen. She was so hectoring, wasn't she? I believe I left her mid-sentence. I am sorry for it, if it meant she chased my husband to her death.'

'I need to go to the police and Benjamin – Mr Blackthorn,' I said. 'I do not know if we have enough evidence, beyond what Lord Laxton confessed to me. Would you testify against him in court, if we needed you to?'

'I do not think I can, as he is my husband,' she said. 'I don't really want to be involved.'

'But you…' I said, and ran out of words.

She shrugged again. 'You can tell the police what you like, but I won't promise to back you up. I'd prefer him to believe he has my affection, for now.' She went over to push the curtains aside from the window, letting in the sunlight. Then she took off her hat and pulled off the hummingbird, leaving two small holes against the white silk. 'Will you take this? I don't want it anymore.'

I took the bird and she put her hat back on, bent down, and held her finger under his nose for a second or two. Then she slipped her hand into his trouser pocket and took out the key to the door.

'How can you live with him?' I asked. I could not think of the words, but he resembled a big squashed spider on the floor, all thin arms and legs and blackness.

'I am who he imagines his ideal woman to be,' she said. 'Beautiful above all, but also stupid, naive, emotional. Hysterical and miserable, if I am not pleased. Full of admiration for him, always. He possesses me and pampers me, as he might a racehorse. He might even love me. Love is not a measurable state, after all. He loves who he thinks I am. I love what he can give me. It works.'

She headed towards the door.

'He is still breathing. I think he'll survive. My aunt admires you, by the way. She says you were entertaining,' she said. 'I don't like women much, as a rule. But you seem to have some gumption. And your fiancé is bang up to the elephant.' She unlocked the door, swung the double doors open wide, handed me the key and went out into the sunshine, leaving me in a room with a hummingbird, some half-melted waxworks and a prone, bleeding Lord.

Chapter Fifty-Seven

I did the only thing I could do, which was leave the room, lock the double doors behind me and go for help. My wrist was sore and aching, I was covered in bruises and dust, but I was lucky. I would heal.

Lady Laxton had already disappeared into the crowd. I stood in the sunlight for a second, wondering which way to go. The world was as noisy and rambunctious as the one I had left, the brass band in full swing.

I had a choice. I could go to Benjamin, who would help me and set the world straight, as he was so good at doing. But then... he would be setting the world straight, not me, and my part would merely be grievous bodily harm on an aristocrat. Or I could go to Constable Carruthers, and tell him what I knew, see if I could make sense of it all for him, convince him I was not making up wild theories.

As I debated, the portrait artist arrived at my elbow, an earnest young man with wild curly hair and a worn corduroy jacket.

'Excuse me madam, you were in the pavilion with her ladyship, weren't you? It's only she walked away at the end, without her portrait, without a word, and she didn't even look at it. Maybe you could take it to her, pass it on? It's only two shillings.'

He handed me the silhouette. It was a good likeness, her profile elfin and delicate underneath her hat. Half in a daze I gave him his two shillings, he put the silhouette in an envelope, and I stowed it in my pocket.

And then I went to see Benjamin, because something about that small exchange had given me my decision. Lady Laxton was right in saying love was different for everyone. If we were to be a partnership in work and marriage, I had to trust Benjamin would not pile in on a case and take away my agency just because he was so very capable of doing so. I had been testing him these past months, without even realising; waiting for him to slip up and put me in my place as nearly every other man I had met would have done, and he had not, by a single hair, ever denied me my freedom or stopped supporting me no matter how madcap my endeavours. I would choose him every time over a man loving me simply for how exquisite I looked.

I went to our detective agency, asked Benjamin to make coffee, and told him all I knew, as quickly as I could, because there was an unconscious aristocrat in the pavilion.

'Shall we go to Constable Carruthers?' he said. 'And send a medical man to the pier while we are at it? Not Dr Spencer; a man I can trust. Who will give Lord Laxton a sedative if he wakes up and looks likely to bluster off into the sunset.'

'Yes,' I said. 'That would be sensible.'

'How are you feeling?' he asked, and he took my wrist in his big hands and ran his thumb gently up the outside, where a bruise was forming.

'I will survive,' I said. Other places were starting to ache, where Lord Laxton had fallen on me, but coffee and Benjamin were a wonderful comfort.

'Ready, then?' he asked, and we went to the police station, stopping briefly at the doctor's house along the way.

Chapter Fifty-Eight

'But what proof is there?' Constable Carruthers asked, distressed. 'You have assaulted a member of the landed gentry because you say he confessed to killing Mrs Withers, but you are not sure if his wife will corroborate? Or can, as his wife? And there is a wild plot about blowing up Hastings as well? I am employed to keep order in this town, not offend those who run it.' The fact Lord Laxton had assaulted me first seemed to be a moot point.

'Miss Hamilton was attacked, he confessed, and her word can be relied upon,' Benjamin said. 'There is also the failed planning application. This may not appear to be an open and shut case, and it may need some piecing together before it goes before a court, but there are witnesses, even if some might need to be persuaded to give testimony.' Big George and Mr Wicken had both not wanted to be involved beyond passing information on, Crazy Ed was likely to disappear, and I was not entirely sure who else had been involved. Mr Gallop was in the thick of it, and I told Constable Carruthers so; but I was no longer certain it could be proved that Dr Spencer had been part of it.

It was not easy, this job. It was herding Mr Wicken's sheep without a dog; no neat conclusion, as in novels, but real life, messy and full of gaps. I did not want the whole house of cards to rely on my female word.

Constable Carruthers agreed to go and speak to the Police Commissioner, who would be more likely to be able to interview

Lord Laxton under caution and could place him under arrest. 'House arrest,' he specified, 'until we understand more.'

'He said he would not be stopped,' I said. 'It worries me there might still be some plan afoot,' but Constable Carruthers was only interested in dealing with the current dilemma.

'I should imagine if there is any such outlandish plan he will drop it now,' he said. 'It would be too easily linked to him.'

After Benjamin and I had given all the details we could share, Benjamin walked me home.

'You have done so well, my brave love,' he said, whispering into my ear by the tree near our house, 'But you must be feeling battered and sore. I wish I could tend to your bruises myself.' He pushed back the hair from my forehead and stroked my cheek with his thumb. 'You have one right here. Are you sure, entirely sure, this is the life for you? This brutal, violent life? I would protect you from it if I could.'

'I cannot see myself doing anything else,' I said. 'Although as I can't always be sure words or my gun or a Lady with a rock will save me, I think I do need to learn better self-defence. How can I learn?'

'I will find someone to teach you,' he said. 'A woman, perhaps, who can fight as underhandedly as a woman might need to. Leave it with me. But meanwhile... don't go rushing about for a while. Until we have sorted this out and Constable Carruthers has got Lord Laxton and his colleagues under lock and key. Do not court danger for a while, I beg of you.'

'Tonight, at least, I need to do nothing but sleep,' I said, and then a lady and gentleman passed by us, outraged at our standing innocently beneath a tree, so we had to go our separate ways.

I slept at first, the sleep of the dead, but at four in the morning the ache in my wrist woke me and then I could not get Lord Laxton's words out of my mind.

'I will not be stopped,' he had said, and I could not believe he could be stopped so easily from carrying out a plan that had caused him to murder a woman who got in his way.

It was only at around six in the morning I finally dropped into a restless sleep again, and barely half an hour later I was woken by stones rattling on my bedroom window.

Chapter Fifty-Nine

It was Big George, his shock of hair dark against his pale face in the moonlight. I opened the window with more of a screech than I wished.

'Sorry, miss,' he whispered, 'But I have to talk to you.'

'Give me five minutes,' I said, and I got dressed as fast as I could in my detective dress, abandoning corset and stays, and shot out of the back door into the garden.

The dawn chorus had begun and there were a thousand chirps and tweets from the bushes around us. We went towards the far end of the garden in the hope no one could hear us.

'I found Crazy Ed,' George said. 'He felt in need of congratulating, so I took him for a pint to the White Horse.'

'And?'

'He's done another job for the toff. This time he's placed explosives so it'll set off without the need for a fuse, so no one'll be near it. But it's set to go off this morning, at eight o'clock. And Crazy Ed was in a talkative mood and wouldn't let me go home, so I had to hit him and he stamped on my foot, so I can't walk far. Took me long enough to hobble here.'

'Where? Where is the explosive?'

'It is on the West Hill Lift. When the first carriage goes down it'll hit the bomb and the town'll go up like fireworks, Ed said.'

We had been muttering to each other under our breath but perhaps it was too loud, because I heard the back door opened again, and there was light coming from the kitchen. George and

I hid behind some rhododendron bushes, but the light came wavering towards us, and I saw it was Hildebrand.

I stepped out and pulled her into the bushes with us.

'Sshh, it's only me,' I said, ducking when she attempted to hit me quite hard on the chin with the heel of her hand (I stored that useful fact for later). 'Hildebrand, it's me, Violet. How did you know we were out here?'

'If you're going to throw stones at windows it's best not to hit all of them,' she said. 'Lucky your father's on the other side of the house. What's going on? Are you working on a case?'

Even in the darkness I could see Big George staring at Hildebrand with a look bordering on awestruck. It was not surprising as she was a pretty sight, and only a few years older than him, but we did not have time to dawdle.

'Yes,' and I explained the bare bones of it to Hildebrand with as speedy a dispatch as possible. 'We need a plan,' I said. 'George, can you hobble to find Benjamin? He sleeps behind our detective agency. And Hildebrand, can you run to fetch the police, preferably Constable Carruthers if he's on an early shift? And bring them both to the West Hill Lift as soon as possible?'

'If we can swap it around,' Hildebrand said, 'It would suit me better. I'm not so keen on constables.' I remembered her previous career and nodded. 'What will you do, Miss Hamilton?'

'Call me Violet, for goodness' sake,' I said. 'I'm going to try to stop a bomb.'

I ran as fast as my legs would take me, feeling afresh the damage done the day before. I ran down the steep London Road and then took a sharp left along the expanse of the seafront, empty and flat enough to feel like a race track this early, although even at my fastest pace I knew it would take me at least thirty minutes. I nearly went head over heels on the downhill slope and had to stop twice to gasp great heaving breaths and allow my legs to regain strength, but eventually, just as dawn was beginning to break, I made it to the lift entrance.

The West Hill Lift was one of two funicular railways in Hastings and St Leonards. Opened only six years before, it saved day-trippers the steep climb from the seafront to St Clement's Caves and Hastings Castle. Run by a gas engine, it worked on a water-balance system, the weight of water sending one smart white-and-yellow wooden carriage down and pulling the other up. Most of the journey was through a tunnel, carved through the hill itself, unlike the East Hill Lift, which ran like a visible scar up the face of the opposite hill.

The bottom entrance to the West Hill Lift resembled a stone gateway to a castle, with an arched doorway and two heavy wooden doors, firmly closed. There was no lift attendant or sign of life within or without. To reach the explosive device I would have to get through the doors, through or over one of the turnstiles inside, and then through the inner door leading to the cabins or the tracks. It would be impossible in the time I had, and for a second I stood, irresolute.

At the top of the hill, a light flashed on. I backed away from the entrance until I could see over it to spy, far above me, the upper entrance to the lift, a hut-like building silhouetted against the skyline. There was a light inside, a lift attendant perhaps, lighting the lamps and getting the lift ready for the day ahead.

A cold wave of horror ran through me. The lift attendant would operate the lifts from the top, and at any second he might send the lift rolling downwards. I needed to stop the lift, not defuse the explosive, but I was too far away to reach him.

I was in the wrong place.

Chapter Sixty

I froze, panic-stricken. Could I create a scene from below, to attract the attention of the attendant? No, he might ignore me as a madwoman. The best course of action was to run up the hill and catch him before he sent the lift down. There were unlikely to be customers so early, but running would take at least fifteen minutes, if my legs obeyed me; meanwhile he might decide to test the lift to make sure it was working, or travel down himself, to set up the booth at the bottom. It was a terrible dilemma, and for a brief second, I faced despair.

And then, looking around desperately, I saw my salvation. There was a giant beast lumbering towards me from the far end of George Street, its head haloed by the yellow-red sun creeping up over the horizon. It was a cart horse. Not just any cart horse, but one led by Farmer Wicken. He must be taking it for one of his morning walks. It was a huge horse, with feet the size of prize hams and legs strong enough to carry full-armoured knights in battle. I ran towards them.

'Mr Wicken,' I said. 'I have no time to explain. I have to get to the top of the lift, up the hill. Can your horse gallop?'

'Marjory?' he said, and he stroked its neck, and the big creature snorted into the cold dawn air and rubbed its nose into the space between his neck and shoulder. 'Yes, I reckon so. Want me to take you up? There's no saddle,' he said, with the blessed calmness of someone already acquainted with my oddities.

'Yes,' I said. 'Yes, please.' There followed some shenanigans as I tried to work out a way to clamber up onto a horse the size of a dragon. I finally clambered up onto a railing and, with a firm shove from Mr Wicken, made it. He leapt up onto the railing himself and then behind me with spry agility, took the reins, then paused.

'Best swing your right leg over,' he said. 'Nobody's about and once Marjory gets going, you'll need a firm seat. It reminds her of her war days and she charges a bit. You might want to take your hat off too,' and I realised that my hat was tangling with his beard, so I removed it, threw it on the ground and swung my leg across, pushing my skirts out the way. Farmer Wicken dug in his heels. 'That's it. Grab her mane, firm-like. Hold on with your knees. Ey-up,' he said, and she surged slowly but powerfully into motion.

We were so high up, it reminded me of being on the roof of the Hydropathic Establishment. I felt a brief surge of terror and then there was something so solid and certain about her, it lessened, to be replaced by exhilaration. We reached the bottom of the hill path and Mr Wicken kicked his legs again, and she began to trot and then to gallop upwards, and I was glad he was there, wiry and strong behind me, to prevent me from sliding off. I entangled my fingers in her mane and clung on to her for dear life, the ground shaking under her strong hooves.

'Lean forward. She fought in a few wars,' Mr Wicken shouted into my ear. 'Poor lady. I think galloping brings it back. I always give her extra hay after.'

I could not see the railway tracks, high up though we were, because so much of them were hidden within the tunnel. Perhaps we would make it yet. Marjory was speeding now, and it would take only a few more minutes to reach the top. Anyone who got up so early would surely choose to walk down, rather than take a lift, and how would they get out the other end, if there was no attendant? The danger then was only that the attendant might test the lifts to make sure they were working.

Finally, we made it to the entrance hut and Mr Wicken helped me down onto the slope of the hill but stayed astride himself. Marjory was huffing and snorting, her breath a steam cloud in the air, and she shook her head from side-to-side as if to try to release herself from her reins. Mr Wicken reached down to pat her neck.

'She's anxious,' he said. 'Needs to trot a bit, to come to herself again. Do you need me?' and when I shook my head, he turned her head further up the hill. 'We'll head home then. Time for her breakfast and a brush down.'

'Thank you,' I said, 'I will repay you,' and he shook his head and lifted his hat.

'Reckon you're tough enough after all,' he said, and trotted off up the hill.

I turned towards the entrance and yelped. Through the glass windows I could see a lady passenger stepping into the upper carriage. Any second now, the lift would go down.

Chapter Sixty-One

I shot inside, shouting. The entrance door was open, but the turnstile stood in my way, and the male attendant, attired in smart blue uniform with brass buttons and a peaked cap, was closing the outer doors to the carriage. The lady sat down one of the pretty red benches inside, looking very prim and proper, with a parasol, and although I shouted at him to stop, he did not, turning to pull the lever to set the carriage in motion.

'You can get the next one, ma'am,' he said. 'I'll bring it up in a few minutes.'

I sat on the top of the turnstile and swung my legs over it.

'No,' I said running towards him as he turned, startled. 'You must stop it. Stop the lift. There is an incendiary device at the bottom.'

'Incendiary…? Miss, you're dreaming,' he said.

'I swear to you, it's true. You must stop them. Lives will be lost – yours, mine, half the town's, if you do not stop it. I swear on my life. Stop the lift.'

He scratched his head. 'It can't be stopped, miss. It only stops automatically, if it goes too fast or a cable breaks.'

'What powers the lift? Can we turn the power off?'

'It's water. There's a tank under each lift, and the weight of the water balances the lift. But miss—'

'If we released the water from the top lift?'

'It might stop it. There's a drain gauge underneath each cabin, where the water tanks are.' He was coming to my point of view now, and he headed towards a little door to the side of the cabin and opened it. It led straight onto the tracks and I clambered out after him.

From here I could see straight down the tunnel. The carriages were nearly halfway, crossing each other in almost balletic motion, the one with the sole lady passenger sailing downwards, the other coming up.

'How long will it take to reach the bottom?'

'A minute or two. Less.' We were already scrambling down the steep gradient, the tracks acting a little like steps. I scrambled faster.

We reached parallel to the lift coming up, and the lift attendant bent under the lift to twist open the drain gauge, but it was still moving, and he was clambering awkwardly after it uphill, and it was obviously stiff. 'It's not...' he said.

'Move out of the way,' I said, and I gestured him with my gun in my hand. 'I'll shoot it.' He clambered to one side, and I shot the drain gauge.

Or at least, I first shot the bottom of the tank, and a tiny trickle of water came out, and then, finally, I shot the cap on the drain gauge, and miracles of miracles it opened, and (I was to find out later) seventeen thousand gallons of water came gushing out in a torrent down the slope. The attendant and I were soaked immediately, even though we were stood to one side. There was a shriek from below as the water hit the open windows of the cabin, and then, gradually, the lift slowed. It looked too close to the bottom, but it stopped. And then, and I had not anticipated this, the lifts began to swop places again, the lower coming up, the higher going down.

Hopefully the explosives would be soaked enough to prevent a spark, but I had to find out. I jumped onto the footboard of the lift going down, hooking my arm through the open window to hold on.

'I will come back!' I said to the attendant. 'I am just checking!' and he nodded at me uncertainly, perhaps wondering if he had allowed a hysterical lady to make holes in his water tank and drench a passenger for no reason.

As the lifts crossed in the darkness of the tunnel, I saw the outraged face of the lady in the opposite cabin, not only soaked but heading back to her starting point, and there was nothing I could do but nod at her.

Shortly before the bottom I jumped off, landing awkwardly, and it was only then I knew my exertions had been justified. There were dynamite sticks strapped to the bottom of the tracks where the carriage would have crossed them, soaked and hopefully now, useless.

I had been right. I had been *right*. I sank onto my knees, realising what had worried me all along; that I was a fool, with foolish notions, and there would have been no bomb, no danger; and I would be relegated to the parlour once more; but I had saved the day. Saved lives. Perhaps I was strong enough. Perhaps I would make a fine detective after all.

I turned to examine the bomb, but then I heard a commotion below me and saw, through the windows, Benjamin arguing with the other lift attendant, who must have arrived in time to open the doors for the lady passenger. It was a passionate discussion, because at one point, Benjamin had lifted the attendant by the front of his buttoned uniform a few inches up into the air. I was pleased to see it was not only me who encountered humdrum difficulties in the execution of detective duties. And it gave me a few seconds to prepare.

By the time Benjamin opened the lower door onto the tracks, I was sitting coolly, one knee crossed over the other, almost lounging; a position appropriate for a detective or a lady spy. Even one hatless, damp and covered in horsehair.

'Violet,' he said. 'Are you hurt?'

I gestured nonchalantly towards the pile of explosives.

'I am perfectly fine,' I said. 'I have sorted out the bomb,' and then I beamed at him with excessive pride, and he smiled back at me with all the relief and affection I could desire.

'I'm glad. I had to lock the lift attendant in his booth to get to you,' he said. 'You have saved the day. You are a genius.'

I knew I loved him then. It was a fierce feeling, a claiming of ownership; this gentleman was mine, was good for me, and I was not ever, fire or flood, hell or high water, going to let him go.

He looked at the bomb and went slightly grey.

'One small thing,' he said. 'It is ignited by this pressure plate here, so it could in theory still go off. Water might not have put a damper on it. Perhaps head outside, preferably a distance away, while I deconstruct it?'

'No, it's all right, I'll watch,' I said.

'Violet—' he frowned at me. I frowned back, ferociously.

'I'll watch,' I said, and I did, although I didn't take it in exactly, beyond watching him detach the metal pressure plate and hearing him talk about a percussion cap, as I was imagining how far our body parts might be flung if the bomb did go off. I would ask him again later.

At last, seconds before Constable Carruthers, Big George and Hildebrand burst through the doors, he laid out the different bits of the explosives, including the dynamite sticks, in a neat line far apart from each other and smiled at me.

'Job done,' he said.

Chapter Sixty-Two

'You have been remarkably impressive,' Lord Brassey said. He was a man of many titles, not least Lord Warden of the Cinque Ports, Knight Grand Cross of the Order of the Bath and Member of Parliament for Hastings, and he summoned me and Benjamin to see him and thank us. He had sideburns and a sharp nose and was thankfully happy to include me in congratulations.

'Thank you,' I said. 'I am pleased to have been of help. I hear the evidence is building against Lord Laxton?'

'Mr Gallop, the head librarian, has confessed all in great detail,' Lord Brassey said. 'He has outlined everything about the first failed explosion, including the argument Lord Laxton had with Mrs Withers before he pushed her. Mr Gallop says he did not agree with Lord Laxton's violence towards her and also did not wish the second explosion to go ahead. He prefaced many of his sentences with the words "As Miss Hamilton knows," so I sense you spurred his confession.'

'He firmly believes I possess a note he wrote outlining the timetable and plans for the evening of the first failed explosion,' I said. 'I have never seen it, but it appears we no longer need it.'

Mr Gallop had apparently crafted a careful note setting all the plans for the night, including details as incriminating as the exact length of the fuse and location of the first bomb, and an address for Crazy Ed. He had secreted the note inside his personal copy of Greek Theology for Beginners and left it on his desk, where in ordinary circumstances, it would have remained, until I came along and briefly purloined it. But I had still never seen the note. It was possible it had fluttered to the ground as I tangled with Constable Carruthers and been swept up by a street sweeper; or perhaps a colleague in the library had found it in the letterbox and thought it nonsense. Wherever it was, it had done a sterling job.

When the tide began to turn on Lord Laxton there were quite a few people who were willing to turn on him. The mysterious Toppings, mentioned in the failed planning application, toppled, and Crazy Ed, disappointed his second explosive had turned into a damp squib, was happy to relate his part in order to receive a more lenient sentence. I put the police in touch with Big George the chair-man and Mr Wicken, both willing to help piece the puzzle together as long as they were not the only witnesses to the evening. The list built up, and now there was plenty of evidence to prove that one of Hastings and St Leonards' most wealthy citizens had been involved in a destructive plot to oust its poorest.

'They were members of the Board of the West Hill Lift,' Lord Brassey revealed now, 'and planned to claim on the insurance when the lift was destroyed. It was a foolhardy, destructive plan, though it might have worked, but for you. I hear you suffered some damage to your livelihood?'

'The contents of our furniture shop were destroyed,' Benjamin said, and my heart lifted a little, because although the detective agency was a joint venture, the antiques side of the business had been, so far, solely his, although I had typed up his invoices and other paperwork. 'Some navvies hired by Lord Laxton, we understand.'

'We are selling our property in the centre of town,' Lord Brassey said. 'It turns out Lady Brassey prefers to reside full-time at Normanhurst. I can direct some of the spare furniture your way, if you wish? It is not in the modern style, mostly Regency and Georgian, nothing of high value, but if you wish I shall arrange it.'

We agreed fervently, aware perceptions of value might differ.

'And there was something about a cousin of Lord Laxton in Scotland, causing trouble, I believe?'

'Yes,' Benjamin said. 'A Mr Fraser in Edinburgh. A second cousin of Lord Laxton I understand, who was persuaded to make life very difficult for me over the past month, in the hope I would be distracted from events here in Hastings. And I would have been, were it not for Miss Hamilton.' He smiled at me and I smiled back, feeling anew the wonder of a man who freely gave me credit.

'Well, I do not think anyone can doubt your reputation now,' Lord Brassey said. 'I will write to some contacts in Scotland to ensure you are not troubled again. Lady Brassey and I are personally grateful to you both, because we were worried our annual Ball would forever be associated with an unsolved death. I am grateful to you for setting matters, and Mrs Withers, to rest.

'I will also do what I can to promote your detective business here and in London. That is, if you wish to continue, Miss Hamilton, and are not merely doing such a dangerous job for a livelihood? If so, I can assist with finding you a more suitable position.' He frowned at me, puzzled, but I was getting used to people's surprise at my profession, and if they thought me too foolish and female to succeed at it, they were wrong.

'I am wholly suited to being a Lady Detective,' I said and smiled at him so dazzlingly he coughed into his hand and looked away.

'Well then, well then. Excellent. We shall do what we can to help you succeed,' he said, grandly. 'Is there anything else I can do to recognise your contribution? A medal of some sort?'

'We would like to ensure the Stade is kept safe for the fishermen in future,' Benjamin said. 'The land on which they pull up their boats should be subject to some kind of statute or law to ensure it cannot be tampered with, and if nature or the hand of man destroys it, it can be reinstated.'

Lord Brassey hummed and hawed a little but eventually

agreed to raise it at a future council meeting, and perhaps at Parliament, although: 'We must not stand in the way of progress entirely,' he said. 'Things cannot always stay the same if we are to embrace innovation and enterprise,' and although Lord Brassey's worldview was not the lunatic grandiosity of Lord Laxton, I could understand why the latter had thought his plan might work.

Chapter Sixty-Three

Although many in town were grateful to us, the fishermen were not hugely so, because it was merely the latest event in a long saga of events designed to push them off the beach, and they were sick of it. But public sympathies were on their side, and the town establishment made many noises, if not written agreements, to say the Stade was secure for their fishing boats in perpetuity. The fishermen carried on their day-to-day business as they always had, struggling with the elements and the vagaries of the sea, and most importantly for them, they were left in peace to get on with it.

It had been my first major case, and I had solved it in just over three weeks. Not alone and not without difficulty. It had not been a matter of striding around importantly and wrapping everything up so neatly it could be explained all at once in a drawing room, as fictional detectives did. But I had solved a significant case and survived, and now most of Hastings and St Leonards knew I was a detective. They had not yet cut me in the street for it.

I had learnt some other things along the way too – who was important to me, that my mother could be understood, if not entirely forgiven; that I could stand up to my father and be respected for it. I had resources and courage to call on if I needed them; and not everyone was who they seemed. It was exactly what I had longed for, once, to learn about life and understand it, and not be trapped parlour embroidering daisies.

The only gap in my reasoning was Dr Spencer. I told the police all I knew, but it appeared he had not known about the plot to blow up the Old Town. He had left the ball with his daughters and gone home and no one, Mr Gallop, Mr Topping, Crazy Ed, implicated him in either of the planned explosions. And looking back across my interactions with him – my therapy session, the conversation I had overheard on the roof of the Hydro, our encounter in the bathing hut – I could not pinpoint anything that clearly implicated him either. Knowing he believed me ridiculous was not enough.

He came to our detective agency early one morning to speak with me. We were still organising the room, as several pieces of very fine furniture had been delivered from Lord Laxton. More people were coming to ask us to investigate cases for them, and it was no good any longer to offer them a half-upholstered armchair or kitchen sideboard to perch on; we needed a clear division between the two spaces, to be equally professional in both. That said, it was unfortunate there was only a very small milking stool available for Dr Spencer to sit on.

He sat on it briefly and then chose to stand, so I stayed standing too. Benjamin was out delivering a mahogany writing bureau to a client, who also wanted him to do a small investigatory task for him; we would have to watch that clients did not muddle their business and ask us to investigate their furniture. I would deal with Dr Spencer alone.

'There may have been misunderstanding between us,' Dr Spencer said. He had clipped his beard closer to his face, which strangely made his whole head look smaller. 'I wish to clear the air.'

'Please do,' I said.

'I have always been passionate about women's health and my vision for a hydrotherapy centre for this town was the fulfilment of my ambition. But I did not know about Lord Laxton's plans and he did not see fit to inform me of them. If he had, I would have been horrified. My role as a doctor is to heal, not harm.'

'Mrs Withers' death was convenient for you, though, wasn't it? After she had called you a quack and threatened to ruin your reputation? I heard you making a crude joke about her being crushed by her hat.'

He blanched slightly.

'I assure you that although some... levity is expected in banter between gentlemen, I have never wished Mrs Withers harm. I had been prescribing Lady Laxton what is called in medicine a placebo for some time, because she did not have any recognised malady, but more generally an inertia of spirits, which I believed would heal in time on its own. You will have noticed she embraces a melancholic air as part of her appearance in society. I do not think it is serious. A placebo is a medicine which is essentially harmless but does not have any significant medical effect.'

'But surely that is misleading?' I asked.

'Such medicines can occasionally have the desired effect simply because the patient believes in them. Patients do not always know what is best.'

'And Mrs Withers?'

'She was going through the change in life which can be a dark and dangerous time for some women. Sadly, the medicine does not yet exist to alleviate the physical and mental symptoms. A calm acceptance of the end of a life stage and approach of old age is best, but Mrs Withers seemed unable to resign herself to it. I prescribed some new tonics but they did not agree with her, and she took against my practice as a result. I was disappointed she wished to spread rumours, but I would never have wished anything but good health for her.'

'Why then did you try to bully me into ceasing to investigate?'

'Bully is a strong word,' he said. 'I was merely concerned your behaviour was dangerous to your own wellbeing. You are of an age with my daughters. However, it appears,' he coughed, and shifted on his feet, 'It appears your actions were grounded in good common sense and this town has much to be grateful to you for.' He stared ferociously at a carved umbrella stand, his sienna beard quivering a little, and I sensed this was as close to an apology as I would get.

'Why do you think Lady Laxton's melancholy is not real?' I asked and he looked startled.

'My wife... Mabel and Felicity's mother... I have said before she died when they were fifteen. It was of a severe melancholy, and although I prescribed laudanum and other tonics, she chose not to... continue. Not by her own hand, but simply by giving up on life and wasting away. Although I had studied medicine for many years, her passing made me dedicate my life to women's ailments, to researching and discovering new cures.'

It was a sad story and a laudable aim, although he did not seem to have achieved a great deal for Lady Laxton or Mrs Withers.

'What do your daughters want from life, Dr Spencer?' I asked, and he drew in his chin defensively.

'The same as most young ladies. To find a suitable husband and settle down. Their mother's passing was difficult for them, but I am confident the taint has not been passed down the family line.'

'Can I suggest...' I was about to make an enemy of Dr Spencer again. 'It might be politic to ask your daughters what they want from life? Whether they want to get married or follow some other path? And if they do want marriage, give them some assistance in finding suitors? They sometimes seem a little... lost.'

'Other path? I know my own daughters,' Dr Spencer said. 'Mabel wants a gentleman who can provide her with pretty things, and Felicity would like to be a helpmeet to a gentleman of intellect. Are you insinuating that I, with my ten years of experience of studying women, do not know what is best for them?'

'I have twenty-nine years of experience of womanhood,' I said, 'and it simply occurs to me that your daughters need listening to, as well as you listen to your patients. Listened to without the need to prescribe, or judge, or to shape a medical solution. Just heard. And supported, in whatever path they wish to take.'

It was too bold a proposition for Dr Spencer and not what

he had come to speak to me about at all, so he left the shop in suppressed high dudgeon shortly afterwards. It did not matter. I had said my piece in defence of his daughters and could rest more easily knowing I had tried. It was beyond my remit as a detective, but I could not help taking an interest in wellbeing of others, from Hildebrand to the Spencer sisters. Perhaps I had more in common with Mrs Withers than I had thought.

There was only one thing left to do, and that was to call on Colonel Withers.

Chapter Sixty-Four

Benjamin and I went together. Colonel Withers was quiet and small in his front parlour, a casualty in a lord's grand plan to change the world.

'I do not think she suffered,' I said. 'Lord Laxton has confessed to pushing her over in anger, and said it was an accident her head hit the capstan. He said it was quick. She went there to save his wife from Dr Spencer's quack medicines, and Lady Laxton is enormously grateful.'

'Well,' Colonel Withers said. 'My wife was always so interested in the welfare of the younger women of the town. I am glad she was trying to help. It is just so very… haphazard an event, isn't it? If she had not chosen to go to the Stade that night, she would still be alive, but half of the inhabitants of the old town might be dead. In a way, she saved them.'

'Yes,' Benjamin said. 'She saved the lives of a great many people, and we all owe her a debt of gratitude.'

Colonel Withers took out his pipe and started to fill it and then remembered there was a woman present and started to put it away again, but I stopped him.

'Please, do not stop smoking your pipe on my account. How are you? What will you do?' I asked.

'I am moving to Bath,' he said. 'I have a sister there, some nieces and nephews, who do not mind if their quiet old uncle comes to stay. I do not want to remain here with the memories.'

'I am sorry for all that happened,' I said. 'I hope you can recover and recuperate.'

'Who knows? But I take comfort in the fact she prevented a

disaster. She can be remembered as a heroine at least. She would like that.'

'She was a warrior queen, saving our town,' I said.

'I should share with you,' Mr Withers said, looking distressed. 'I should say, because you, by the nature of your profession, are more open-minded than most and will keep a confidence… my wife and I had… have a daughter. She ran away with a gentleman not of her station, when she was only eighteen, and my wife was deeply upset by it, by the… insult to us. I believe that's why she took such an interest in the young ladies of this town, in keeping them safe from unsavoury influences. In protecting their good name.'

'I am sorry to hear that, sir,' Benjamin said.

'Although our status in society meant a great deal to my wife, I am not so worried about what people think,' Colonel Withers said, 'My daughter still lives happily with a butcher in Essex, I believe. I have grandchildren I have never met. I hope my wife would not begrudge me the realisation that life is too short to avoid one's own flesh and blood.'

'Indeed not,' I said. 'I think perhaps she might have come to that realisation herself soon, had she lived.' I was not sure it was true, but I sensed he needed reassurance.

As I stood up to go, he had one more favour to ask.

'I am not taking all my furniture,' he said. 'I heard there was some destruction of your antiques shop. Would you like whatever I leave behind?'

'Yes,' Benjamin said, 'yes, please. You are a good man.'

'We need to be,' Colonel Withers said. 'In this world, we need to cherish the good people. Some of them are not around for long enough.' He coughed and lit his pipe, blinking and we knew it was time to leave him in peace.

Chapter Sixty-Five

Spring was full established, sun more common than rain, and one sunny day I arrived home to find a beaming Mrs Beeton and my father, holding hands in the front parlour.

'We are engaged!' Mrs Beeton said. 'I hope you do not mind. I know your mother is still alive and will hopefully be for some time. Lucas has explained it all, and I am afraid we are about to commit *bigamy*.'

The two of them looked like naughty children caught stealing biscuits, but my father was the happiest I had ever seen him. I found out later he had plucked up his courage to go and see Mrs Beeton, telling her it was the existence of his very live wife that had led him to sever contact with her.

My father shifted in his chair, guiltily. 'You may not approve, but we have decided it is the only way for us to be together. We will be married in our own eyes. I know you may have strong opinions about right and wrong and the offence we give to your mother, but...'

'That doesn't sound like me at all. Don't make me your judge and jury,' I said. 'I couldn't be more delighted for you both. The word bigamy will never cross my lips. As far as I am concerned you are perfect for each other.'

'If we are ever found out it will severely affect all our reputations,' my father said, clutching onto Mrs Beeton's hands as if he would never let them go.

'Reputations are severely overrated,' I said. 'Mine is very dented already. I am going to try to put happiness first for a while.'

'I have brought some fresh scones and cream,' Mrs Beeton said. 'And a bottle of the ale you both like so much. Do you have any jam, perhaps, and we can celebrate?'

We all had ale and scones together in our tired little front parlour that Mrs Beeton warmed up with her joyful presence, and it was the perfect combination.

Chapter Sixty-Six

Five months later, Benjamin and I were married by the Reverend Bartle in the church I had attended since I was ten.

It was a small congregation, but it included my father and Mrs Beeton, Benjamin's stepmother Agnes and his stepsisters and brothers, Miss Turton and Mrs Monk, Mackenzie, Mrs Cherry – wool shop owner, whose case I had once solved – Hildebrand, Mr Wicken and Big George. It was perhaps not a high society wedding, but it included the very best of those I knew in society. Lord and Lady Brassey had offered to attend, grateful to us for our role in saving the town, but I had explained it was a small, private affair.

It was too much of a risk to invite my mother, but we promised to stop by on our honeymoon, which was to be a small tour of Derbyshire. Not for long, because we had work to do. Ever since I had said at the Pierrot show we did cases at reasonable rates, we had been rather busy. It appeared there were a lot of problems bubbling under the surface in our seaside town.

I was unaccountably nervous, but when Benjamin took my hands in his, I felt reassured as always.

'Remember,' he said, bending down to whisper in my ear, 'this is just an extension of our working partnership. With extra intimacy,' and I gave a small gurgle of laughter, because he was being funny just to relax me.

'Behave, Benjamin Blackthorn,' I said, looking him in the eye, 'I am not going to laugh through this ceremony. It is a very serious matter, marrying me.'

'I believe it, Violet Hamilton,' he said. 'Even though I am only marrying you so we can share our bathwater.'

'Shall we begin?' the Reverend said, and I smiled at him too, because he was taking this very seriously indeed and already had a tear in his eye, as if I was his own daughter.

At that moment, the doors to the church burst open, and a man came crashing through.

'Blackthorn? Hamilton?' he said. 'I need a detective,' and then he fainted away flat on the floor of the church, his feet sticking out from behind the last pew.

Benjamin sighed and turned to the congregation.

'Mackenzie, can you kindly check on the gentleman for the moment? We have some business to complete here,' and then we turned back to the front and the Reverend continued with the ceremony.

Life was going to be interesting.

Acknowledgements

I Have already thanked all those family and my friends who helped me write *No Life for A Lady* and now I would like to thank them again, for tirelessly and selflessly championing it to the extent of photographing it on beaches abroad, in front of castles and in the jaws of dinosaurs. Such dedication is invaluable.

I have been so honoured and delighted by all the reviews too and am pleased to know that people are looking forward to this sequel. The wobbly early days of being an author have been made wonderful by this support.

For my second book, I would like to dig deeper and thank the editor of my student newspaper for asking me, in the brown gloom of a university lift one evening, not if I would like to go out with him but if I would like to edit the newspaper after he had gone. As an eighteen-year-old nurturing a giant crush for a beautiful man, I was mildly devastated, but it didn't take long to realise he had given me the greater gift of a belief in my writing. In that crazy, wondrous year, in between securing seminal advertising from Tetley tea and Viz magazine, I wrote everything from book and film reviews to news articles and features, including an interview with the Bay City Rollers revival band. I will never forget the joy of seeing my writing in print.

Next, I would like to thank the editor of the Wiltshire Gazette & Herald, who saw beyond my woeful grasp of shorthand to send me on a paid journalism course in Hastings and St Leonards, where I learnt the brutal tenets of the profession and was inspired enough to set my two books there nearly thirty years later. Each week we were sent out to cover a small patch of town with the threat of being barred from the course if we did not secure two stories. Although I was thrown out of a joke shop and frequently trod the streets with a weary sense of despair, it gave me a fine sense for storytelling. My cutting-edge scoop on stolen spectacles very nearly made it into the Evening Argus.

I've since had a long career in PR, and while I didn't love the people who edited my press releases into pointless oblivion in the early days, I have been privileged to have the chance to craft stories about many, many wonderful things, from Egyptian mummies to dinosaurs and from Picasso's pots to King Henry VIII's gardening manual. It taught me an economy of words and an ability to get to the point that I'll never forget; you will never persuade me to write obscurely purely to make a reader think I'm bright, while they wonder what I'm on about.

That said, writing this second book was hard, and it took me a while to realise what I was on about myself. I'm there now though, and it's glorious to have a book that was hard to carve but feels like Michelangelo's David, to me at least, not that I have ever felt a marble statue. That might get me arrested.

Hastings and St Leonards, so rich in history and such a glorious backdrop for adventure, delivered me bucketloads of atmosphere again. Every time I think up a story and research the town to check it if something was possible, I find nuggets of truth to back it up. The fishermen have long had to fight for their space on the beach; the artist Marianne North lived at Hastings Lodge; invalids were pushed around all over the place in bath chairs, and unregulated medicine and its advertising presented society with significant challenges well into the 20th century, despite campaigning by the BMA. And electric corsets did exist. I can show you the advert.

Thanks to my publishers for all the work that has gone into making this second book happen – it's been a blast. And to my agent Diana Beaumont again, for championing me so supportively throughout the year. As I've discovered, she is one of the best.

Thanks finally to my wonderful readers too – I hope this book carries Violet's legacy on to your full satisfaction. And hers.

About the Author

HANNAH DOLBY'S first job was in the circus and she has aimed to keep life as interesting since. She trained as a journalist in Hastings and has worked in PR for many years, promoting museums, galleries, palaces, gardens and even Dolly the sheep. She completed the Curtis Brown selective three-month novel writing course, and she won runner-up in the Comedy Women in Print Awards for her novel *No Life for a Lady*. She is from Edinburgh and lives in London.

You can follow Hannah on Twitter @LadyDolby.